THE WORLD WIDENS

The Belandria Tarot Book 4

By Alex McGilvery

The World Widens

Beta Reading

Emily Gilson

Sarah Hamill

Proofreading

Tammy Hadaway

Tarot Cards for readings the end of the book: Karla Pearce

CHAPTER 1

SLOW PROGRESS

Leandra winced as Trader Hurve grew louder and less coherent while his face reddened. The justicar beside Leandra wiped the man's spittle from his face with a kerchief.

"I think I understand your complaint." The justicar rapped on the table, cutting the trader off in mid-sentence. His face would have made her laugh if she weren't already trembling with anger.

Calm yourself. The coin around her neck, one of four magic items created before the exile, sounded pleased.

You said by striving to be fair in all our dealings, we'd be accepted.

So I did, and if you calmed down and looked at the situation objectively, you'd see the fruits of your people's labours these last six years. The sensation of hands cuffing the back of her head made Leandra grit her teeth, but she focused on the crowd around her. Over the years she'd attended too many of these tribunals, hearing claims of how the Rehego cheated honest people.

The crowd watching didn't have the avid look of people

wanting blood. They looked more embarrassed than angry. She thought back through other meetings. The mood of the crowds had been shifting even if the nature of the complaints hadn't.

"Justicar," Leandra leaned over to speak quietly, "perhaps we might hear from others who have traded with Simeon recently. Surely if he cheated one person, there might be others."

The justicar looked at her with raised brows but nodded sharply.

"I am asking any others who have traded with the Rehego Simeon to come forward with their complaints."

A big man moved forward through the crowd with surprising delicacy to stand in front of the table.

"You will testify under oath to the king. Lying to a justicar's tribunal is the same as lying to the king."

The man grinned. "No one's accused me of being anything but honest, sometimes too honest for some." The crowd chuckled. "I'm Stan, have a farm just out of town."

"Very well. Give your testimony." The justicar dipped his pen and poised it over his paper.

"You asked for complaints, sir, but I stand here you to tell you I have no complaints, least not about Simeon. The folks will tell you I like my fiddle music, but things happen, and my fiddle got damaged. My young'un was devastated. When Simeon come by, she brought every last penny and asked if he'd fix the thing. Never a whisper to me. He took it back to his wagon for the night, then returned in the morning to give it to her." Stan took a deep breath.

"You can imagine my shock when she traipses in with my fiddle, better than I ever seen it. When she told me what she'd done, I went to Simeon's camp to offer him more money for his work. He refused. He'd made his bargain with my daughter and that was that. Simeon did offer to sell me a tin whistle, though not for nearly what I wanted to pay, then he sent his daughter to teach my girl how to play it." A stubborn look came over Stan's face as he crossed his arms. "That's the kind of man Simeon is. Sharp as a knife when he's trading, but aren't we all? But fair as any trader I know and fairer than some." He sent a smouldering glare at Hurve.

"The man's got a grudge against me over a trade!" Hurve

shouted. "You can't listen to his stories."

"I ain't got no beef with you." A voice from the crowd yelled back. "I'll take oath to say so and that I agree with Stan." A stout woman pushed her way forward.

The justicar waved her forward and took her testimony, then that of a crowd of others. Leandra's anger faded and her heart swelled with pride at how Simeon had made himself a part of this community. The sun had sunk low in the west by the time the last person spoke their mind.

"The day has been long," The justicar announced. "I will give my decision in the morning. I would remind you: the king's justice does not allow for action against either party of the complaint. There will be no trouble tonight."

"Sir," Gearges, the thin young man who was the town's representative on the panel, stood. "We've been a free-town for three years, and we take our duty to keep the king's peace seriously. There will be no trouble."

Leandra stretched to work out the kinks, made worse by her anger, then she headed over to the inn to join Cameto in the tavern. She picked up her son to hold him on her knee. He grinned and clapped along to the music Stan and his daughter played.

"Raphael has good taste." Cameto leaned over to brush his lips against her neck, making her shiver. "Indeed. His grandfather would be proud of him." She leaned her head on her husband's shoulder. "I never thought about family, too focused on my power games. I wish I could tell that angry young woman how happy she'd be."

Cameto put his arm around her and squeezed.

The justicar sat with his still-full glass of wine in front of him, tapping his toes to the music. Wolflem's mayor, surprisingly young, drummed a finger on the table.

These are good people.

They are, the coin responded. *Good people respond to good people.*

I am glad I followed your advice.

As am I. Conflict can be an opportunity for profit, but peaceful trade is much healthier for all sides.

***

"Very well." The justicar stood and straightened his notes. "Allow me to summarize the situation so any correction can be made before I give judgement.

"Trader Hurve states that Rehego Simeon grossly overcharged him for a shipment of tanned leather. He also complains that the leather was of a substandard quality beneath the one fine skin he examined. In support of his first complaint, Trader Nothrin has come forward stating that he would have charged a quarter less for the same leather and guaranteed the quality." He looked around for any dispute. No one moved, so the justicar picked up the next paper.

"I will deal with the second complaint first as it is the easiest. Trader Hurve states the goods are not available for inspection as he sold them at a loss, just to get rid of them. Since it is impossible for the tribunal to determine the quality of the goods. the second part of the complaint is set aside. It is a complainant's duty to keep proper evidence to support their statements. I am not in the position to decide if this person's testimony is more true than that person's."

"He's a waggoneer, and you're putting him on the same level as me? Everyone knows they are—"

"Silence!" The ice-cold edge in the justicar's voice made Trader Hurve's face pale. "I am not here to judge between Rehego and Belandrian but on the facts of a trade." He put a clear emphasis on Rehego.

"The question of quality is closed. There is no judgement against either party." Another shuffle of pages and the Justicar frowned. "In regard to the first part of the complaint. There is supporting testimony to the unreasonably high price. I would have preferred to hear from more than one source, but Wolflem is isolated and I understand the difficulty of convincing traders to take time to come with their insight to such a tribunal where they make no profit. In this case, I find for the complainant as Simeon could provide no support to show his price was indeed fair."

Leandra stiffened and bit her cheek to keep from arguing. The crowd muttered, but their black looks weren't directed at Simeon.

"For recompense, Trader Kalmin will sell the leather he has testified is in his warehouse to Simeon for the price he stated was the fair price he would have asked from Trader Hurve. After that sale, Simeon will pay the difference in the prices to Trader Hurve. Given the distances involved, I am granting one week for all parties to fulfill their parts in the judgement. In the king's name I—"

"Wait!" Trader Kalmin, as thin as Hurve was fat, stood up and waved his hand. "You can't tell me what price to sell my goods at."

"You testified under oath to the king that your price was fair and customary." The justicar frowned. "Are you telling me that wasn't true?"

"No, no." Kalmin's face went grey. "But I need time to get the goods organized."

"Again I remind you of your testimony, that the leather in question was in your warehouse, ready to sell to your fellow trader."

Kalmin looked around frantically, then slumped to the ground.

"Let me through." Simeon ran to the man and rolled him on his back, listening to his breath and feeling his pulse at the wrist. "Istella, the belladonna." His wife ran forward to hand him a tiny pouch. Simeon used a tiny spoon tied to the pouch to put a minute amount under the fallen man's tongue. Even from where she sat at the table, Leandra saw the difference in Kalmin's breathing and colour. Simeon sighed and leaned back.

"Sir, it would be unwise for this man to travel at this time. I am willing to wait for his recovery."

"I'm not. I want my money now." Trader Hurve stomped forward. "How do we know you didn't poison him?"

"Oh for crying in a bucket!" Gearges smacked his hands on the table. "I will travel to Trader Kalmin's warehouse. The justicar can send someone to witness, and we'll bring back the leather, then you can get your money." He scanned the crowd. "Council meeting now, we have a quorum." The stout woman came forward along with a few others. Stan waved.

"I'm in conflict of interest, I'll not vote."

The people huddled around the young man as other men carefully carried Kalmin to the inn, followed closely by Simeon and his wife. Then Gearges returned to his place at the table.

"Justicar, since you have given your judgement, let me give

the council's decision before I leave. I will not comment on the case, as it has been resolved by the king's justice, but I will state that we as a free-town value every person in our community equally. Trader Hurve's animosity toward the Rehego is well known and will no longer be tolerated. Once the week has passed and Trader Hurve has his money, he will have another week to leave this town and remove all his goods. Neither he nor his associates will be allowed to trade anywhere in Wolflem's jurisdiction."

"You're throwing me out?" Trader Hurve's voiced squeaked and his face went purple. "The judgement went against the filthy waggoneer."

"To be honest, the trade with the Rehego would be a greater loss to our community. You have had little if anything to do with running Wolflem, using your warehouse in our town to avoid taxes the nobles would ask you pay. Under our charter, we have the right – no, the duty - to remove anyone detrimental to the town."

"Trader Hurve." The justicar glared at the man. "Surely you acquainted yourself with the law before moving here. The council of a free-town has the same rights and duties within their region as a noble. The king will not force them to allow you to remain any more than he would force a noble to keep someone sent from their estates. Be thankful they have given you a generous amount of time. It would be within their rights to evict you immediately."

***

Before the end of the week, Gearges returned to Wolflem accompanied by Kalmin's eldest son. The justicar convened the tribunal in the inn as rain pounded the fields outside.

"Sir Justicar." The son went to his knee. "I wish that I had known what my father planned; I would have put a stop to it. As it is, I have petitioned the guild to revoke his license to trade. Still, I am aware his goods are forfeit to the crown for his perjury. We have never traded in leather since I got my license ten years back. A great many people's livings depend on our trading house. For their sake, I ask for clemency. We will instead offer to pay a fine in the amount of the value of the goods contained in our warehouse."

"Sir Justicar." Simeon stood up. "I have traded with this man, and I believe he is honest in his declaration. Our country needs good trade. The loss of this business would leave a hole hard to fill.”

“You just don’t want to lose a trading partner.” The son looked over at Simeon and grinned.

“No, Thoms, I don’t.”

“Very well.” The Justicar smiled slightly at the men. “Trader Kalmin alone will pay the cost of his perjury. It is beyond my purview to make any statement beyond that, as he will face trial in Belopolis. I will require your trading house to pay Simeon the value of the leather goods which should have been present. I will leave it to you to discuss how to arrange it.”

Two of the Justicar’s men dragged Trader Hurve in front of the table.

“Caught him making a run for it,” one man said.

“Trader Hurve, you will be tried for perjury against the crown. The king’s justice depends on those who testify keeping their oath. It isn’t my jurisdiction, but I will suggest that Wolflem take all your property and goods as forfeit, as is their right.” Hurve hung his head.

“Sir Justicar,” a woman in the finest clothes Leandra had seen in the town stood forward. “I have the misfortune to be Hurve’s wife, Gellica. As a result of his greed and stupidity, I and my children are homeless. What will happen to us?”

“Did you know of his perjury?”

“To my shame, I did. I argued against his plan and lost.” She put a hand to her face. “He threatened to tie me to my bed if I tried to leave the house. I feared for my children.”

“You may be asked to give testimony in Belopolis, but no action will be taken against you or your children. Clearly, you were coerced into remaining silent.”

“Gellica, you’ve always been generous with us, even at risk of angering your husband.” The stout woman councillor scanned the room. “We of Wolflem will not turn away any in need.”

“I have no money nor much in the way of skill to offer.”

“Do not worry about that at this time,” Gearges said. “Janis will see that you have what you need if you wish to stay.”

“I do.” Gellica lifted her chin.

“Let’s go and see what needs to be done.”

The justicar sighed and leaned back in his chair. "It is good to see people taking care of each other for a change."

"I hadn't thought of it, but you would mostly see the worst of people." A twinge of sympathy ran through Leandra.

"I suspected they were conspiring, but without proof, I could not act on it."

"So you chose as restitution something which depended completely on their testimony being honest." Leandra laughed. "I like that, it is something the Rehego might do."

"I have to admit years ago, I was distressed at the influx, but I was used to dealing only with those who'd broken the law. Over the years, I have seen the Rehego discipline their own with more firmness than I would dare. More than one free-town owes its prosperity to a good relationship with your people."

"You are always welcome at our fire." Leandra rolled her shoulders to rid herself of the last of her tension.

"I'm honoured."

"There are a number of towns which have banned the Rehego over the years. If any of them wish to change their mind..." She drew a sign with her finger on the table, and the justicar copied it with his pen. "This is a welcome sign. We will not hold any grudges. Belandria is our home now."

CHAPTER 2

LESSONS LEARNED

Prenny blocked the staff at the last second. The vibrations made her shoulders ache. She gritted her teeth and spun her own staff in attack, but her opponent pushed it away with a sneer and jabbed at her knees.

"Point!" the soldier judging the contest shouted.

Blast. Prenny cursed herself. If they were using fists instead of staves, she'd beat him bloody. But she was *noble* now, and fistfights were undignified. Or so all her tutors kept telling her.

His staff smacked her ribs, and even through the mail and leather it hurt.

"Point." The soldier sounded bored. For all her efforts, she'd failed to land a single blow, just like every other time.

"Come on, bandit's brat, hit me." He stood, his arms wide, staff held out to the side. She didn't take the bait.

"Better a bandit's brat than a brainless lump with nothing better to do than beat up on girls."

He snarled at her and attacked. His staff found its way past all her attempts at defence. Prenny backpedalled, then tripped. Her staff rolled to one side. His moved like lightning, and she cringed.

"HOLD."

Prenny's heart thumped as she gasped in painful breaths. The wood staff froze an inch from her breastbone.

He made a spitting sound at her and turned away, throwing his staff to the ground.

She fought unsuccessfully against the tears.

The Marshal's voice continued in the background, but she didn't pay attention to the words.

"It's all right now." Princess Thuria, called Fury by everyone, lifted Prenny to her feet. Though Fury was ten to Prenny's sixteen, they stood eye to eye. "I'll take it from here."

"I have to—"

"You have to let your friends help. My mother will have a word with your tutors, and I," Fury strolled over to pick up Prenny's staff, "will have words with these noble sons." She made noble into a curse.

"Come on." Nikay tugged Prenny to the side of the courtyard. "She's been gunning for this since we heard what was going on. Don't spoil her fun."

"That was hardly a fair contest." Fury sounded oddly like Prenny.

"Anyone knows you have to expect a few bruises when training." Prenny thought his name was Doniel, but it didn't matter. He had a noble father, so he could do what he wanted. "You are too weak."

"This wasn't training though, was it?" This time Fury's voice carried her customary snap. "This was another one of your stupid duels because you imagine you're insulted by Lady Prenny's presence."

Doniel spun and turned white. "Your Highness." He bowed deeply.

"Don't *highness* me. Pick up your stick and face me. I am insulted at how you have treated my friend."

"But, you're in a dress…" Doniel sputtered.

"Lalith, bring a dress for him. Let's make it fair."

Sam, the Marshal, looked like he was hiding a smile.

"I will judge this contest." He looked at the soldier. "You're going to be busy packing. The king is sending more soldiers to the northern mountains. You will be with them." The man dropped his shoulders and left the courtyard, feet dragging.

Lalith had returned unbelievably quickly with a dress. She handed it to Doniel.

"I am waiting." Fury's finger beat a rhythm on the staff.

Doniel looked around at his friends; they all shrugged. The Marshal's face held no sympathy.

"Oh right, never mind. You'd just trip in the skirts." Fury held up her staff. "I'll count to ten, then we begin. One…"

Doniel ran and snatched up the staff, getting to a ready position just as she reached ten.

Prenny knew Fury was fast; even she had no hope of keeping up anymore. The princess trained with the Marshal because there was no one else in the capital who could give her a challenge.

She still underestimated her friend. Fury covered the distance between her and her prey in a blur. Prenny couldn't follow the staves except by the sound of them colliding. Doniel had a desperate expression, but Fury grinned.

"Not bad, a little slow, but you know the basics." Fury wasn't even breathing hard. "Let's find out what you know." She planted her staff and vaulted over her much taller opponent, somehow rapping him on the shoulder before she landed. When he spun, she jabbed her staff between his knees, sending him to the sand.

"Point and point," the Marshal called. "How many points in the match, Your Highness?"

"How many hits do you normally go to?"

"Ten," Prenny called out before he could lie.

"The finals of the championship are only to five." Fury spun her staff and pointed it at his face. "You must be quite something. Well, I don't have all afternoon."

Doniel might as well have been standing still for all the good his defence did. In seconds, the Marshal called the match, and Doniel staggered back and fell to the courtyard. Fury walked over to him and offered her hand.

"A real noble is gracious in victory." She hauled him up as easily as she had Prenny, then planted her staff in the sand. "The game is over. If you want to fight Lady Prenny, you need to beat me first. Whatever imagined slights are making you challenge her, get over them, or go back to your estates. There is no place for bullies in the palace. You want to train here? Well, now your training includes learning diplomacy and tact. You are going to be watched and judged on your ability to think past your offence." She waved her hand. "Dismissed."

The boys stampeded out of the courtyard as Fury returned to Prenny's side.

"I…" Prenny hung her head. "I should have asked your advice earlier."

Fury wrapped her arms around Prenny. "You had people giving you outdated instruction. That will be remedied. Nobles think they are above everyone, but we need to work together. The day Nikay was born, it was the common people of the city who stopped the legionnaires. If they can't change, we'll push them aside."

"A little forceful, don't you think?" Sam drawled from where he leaned against a wall.

"I didn't force him to wear the dress." Fury pointed at the Marshal. "I really wanted to, but I have to take my own advice. We can't be placating the houses, but neither can we antagonize them."

"Granted," he shrugged and put a hand on Fury's shoulder, "and you didn't break any bones."

"Next time I might." Fury said. "Sam, there is no way this should have been allowed. These so-called 'duels' have been tolerated as an outlet for the idiots, but when they became a campaign against a sworn heir, it comes dangerously close to treason."

"Lady Prenny, if you are attacked, use every weapon at your disposal. Holding back because of someone else's idea of honour will only get you killed." The Marshal nodded at Lalith. "Lalith will check your injuries, then help you dress. Council meets in an hour."

"Council?" Prenny's mouth went dry.

"As Fury rightly pointed out, you are a sworn heir. That gives you the right to sit in council as your mother's representative."

***

The dress Lalith chose was surprisingly comfortable.

"Think of it as armour." She whispered Lalith's advice to herself. Her escort gave her an encouraging smile. He'd told her since this was a formal meeting, she needed a guard. Prenny nodded, and he pulled the door open.

"The Lady Prenny."

Prenny didn't know if it was the booming voice or her name that riveted every eye in the room on her. She walked with shaking knees to the chair with the Northern Duchy's crest embroidered on it. A sheaf of wheat, a deer, mountains in the background. It looked like no other crest. Prenny loved it.

"Welcome, Lady Prenny." Rodrigo smiled at her. She didn't see him much, but he was always kind.

"My thanks, Champion. How is Aimee? I haven't seen her in a while."

"She is attending school. I think it's carpentry this week." He smiled proudly. "She wants to learn everything at once. I will let her know you were asking after her."

"Good to see you, dear." Lady Marriette inclined her head but had a mischievous glint in her eye. "We could use your input."

"Me?" Prenny squeaked, flushing red before dropping into her chair.

One of the younger members chuckled.

"Don't worry, Lady Prenny. My first day in Council, I tripped while standing for the king and fell on my face. I am Lence Graine." He bowed in his seat. "It will be pleasant to no longer be the youngest in the room."

The others introduced themselves with a mix of genuine welcome and patronizing smiles. A rap of a staff called the room to silence. Everyone stood.

Prenny didn't trip. She gave her curtsey without flourish, but none of the others made a fuss either.

King Harald took his seat and relaxed as he looked around. His mouth twitched when he saw Prenny.

"Lady Prenny, thank you for accepting our invitation. We desire your advice." He winked at her, and Prenny couldn't help but smile back. "Very well, to business then. We have been discussing the issue of our northern border. As you know, with the success of Lady Joan's guidance, the duchy has grown northward and has begun to bump up against the mountain tribes. There have been raids and bloodshed by both sides."

"My mother has said as much in her letters. She's asking people not to move any further north until the situation is resolved."

"Thank you, that is wise." The king spoke as if he didn't already know that and more of her mother's thoughts. "You have a unique background which may help us in our discussion."

"Your Majesty?" Prenny's palms went damp, but she refrained from wiping them on her dress.

"You grew up in a community which was outside the rule of our law. Then you graced us with your loyalty. Your story is close to the situation of the northern tribes. We would like your opinion on what made the move from bandit to loyal subject possible."

"I ain't thought of that in some time." Prenny gasped and put her hand over her mouth.

"Don't apologize," Lady Marriette put a hand over Prenny's. "Asking you to think of your past will necessitate you thinking the way you did when we first met."

"Thanks, Lady Marriette." Prenny put her hands on the table and breathed deeply and tried to organize the chaos in her mind. The silence around the table unnerved her and made it harder to think.

"Guess, I'll jus' have to talk an' hope ye c'n understand me." Prenny kept her eyes closed so she didn't have to see the look of disgust on her audience's faces. "What kept us out was thinkin' there weren't anything but a noose for us. Chancy made sure we hated the nobles. Most of us had good enough reason to anyway. Ain't much reason in talking if y'll hang for it. Lady Joan and Lady Marriette offered somethin' new. Give us cause to trust ye."

She brushed a tear from her eyes. *They'll never talk to me again.* A hand put a kerchief in her hand. Prenny opened her eyes to see one of the older councillors smile at her.

"I'm Lord duSarche. You support my first point: language is important. When I'm hearing from my fishing villages, I need to understand them as they speak, not try to make them sound like me. Lady Prenny's experience will be invaluable."

"It makes sense that they wouldn't want anything to do with people they think want them dead."

"Just common sense," Lence said, "our whole society is based on making life better for everyone. If they don't think we'll help, why bother?"

"There's another thing." Lord Torrance rubbed his chin. "We don't know what is being said about us. We know that we're all kind and loving people, but they haven't had the opportunity to learn that yet."

The people around the table chuckled at his ironic tone.

"We have a place to start a different response to sending soldiers north. Soldiers are trained to fight, not negotiate." King Harald leaned forward on his elbows. "Do we have anyone we know who speaks the language of the northern tribes?"

"I have some people. They were captured on a raid in my father's day. I offered to let them return home, but they said they wanted to stay. They still speak their own language at home." Lence made a note. "My mother was from the north, so we often sent men up. I remember wanting to go, then being fascinated by the people from the mountains when I learned about them."

"I would like to learn the language." Prenny surprised herself by speaking up. "Since I'm from the north."

"Very good, Lady Prenny." King Harald looked around the table. "Any others?"

"I already speak a little." Lence lifted a hand. "Wouldn't mind learning more."

"As Chancellor, I will learn." Lady Marriette smiled. "I will suggest we offer the opportunity to our young people. If I can practice with Nikay, we'll both learn faster."

"I'll have to go to the classes in self-defence." Lord Torrance winked at Lady Marriette.

"We will leave it to Lence to organize the teaching." King Harald tapped the table absent-mindedly. "We'll need to think about what we offer and how to get past whatever opinion of us they have at present. From our history, we doubt it is pleasant." He nodded at Prenny. "Lady Prenny can continue to educate us on what it feels like to be on the outside and what is needed to bring her in."

Prenny reddened and clasped her hands to stop them from trembling.

"I will do my best, Your Majesty."

"We are sure you will, ye ain't never b'n a quitter." King Harald stood while Prenny was trying to close her mouth. He had left the room before she scrambled to her feet.

The rest of the council filed out, talking animatedly. Prenny dropped back into her chair. What had she gotten herself into?

CHAPTER 3

THE CALL

It is time, my daughter.

Lydia sat up in her bed, her heart breaking. There would be no point in arguing with that voice. She'd vowed she wouldn't.

"Does it have to be now? Who will care for Fury and Nikay?" Lydia wiped tears from her eyes.

It is time. A caress ran down Lydia's back. *It's all right to grieve.*

"Will you give me the words?" Her voice broke and tears dampened her face again.

I will be with you, child.

Lydia didn't change out of her nightdress, only wrapping a robe around her before walking out into the corridor.

"Late to be walking the halls." The guard outside her foster parents' door looked concerned. "Are you all right, Princess Lydia?"

"I must speak to the king and queen immediately." Lydia wiped at her face with her sleeve.

The guard stared at her, then knocked on the door.

"Since it's you asking." He shifted nervously.

"They will not be angry with you." Lydia put her hand on his arm.

"What is it, Hamon?" The king's voice came muffled from the other side of the door.

"The Princess Lydia wishes to speak to you. She wouldn't wake you lightly, Your Majesty."

"Thank you, Hamon, send her in."

Hamon opened the door and waved her through.

Lydia had been in this room a handful of times in the years since the royal couple had brought her to Belandria and treated her as their daughter.

The subtle scent of the Queen's perfume calmed Lydia's heart. She'd had nightmares the first year here. Something looking for her, wanting her back. The queen had sat rubbing Lydia's back, telling her she was safe.

Sara sat up in bed, the quilt wrapped around her. Harald lit candles, wearing a tattered robe.

"What is it?" The queen patted the bed beside her.

Lydia's grief overwhelmed her, and she wrapped her arms around the woman she thought of as her mother. Her father's strong arms held them both as Lydia shook with her sobs.

They sat like that until the storm passed. Lydia sighed and hiccupped.

"I woke in the night." Lydia closed her eyes hearing the words in her head. "It's time."

Her mother gasped and squeezed Lydia tight, then let her go.

"I always knew this day would come, but I hoped…"

"Me too, Mother." She allowed herself the word this one time. All her life it had been Harald and Sara to keep it clear she wasn't an heir.

Harald groaned and put his face in his hands. Lydia hugged him.

"I love you, Father," she whispered, "and you too, Mother."

"When?" Harald straightened and wiped his face.

"My ship leaves with the tide," Lydia said. Her words drove it home. It was real: she was leaving everything she knew and loved to travel alone.

Not alone.

The king opened the door a crack.

"Hamon, we need a maid to pack what Lydia needs for a journey. Keep it practical and low-key. It will be cold where she's travelling, so winter gear is essential."

"As you wish, Your Majesty." Hamon whistled quietly, footsteps approached the room. Harald closed the door, cutting off the quiet conversation.

Her mother climbed out of the bed and rooted through a drawer.

"Ah, there it is." She handed Lydia a dark, metallic ring with only the slightest sheen. "This has been passed down in my family for generations. I could never find out what the markings meant." Sara slipped it onto Lydia's finger. "Thuria will have a great deal of old family jewellery, more than she wants, likely. I want you to have this."

The ring already felt right on her hand. Lydia twisted it, looking at the angular marks on it.

"I feel foolish giving you this," Harald put his hand on Lydia's shoulder. "Being who you are, but…" He put a small book in her hand. "This is the Bible I studied when I was a youngster. You may find a few irreverent comments in the margin." Her father smiled crookedly, and Lydia held the book to her chest. A combination of sadness and joy wrestled within her.

"Why is Yennet packing up Lydia's room?" Thuria stomped into the room.

"Sister." Lydia pulled Thuria into a tight embrace.

"What's going on?" Thuria's voice went higher.

"It's time for me to go," Lydia said, not letting go. "I'm going to miss you."

"You can't leave. You can't." Thuria pushed Lydia away, backed up and ran out the door, leaving Lydia's empty arms reaching.

"Your things are ready." Yennet stood in the doorway. "The coach will be ready in a few minutes." She raised an eyebrow. "You might want to get dressed."

***

Lydia shivered in the damp air. It was still summer, but the mornings were cool. Yennet put a cloak over Lydia's shoulders. "It has hidden pockets with some useful things. You'll find them when you need them." She held Lydia's eyes with hers. "Don't trust too easily, but when you do trust, trust completely."

Her face reddened. "Honestly, I don't know what it means. My gran said that to me, but it is the only wise-sounding thing I can tell you."

Lydia laughed and hugged Yennet.

"Thank you, look after my mother and sister for me."

"Always."

"Ready?" King Harald stepped outside with Sara at his side. He swept Lydia up in a hug. "We will always love you, wherever you go. You will always be welcome here." He set her back on her feet, then turned and left. Sara put her hand on Lydia's cheek briefly, then followed her husband.

Heavy-hearted, Lydia let the coachman help her into her seat. She still clutched her father's holy book. The coach started away, rocking so she had to hang on. Not wanting to drop her book, Lydia explored her cloak and found a pocket to slip the tiny volume into.

The coach stopped and shouting sounded from outside. Lydia opened the door to find out what was going on.

Fury stood in the gate with her staff and a stubborn expression.

"I won't move until I talk to Lydia."

The driver muttered.

"It's all right," Lydia said to him.

Fury ran to the coach with the speed that always took Lydia's breath away.

"Lydia, you can't leave, not until I say goodbye properly." The princess clambered into the coach and hugged Lydia. "Fury in me, told me it had to be." She wiped at her eyes, then handed Lydia a necklace. An odd-shaped blue stone lay in her palm, wrapped in silver wire. A silk cord puddled around it.

"I made it." Fury blushed. "I wanted to give it to you, but I was afraid you'd laugh."

"It's beautiful." Lydia lifted it to look more closely. "There is nothing in the world you could give me that would be more precious."

Fury clasped Lydia so tightly she struggled to breathe.

"I'm going to miss you terribly, Sister."

"And I will miss you too." Lydia hugged Fury, ignoring the driver's irritated harrumphing. "Be slow to trust, but when you trust, trust completely."

"What?" Fury pulled back to stare at Lydia.

"As your older sister, I thought I should give you some wise advice. It is something Yennet said to me."

"I love you to the end of the world and back." Fury jumped out of the coach and streaked away across the lawn.

"Finally," the driver grumped.

"Driver, you would be best to keep your words to yourself. That girl is going to be your queen someday." Lydia slammed the door shut, then giggled. She'd never spoken to anyone in the palace that way. Now, on the last day, she acted like a princess.

The ride to the port was both too long and too short. Lydia directed the driver to the dock, had him unload her bags, then dismissed him. He glowered at her, but Lydia refused to turn away. The driver reddened and slapped the reins harder than he needed, setting the coach in motion and almost colliding with a wagon carrying others onto the wharf.

"What do you want, miss?" A sailor, younger than she, stood at a respectful distance.

"I need passage on this ship." Lydia reached down to lift her bags.

"Leave them here for the moment," the sailor said, "I'll keep 'em safe. You'll want to talk to the captain. Up the gangway, then turn to the bow. He'll be talking to the first mate."

Lydia walked up the ramp, faint memories of a trip across the ocean when she was young. The tar and wood smell brought them back more clearly.

"Captain?" Lydia addressed the man doing all the talking. He nodded at the other man who went off giving orders.

"I'm the captain." He stood only slightly taller than Lydia but had to be twice as broad. He looked stern, but Lydia liked him.

"I need passage on your ship."

"We sail in less than an hour. We'd have to rearrange too much to accommodate you."

"I don't need accommodating, Captain. A curtain across a corner will be enough."

"I don't know. I have passengers booked already. They have the one cabin, and I won't put a girl amongst the men. They wouldn't do anything to you, but it would make them uncomfortable."

"I'm travelling in God's service." Lydia's face heated at the claim.

"God should make better plans." The captain frowned at her. "Is God going to pay your passage too?"

"No, the king has sent money for that."

"The king? You keep high company."

"Lydia, I thought you'd be in the cabin already."

She spun around at Rodrigo's voice behind her. Milene and Aimee stood with him.

"She's with you?" The captain waved a hand. "Why didn't she say so?" He stomped off.

Rodrigo took Lydia's arm and led her to the cabin. The entire space would fit four times into her room at the palace, but it was cleverly organized to feel bigger. The young sailor brought up her bags, then Rodrigo's on a second trip.

"I'm Bill." The sailor pointed to himself. "It's my job to make sure you have what you need. The captain and the rest are busy, so call on me."

"Thank you, Bill." Rodrigo nodded at the sailor. "We will endeavour to stay out of the crew's way."

The young man left, and Lydia sat on a bunk while Aimee checked out every corner of the cabin. Milene watched with a bemused look.

"How did you know?" Lydia asked. "I only learned this morning."

"I try not to question these things." Rodrigo shrugged and sat across from her. "It makes me queasy."

"It's good not to be alone."

"If there is one thing I've learned," Rodrigo stretched out on the bunk, "it is that we are never alone."

CHAPTER 4

NO OPPORTUNITY LIKE A NEW ENEMY

"Disturbing news." Leandra tapped the letter on her knee. Raphael poked the fire with a stick while Cameto stirred the mushrooms in the pan.

"New territory comes with new problems." Cameto gave their son a longer stick and moved him away from the fire. "The king gave us the land to settle but no guarantee it would be easy."

"So, what do we do about the raids on our people?" Leandra closed her eyes to visualize the plateau. "Reports suggest the problem is the southwest, near the desert."

"That would explain why they're raiding. Not much in the way of resources in that corner."

"I'll send a letter to the king to let him know the situation. We'll send it at the next town. Then we head to the grasslands."

"What do you have in mind?" After a last stir, Cameto scooped the mushrooms onto plates and pulled tubers out of the coals.

"We're Rehego; we haven't fought a war since the exile. I don't want to start now." Leandra took her plate and breathed in the rich smell of the food. "We will start by talking with them. The Rehego are no longer warriors, but we are the best traders in the world." She dug into her supper, savouring the flavours.

***

Five years before, Leandra and Cameto had travelled through the plateau. She'd forgotten how big it was. The waves of grass ran as far as she could see. A hint of distant blue mountains in the west was the only relief from the plain. They'd been rolling a week since the letter had been put into her hands. At Wolflem she'd bought an old wagon and filled it with food and water jugs. An ox destined for the butcher completed the ensemble.

She had Raphael running back to peer through the window in the door to make sure they didn't pull too far ahead of Cameto.

They stopped for the night and, after supper was done, lay on their backs to look at the stars.

"Last time when we left the plateau, I was carrying Raphael." Leandra reached over and brushed her husband's face. "Maybe it's time to give him a little sister."

"You'll get no argument from me." Cameto rolled on his side to pull her to him.

***

The grass didn't end, it faded, growing shorter, more ground between the plants.

"This will do." Leandra stopped the horses and set the brake. "Cook extra tonight, we'll need it."

Raphael slept in his bed and Leandra leaned against the wheel of their caravan to admire the night. Shadows moved silently toward them. Leandra drew the last part of the rune she'd spent a week placing on her and Cameto.

"Come join us at the fire. There's plenty of food."

The night went utterly still, and for a few beats of her racing heart, Leandra thought she'd miscalculated. Then a figure in a mottled robe walked into the firelight.

Leandra held up her open hands as did Cameto.

"The fire is sacred; no harm will come to you while you are our guest." The person in the robe held out their hands, then

24

deliberately dropped the knife out of their right hand.

"How our language you speak?" The warm contralto voice made Leandra smile.

"I'm counted as wise among my people."

Their visitor sat gracefully and pushed the hood of her robe back. Rehego were known more by the bones of their face than colour of skin or hair. Leandra was dark, Cameto fair, but she'd never seen someone with skin like their visitor's. Either nature or paint drew lines on her face giving her a cat-like appearance, her hair streaked with colours.

Cameto filled a bowl and handed it and a spoon to the woman. She sniffed at the stew, then tasted it and sighed.

"Why don't you ask the rest of your friends to come too?" Leandra leaned forward, half in earnestness and half in curiosity.

"How not alone do you know?" She hardly slowed the motion of her spoon to talk.

"There are two behind you in the shadows, where fire blinded eyes can't see them, and another two checking out the wagon with the ox. I'd prefer the one poking at the door to our home not wake my son.

The woman trilled softly, and the five walked into the light and sat. Cameto handed out bowls and put water on for tea.

"To rob you we come, but welcome we get." The one to the left of the woman pushed back their hood revealing a man with bold black and white stripes in his hair and on his face.

"This is why am I here." Leandra straightened. "I heard from my people, so I came to see for myself and talk with you. The plateau is large, enough space for us to live peacefully."

"Warriors would not talk of peace." The man frowned at Cameto.

"We are not warriors," Cameto shrugged theatrically. "Not for more generations than I can count. We are traders, merchants."

"Why should we not take what we want from you traders?" Another man shrugged off his hood, revealing bright red hair over a dark-skinned face.

"You weren't one of those looking at the other wagon. Ask your fellows what is on it."

A quick conversation ensued with expressions of disbelief

and waving of hands.

"Food and water, some cloth." The red-haired man curled his lip. "What of it? It is ours now."

"Of course." Leandra smiled broadly. "We brought it to you as a gift."

Five pairs of eyes fixed on her, and a shiver ran down her spine. Something about gifts was important, but she didn't know why or how yet.

The fire cracked and snapped as Leandra let the silence hang between them.

"If we accept this gift, what are we bound to?" The last person pushed back their hood, their face covered with swirls and their blond hair curled tightly.

"To talk." Leandra let her stomach relax a little. "Nothing more."

Another conversation erupted with the three men appearing to oppose taking the wagon, the woman in favour. The last person pushed back her robes, and Leandra couldn't hold back a gasp. She was like a marble statue come to life, but with blazing blue eyes. The argument cut off and all four bowed low.

The woman picked up her bowl and tasted the stew before smiling, showing sharply pointed teeth.

"It is clever, how you learn our language. Is it able for me to learn yours?"

"Yes." Leandra bowed from the waist. "But it requires time and trust."

"I will stay. Mahaloun will guard my dignity. The others will travel to fetch one who can talk."

The black and white man, Mahaloun Leandra guessed, stayed seated. The other three stood.

"Your fire we enjoyed." The woman picked up her knife then led the others into the surrounding night.

"Strange people to welcome thieves with softness." The woman held up her bowl, and Cameto refilled it, topping up Mahaloun's as well.

"We have a saying." Leandra accepted a bowl from Cameto before he filled his own. "There is no opportunity like a new enemy."

The woman frowned and leaned over to whisper with Mahaloun.

"I do not understand." The woman drew a knife. "Enemies are for killing."

"But new enemies may become new friends. There's no profit in a dead man."

She stabbed the knife into the ground. Cameto winced and Leandra elbowed him. Mahaloun laughed, looking relieved.

"He doesn't like to see a weapon cut the earth." Leandra nudged him again.

"It is hard to know what it slices." Cameto grimaced.

"We will rest apart, but not far. Mahaloun will watch."

***

While they waited for the others to return, Leandra showed the woman the runes enabling her to understand and learn the other's language. The woman was intrigued but not surprised. They practiced by talking of inconsequential things - the way the grass moved, Raphael's insatiable curiosity about Mahaloun. He even went to the extent of using ashes to draw lines on his face. Neither of their guests paid any attention at first, but toward the end of the week, the woman called Raphael over. She scrubbed his face clean, then took a pot and brush from under her robes and painted the boy's face with delicate lines which made him look both adorable and fierce.

"The elder may be pleased." The brush and pot vanished beneath her robes.

That evening five figures appeared out of the grass. Three whom Leandra recognized had their hoods down already. One of the others leaned on the last as if they were elderly. When seated, they too pushed back their hoods. The elderly one was a man with faded stripes on face and hair. The last was a person with a shaved head and skin as black as their guest's was white.

Raphael jumped up to bow deeply to the old man.

"Welcome to our fire." He announced proudly.

"Come, child, let me see you clearly." Leandra translated softly for Raphael.

Raphael knelt and gazed up at the man.

"Did you paint your face to humour an old man?"

Leandra translated again, and Raphael turned to look at her, his face scrunched up in puzzlement.

"Tell him what's in your heart." Leandra smiled at him.

"I want to be strong like a cat, so I can protect my mother like Mahaloun protects the white lady."

The white woman put her hand over her mouth, but Leandra was sure she heard giggles as she translated.

"An honourable desire." The old man smiled and patted the ground beside him. Raphael sat and snuggled against the old man.

He chattered away through the meal. Leandra gave up trying to keep up the translation, but the old man nodded as if he understood every word.

Soon after Cameto collected the plates, Raphael had curled up and was snoring gently.

"My warriors told me, but I had to see with my own eyes." The old man smiled at Leandra. "You may call me Xianju; my strength is Hojiam." He put his hand on the black person. "You have met Lupji," the red-haired man nodded, "Pounjou," the one with the swirls lifted a hand, "and Teekja." The woman they'd met first bowed to the ground, and when she straightened, tears glistened on her cheeks. "The last is well-named by the child. Vazee, in our language."

The woman inclined her head, smiling slightly.

"I am called Leandra, once the white heir, now as close to a ruler as my people will allow." She put her hand on Cameto's shoulder. "My heart and right arm, Cameto." *Names are gifts to these people.* "You've met my little kitten."

"We have come to talk, Leandra, white heir to your people, as you have asked."

"You grace us with your presence, Xianju. I can see how you are regarded by your people. As they will have told you, the wagon we brought is a gift to your people. By coming to talk to us, you have met all obligation of the gift."

"I bring a gift in return." Xianju put his hand out, and Hojiam placed a midnight black object in it. "I offer it in token that our talking be honest."

Acting on instinct, Leandra walked around the fire and knelt in front of the old man. He put a huge claw into her hand. "This is a claw from the great black cat of the jungle. More than anything else, it announces who we are."

Impulse made Leandra tuck it in under Raphael's arm.

"I will pray my kitten grows to be worthy of the gift from the black cat of the jungle."

The visitors turned to Raphael's sleeping form and bowed, even Xianju and Vazee.

What have I done to you, my darling?

CHAPTER 5

A NEW PATH AT SEA

Lydia failed completely to hide her laughter as Aimee wheedled Rodrigo into wearing the hook she'd smuggled onboard. Milene wasn't even trying.

"Come on, Papa." Aimee held up the hook with sleeve and buckles dangling. "It will be more useful than what you have now."

"It will look ridiculous. We need to stay out of sight. Me looking like a pirate won't help." Rodrigo put his stump behind his back as if he feared Aimee would put the thing on him without him noticing.

"Remember the beard and haircut?" Aimee didn't quite pout. "You said it was to distract people from seeing you. This is the same."

"You may also remember I shaved the beard off as soon as we set sail."

"I worked hard on this." Aimee pushed it at Rodrigo.

"You made it?" Rodrigo's jaw dropped.

"No, a blacksmith made it." She rolled her eyes. "I *designed* it. The blacksmith laughed at me, so I made one of cloth and wood to show him it would work. He kept the one I made." Aimee put out her hand. "Give me your arm. Try it. If you don't like it, throw it overboard." Now she pouted in earnest, her lips trembling, eyes shining with unshed tears.

Rodrigo sighed and put his arm out. Aimee jumped up and down, pout and tears forgotten. She slid the sleeve of his shirt out of the way, then wrapped his arm with gauzy fabric. "This will keep it from slipping off if you sweat in the heat and keep you warm if it's cold."

Rodrigo looked at the fabric curiously. "I haven't seen anything like this before."

"Don't wrinkle it, Papa." She adjusted it carefully, then put the leather cuff on and tightened it. "See, no holes. It must be exactly right. Too loose and it will fall off, too tight and it will hurt your arm. You can adjust them with one hand like this…"

Lydia peered over Aimee's shoulder admiring the ingenious design.

"Won't the teeth eat through the leather?"

"Eventually." Aimee didn't look up from her adjustments. "The straps are easy to replace." She backed. "Try moving your arm about."

Rodrigo swung his arm with a strange look on his face, then adjusted a couple of straps and repeated the process until he nodded and started to slide his shirt sleeve down his arm.

"I need to show you the rest."

"The rest?" Rodrigo sat down and stared at Aimee. "Just how long have you been working on this?"

"I made the first drawing on the ship, but it took a few years to get the cuff to work. The rest was easy."

"Years…" Now tears shone in Rodrigo's eyes. "And I argued, saying it was silly."

"It's all right, Papa." She kissed him on the cheek. "It's more fun when you argue."

"That's our daughter." Milene lay on the floor with a grin on her face. "Our four-thousand-year old daughter."

"Four-thousand-and-*thirteen*." Aimee glared at Milene, then blew her a kiss.

"Wouldn't it be four-thousand-and-five?" Rodrigo fussed more with the straps.

"That makes me sound like a child!" Aimee frowned at him.

Lydia fell back on her bunk and roared with laughter. Aimee landed beside her and howled like a desert animal.

"What does this do?" Rodrigo tugged at something; it slid out and his eyes widened. "A knife?" He tested the edge with his thumb. "A very fine one too."

"That was my idea." Milene sat up to put a hand on Rodrigo's knee.

"You knew about this?"

"Of course." Aimee sat up. "I had to get a little help."

"How long?"

"Aimee showed me the first drawing on the ship. We've had some lively debates over the years."

"What did I do to deserve you?" Rodrigo swept Aimee into his arms and hugged her. She wrapped her arms around and squeezed until he ooffed, then wriggled free.

"Watch this." Aimee gripped the ball on the point of the hook and twisted it sharply. It came off with a click. Rodrigo sheathed the knife to look closely at the wicked point the ball had hidden. He put it back on, then peered at the joint.

"I can barely see it, and I know it's there. That's a very talented smith."

"He should be. He makes the king's armour and swords."

"Harald was in on this?"

"The smith might have mentioned it. He said he had to get permission."

"Did anyone not know?"

"I didn't." Lydia giggled from her bunk.

"One last thing. The smith's idea." She gripped the hook, pushed toward her father and twisted the opposite way to the ball. After a louder click, the hook came off in her hand. It had a loop on the end. "The hook goes over a pin, but there's a spring, so you have to push, then turn." Holding it up, she poked her finger through the loop. "You can put a rope on this, and it will hold twice your weight." She rolled her eyes and huffed. "He made me promise to say this. You might find it handy." Aimee put her hand over her eyes as Rodrigo snorted.

He put the hook back into place and checked for wobble. "If someone could match the looped end exactly, they could make a different attachment."

"I didn't think of that." Aimee widened her eyes comically, then reached in her bag to pull out a short piece of steel with a loop on the end. "But the smith did. He was smart for an old man."

"Hey, what does that make me?" Rodrigo put the hook over his heart.

"My Papa and the Rehego Champion." Aimee declared putting her hand over his heart.

"And, I think, the luckiest man in the world."

***

The hook became a favourite subject of discussion. The captain and crew were fascinated by the intricacies of it. When Rodrigo proudly explained how Aimee created it, it wasn't uncommon for someone to show her something and ask what she thought about it. Bill particularly was fascinated by her description of the process of trial and error over the years.

The weather stayed fair for sailing, and they made good time. Lydia smiled at how Rodrigo straightened and walked differently with the hook on. No matter how much he tried to lift, it didn't slide off his arm. More than once, she caught Aimee watching her father with tears in her eyes.

"You saved his life," Lydia whispered to her one day. "He thought he'd accepted losing his hand, but look, see how his eye sparkles and he walks like a wolf on the prowl."

Aimee wiped her eyes. "That's silly. He knows he's more than a missing hand."

"He did, until his daughter gave him a new one. It isn't just the hook; it's that you made it."

"I don't understand." Aimee looked at Lydia. "It's still a hook."

"Some things are meant to be felt, not understood." Lydia gave Aimee a hug. "I wish I'd gotten to know you better before. I would love to have been in on the surprise."

"I liked the palace and the people, but it wasn't my place."

"I grew up there, and sometimes it still didn't feel real." Lydia sighed.

"What's it like, knowing you're going to be the Holy Mother and talk to God?"

"What's it like being four thousand and thirteen?"

"Confusing when I stop to think about it."

"Same with me. Before I can be Holy Mother, I must be Lydia, so I work on Lydia, and don't worry about the Holy Mother."

"Sail on the port side." The lookout's voice shook, and a chill ran down Lydia's spine.

"Go find your father and keep him safe. He's going to need you." Lydia watched Aimee dash away, then went to their cabin. She put on the cloak Yennet gave her, checked to be sure the holy book was safe in its pocket, and that her necklace was tied securely. Lastly, Lydia dug to the bottom of her bag and hauled out the leather satchel which gave her bag its weight. Her shoulder ached already, but she stepped out of the cabin and walked to the bow.

"We can't outrun them." The captain spat over the side. "We'll have to pay their toll." He glared at Bill. "Get the passengers in their cabin."

"Remember how you said God needed to plan better?" Lydia shaded her eyes and peered at the rapidly approaching ship.

"Papa, come back." Aimee hauled at Rodrigo's arm. "I need you."

"I can't let pirates attack the ship."

"They won't attack unless we do something stupid." The captain spat again. "Easier to collect their toll and leave us to sail on so they can stop us again another time."

"I see." Rodrigo's eyes became calculating.

"Champion." Lydia put her hand on his shoulder. "This is not what you are for. Wield your passion for your people. We will meet where the grass grows tall." She pointed ahead of them. "Beyond the mountains to the east, you will meet the tribe of the sword as the Rehego are the tribe of the coin."

"What of the rod and the cup?" Rodrigo whispered hoarsely.

"You know the fate of the people of the cup. Those of the rod lived but are scattered beyond gathering. You've met them. The time of the Four is ending."

"Thank you, Mother." Rodrigo bowed deeply. "May your road be safe."

"Find peace around the fire." Lydia pointed toward the cabin. "Milene is waiting for you."

Aimee dragged Rodrigo at a run to the cabin.

Lydia stood at the rail until the ship arrived, a wolf to the captain's horse. She closed her eyes and sought the peace she'd wished for Rodrigo.

"Ho, the ship." A man in mail with dark red hair tied behind him, streaks of grey in his beard, stood at the bow of his heaving ship as if it were a rock. Other men hauled on oars to bring the ships together.

"Let the sail go slack," the mate ordered. "Heave to."

The captain shouted. "Do you still like the wine?"

The man on the other ship grinned. "You think you will buy passage with a bottle of wine?"

Bill staggered over to the captain with a barrel his arms barely wrapped around. The captain lifted it from the sailor and held it easily.

"I don't know if they call you The Red for your hair or your taste in wine." When the ships slid together, the captain handed the barrel to the man in the wolf-ship.

"Let's see what else you have." He passed the barrel off and made ready to jump aboard.

"It isn't your hair or the wine that names you Red," Lydia said and shuddered, "but the blood you've shed."

The man stopped like he'd been struck by lightning.

"Are you a witch?" He put his hand on his sword.

"No witch, Red One, I'm here by God's hand."

"The weak God of the southerns?" He laughed.

"Weak?" Lydia sighed. "There is more than one kind of strength. You are here to take me on the next step of my journey."

"Really?" The man laughed, but his men muttered behind him. "And where would we be taking you?

"Wherever your ship is going." Lydia dropped the satchel on the deck. Every eye on the wolf-ship stared at it. "With this I am paying my passage. In return, you will let this ship continue in peace."

"And why shouldn't I take both you and ship together?" Red leaned forward again. Lydia swept up the satchel and held it over the side.

"Because if you step foot on this ship, I will drop the satchel into the deep. There is gold enough here to buy this ship twice over." Lydia's arm shook with the strain.

"Done." The man jumped back to his ship, and Lydia hoisted the satchel onto her shoulder.

"Captain, thank you for your service. See the rest of my goods get where they need to be. May the winds stay fair in your sails." She stepped up to the rail, handed Red the satchel, then accepted his help moving from one ship to the other.

"Lads, put the wench in the back."

"Do you go back on your word so quickly?" Lydia met his eyes, forcing her shaking knees to hold her weight. "I gave you the gold, not myself."

"You're a bold one." Red took her chin and held her tight. "I am a man of my word. You are a passenger until we make land. Then you are on your own."

"Agreed." Lydia shivered. The air that felt warm on the Belandrian ship froze her bones on this wolf-ship.

"Laef." A younger blond man stood. Red gave him an order in an oddly fluid language. He took her arm and led her to the stern where he picked a fur-lined cloak and draped it around her.

Red shouted something else to the men, and they hauled at the oars to turn their ship.

Lydia didn't know what was worse, the rough laughter of the men at the oars or the look of pity on Laef's face.

CHAPTER 6

BECOMING THE LADY

"Thank you, that is enough for today." The king stood and the council jumped to their feet. "Lady Prenny, if I may have a moment of your time."

Prenny's gut clenched, maybe she'd been too forward with the discussion of how language changed from noble to commoner. Some of the things she'd said could have offended someone…

"Prenny, dear," Lady Marriette whispered in her ear. "Relax, the king has no compunction about disciplining council members at the meeting. He simply wishes to talk to you."

"Why would he want to talk to me?" Prenny wrinkled her forehead, and her unease travelled from her gut to her chest. Marriette wrapped her arms around Prenny.

"You are the heir to the Duchess of the North."

"I keep forgetting that." Heat travelled up her face. "I mean, I still feel like Prenny, the bandit's brat."

"Oh, she's still in you, but there's also the Prenny who risked her life to aid the kingdom and the one who worked hard to learn to read and write and understand the bigger world around her. Not to mention, Lady Prenny, whose voice is a valued addition to council.”

“What? Me?” Prenny shook her head.

“Yes, you.” Lady Marriette smiled and stepped back. “Many of the councillors are as unaware of the rest of the world, as you were in the forest. You are educating them. Already I’ve heard how a few have been able to resolve long-standing problems because of what you’ve taught. Belandria is changing, and you will be one of those who lead the change.”

“Now I’m truly terrified.” Prenny put her hand on her heart, but she gave a weak laugh. “I’d better not keep the king waiting.”

Heart racing, she pushed open the door the king used to come and go from council. He sat at the corner of the table, a teapot and two cups in front of him.

“Here, sit down, Prenny. Pour tea if you’d like.” He shuffled through papers, setting most of them aside but keeping a handful in front of him.

Prenny poured tea into each cup, then added cream and sugar to hers.

The king picked up his without looking away from the paper in front of him. “Ah, that’s good.” He slid the small stack out of the way. “How are you enjoying council?”

“It isn’t what I expected, Your Majesty.” She sipped at the tea to give herself time to think. “I expected a lot of stuffy old men, arguing about things I didn’t understand.”

The king roared with laughter. “That is a perfect description of what it was like when I started as King. I was terrified.”

“You?” Prenny stared at him.

“Me,” the king sighed and stared into his teacup. “I wasn’t a very good king until Marriette came along and shook all my assumptions. I’m sure you’ve heard the story.”

“Lady Marriette told us in the wagon as we travelled from the bandit camp to my mother’s village.”

“In the same way she overturned assumptions then, as Regent, you and your generation will challenge us old men to think differently.”

Prenny’s head spun, and she held onto the table to keep from falling out of her chair. The king put his hand on her shoulder, and his strength bled into her.

"I'm too young, just gave my oath this spring." Even with the king's strength, she shook helplessly. "What if I do the wrong thing?"

"We all do the wrong thing at times. I'm sure you'll make your share of mistakes, like letting foolish young men push you around. Fury told me the story. I have to admit to wishing I'd been there to watch." The king gave her a gentle shake. "We do what we must, knowing it might be wrong but trusting God to set it right."

"I think I know what you mean." Prenny took a deep breath and drank more of her tea.

"I have a favour to ask of you." The king picked up the small stack of paper. "It is coming up to the time for the king's representative to audit the free-towns. Most of them are doing well, better than I expected, to be honest, but a few are struggling. The man I send to do the audits is very conscientious, and it bothers him that he can't get a handle on what the problem is with those few villages. This year, I'm sending a different person to the ones who are doing fine." He tapped his finger on the larger stack. "I would like you to accompany Yurgens to these few. You will represent the council in this matter."

"What!" Prenny squeaked and grabbed the table again, trying desperately to breathe past the beast raging in her chest.

"You are uniquely qualified, Prenny. I don't expect you to make decisions, but I'm hoping you will show them that we in the capital care about their welfare. If there are things you think will help the situation, talk it over with Yurgens. If need be, send a letter to me asking for council."

"Your Majesty, if I can help in any way, I will."

"That's what I was hoping to hear. You have a courageous heart, Lady Prenny." He slid the small stack of paper to her. "You can read these and get a feel for what the problems are. I will inform Yurgens you will be travelling with him and in what capacity. You have a couple of weeks before you leave, so take some time to ask advice from those you trust."

Prenny picked up the papers. They were cramped with

spidery writing; she'd have to get Lydia to help her. Only Lydia had gone, vanished overnight, and Fury refused to talk about it.

"Do you think Lady Marriette would be willing to meet with me?"

"Of course. She has a great deal of respect for you. Lady Marriette was the strongest voice in council in favour of making you heir. I trust her judgement completely."

"A couple more things." The king pulled something out of his pocket. "You need something to show you are representing the council. This ring should fit, I had it made by the same goldsmith who made your ducal heir's ring. Belandria's crest is engraved on it. You can use it as a seal if you wish."

Prenny slipped it onto her left hand.

"Since you will be travelling with a man, even someone as respectable as Yurgens, I will be sending a maid along with you. She will help with choosing your dresses and whatever else you need. Halonde has assigned Yennet to the task. She will come to your rooms tonight to talk about what you wish to bring."

"Thank you, Your Majesty." She twisted the new ring on her finger.

"That's settled then." The king stood and gathered up the remaining papers. Prenny stood up and curtsied.

After the king left the room, Prenny carried the papers back into the council room.

Lady Marriette sat at the table writing on something.

"How did it go, dear?" She patted the chair beside her. "Come tell me about it."

"I wanted to talk to you anyway." Prenny sat down and took a deep breath, then dove into an explanation of the king's request.

***

Two weeks passed in a heartbeat. Prenny's head was full of advice from people she'd sought out and those who gave her their opinion without her asking.

Fury came to Prenny's rooms the night before they were to leave.

"You be careful." Fury put her hands on her hips. "Don't let anyone push you around. Father is sending you, so don't try to be anyone else. A long time ago, Lydia told me to stop trying to be what everyone wanted."

"Where did she go?"

"She was called away in the middle of the night." Fury slumped on a chair. "I sort of knew she had a special job, but it never occurred to me she'd leave."

She sniffed and rubbed her eyes. "I miss her. I want to know she's all right. She was like my older sister."

Prenny went over and hugged Fury. "You were my first friend here. If there is ever anything I can do for you, just ask."

"Come back." Fury gripped her tight. "Come back. I don't want to lose another person."

"I plan to come back." Prenny ran her hand over the princess's hair.

Fury backed away and brushed the tears from her face.

"I brought something for you." She dug a wide bracelet from her pouch. "Wear this all the time."

"I will." Prenny slid it onto her right arm and turned it around. It was made of hammered tin. A glass chip formed the eye of what Prenny decided had to be a dragon. "Thank you."

"Watch." Fury pushed on the dragon's eye and pulled to the side. The dragon came away from the bracelet forming the hilt of a tiny blade. "The smith was working on it. I asked if I could have it, and he gave it to me." Fury rubbed her eyes. "The Fury in my head told me to give it to you. Don't show anyone how it works."

"I promise." Prenny took the little knife from Fury and returned it to the bracelet. She practiced a few times under Fury's watchful eye. Then the princess left and Prenny went to bed to try to sleep.

* * *

Yurgens spent his time in the coach reading and re-reading reports he kept in his lap desk. Prenny stared out the window at the passing scenery. They headed north, not far from the coast.

"All the places we are visiting are in the north?" Prenny turned away from the view. It hadn't changed since they'd set out that morning from the first inn they'd stayed in.

"Yes," Yurgens said. "I'm relieved you have done some preparation. When the king suggested this, I had my reservations." He glanced over at Yennet who sat sewing on a dress. "But I've heard that you work hard in council and have been willing to listen to advice."

"Do you have any advice?" Prenny folded her hands to keep from fussing. This man probably had grandchildren older than her.

"Your task is different from mine." He put the papers away and closed the lid of his desk. "I am to determine how well the villages are doing economically and decide a fair amount for them to pay in tax." He rapped the desk with a knuckle. "I accomplish that by comparing their current situation to past years. Small changes can make a big difference, so I pay great attention to the details. If I understand your work correctly, you are assessing their social success, or lack of, and then attempt to perceive what is holding them back." He sighed and slid his eyes over to Yennet again.

"I think you have the more difficult task," Yurgens said. "You won't find your answers in numbers. However, if the king feels you are up for the task, then I will trust that you are. I have worked since the days of the king's father, and I will admit King Harald has a much better understanding of his people than his father. So if I were to give you advice, it would be to trust the king. He chose to send you for a reason. Don't worry about becoming Lady Prenny. You are already the Lady Prenny the king needs."

CHAPTER 7

A FORK IN THE ROAD

Leandra watched Raphael play with the black claw, completely unconcerned with what it might mean.

"You all right?" Cameto came up and put an arm around her waist.

"Too much is falling into place too easily." Leandra leaned against him. "I don't trust it."

"Isn't it a good thing? They are happy to talk."

"We haven't said anything yet. I don't even know what they call their people. Xianju spoke of jungles, but they came out of the desert. I don't know how far we'd have to travel to get to a jungle."

"Far." Cameto tilted his head. "The south shore of the Lower Sea is desert, and rumours say it's at least a month's journey to the other side of the desert. The people call it the Sand Ocean."

"Yes, we must leave soon. The winds will change, and the desert will be impossible to cross." Vazee frowned slightly. "Lupji, Pounjou, and Teekja will stay to guard your home."

Leandra's mind went blank. Cameto beside her talked to Vazee.

"May I suggest I stay with those three and introduce them to more of our people? Sharing around a fire is the best way to learn of each other."

"But…" Leandra tried to force her mind to put words together. "How long?"

"The trip to the oasis is only a week, but the storm season lasts for three moons."

Breathe. The coin sent a jolt through her. *You should have expected this.*

You're right. Leandra closed her eyes and felt the ground under her feet. It connected her with her people, whether in the grassland or in Belandria or even farther away across the ocean.

"We can leave as soon as you are ready." A wind shifted in Leandra's soul. She was once again risking her life and people. Change as great as the shattering of the empire hung over her.

Raphael chased Hojiam in a wild game of tag while Xianju laughed. She detected no malice in them. In their own way, they were honest. Since she had started this, she needed to match their honesty.

In less than an hour, Leandra was saying her farewell to Cameto. The runes she'd put on him would last months longer after she made a couple of adjustments. Vazee watched with great interest.

"The runes draw power, usually from the one who draws them. It prevents us from using them foolishly, yet once drawn, it can be possible to have them draw from a different source. In this case, Cameto has agreed to carry the burden. These ones don't take much, so he'll hardly notice it. As he learns the language and the need fades, so will the runes."

"Ah, you are huangoki." Vazee tilted her head and studied Leandra. "You are brave."

"I don't understand the word you used, even with the rune, but power should come with a price, and the user of the power should be the one to pay."

Leandra thought of the ritual she'd worked toward for years, and the idea sickened her now. She didn't think it made her weaker. How she worked now was much more in line with the Balance.

Thinking of the Balance reminded her of Rodrigo. She put a

finger on the Balance to feel his presence.

"Cameto!" Leandra turned to clutch at him. "Rodrigo is on a ship heading to the empire."

"He knows what he's doing." Cameto held Leandra until she stopped shaking.

"Head toward the capital. You'll need to represent the Rehego on the council for now. Introduce our new friends; they are guests of the Rehego." She slipped the coin in its silk pouch into Cameto's hand. "Keep them safe."

"I understand, my Queen." Cameto bowed and kissed Leandra's hand. He jumped on their caravan with Lupji sitting beside him. Pounjou and Teekja were in the back. They were rolling away before Leandra took the reins of the wagon.

***

The wagon crunched over the desert rocks. Mahaloun guided them around any sections of loose ground or sand which could bog the wagon. Xianju, Hojiam, and Vazee perched on the load, taking turns teaching Raphael a game with string.

"We're travelling slower than I'd planned." Mahaloun peered east. "We may be chewing on dust before we arrive."

"I have kerchiefs for Raphael and myself. I'm guessing you are better prepared than we are."

"If everyone packed what they were told to." Mahaloun smiled and cast a glance back at the giggling party on the wagon.

As Raphael snuggled up to Leandra, he chattered on about the day. Hojiam had pointed out snakes and lizards beside the path. Vazee told him stories about the plants. Xianju recited legends from the jungle. Even without the runes helping him, Raphael knew the language almost as well as Leandra.

"Mama, is Hojiam a boy or a girl?"

"I don't know." Leandra squeezed him. "Does it matter?"

"Isn't everyone a boy or a girl?" Raphael wriggled so he could look in her eyes.

"I don't think so." Leandra paused as she tried to decide how to explain. "Some people are all boy or all girl, but others are more in between. What's important is not what we want to call them but what they want us to call them."

"Oh." Raphael stayed quiet so long Leandra thought he'd

gone to sleep. She was looking up at the stars, deep in thought, when he spoke up again. "I'm a boy, right?"

"Is that what you want?"

"I like being a boy." Raphael snuggled closer and this time truly slept.

Leandra hadn't paid attention, but Raphael was right, Hojiam and Pounjou were both referred to by a pronoun which neither Belandrian nor Rehego had, a personal neutral. She could see how it would be useful. She knew more than one Rehego who might have been forced to be something they weren't happy with simply because there was no other choice.

It wasn't just gender. The language of their new friends was much more fluid; things weren't locked into one state. Words changed depending on how certain the label was. Rocks didn't change much, but the words for plants shifted in ways she hadn't figured out yet. It made sense for the way they talked about themselves to be even more changeable. It would explain the importance of names.

She brushed Raphael's hair. He'd alerted her to a possible minefield. Slept found her as she considered the ramifications of what she'd learned.

***

"The sands are shifting." Mahaloun pointed to a cloud on the eastern horizon. "It looks far away, but it will be here by morning."

"How far are we from the oasis?" Leandra resisted the urge to slap the ox into a faster speed.

"Two days." Mahaloun shook his head and looked back at the others. "We may have to drive through the night. Hojiam will take the reins. They have better night sight than the rest of us."

"Perhaps ask them to come forward, and I'll show them how I drive the wagon."

"I expect they know well enough, but it won't hurt." Mahaloun shrugged and hopped off the bench to wait patiently while Raphael and Hojiam finished a discussion on a mouse he'd seen in the shade of a rock. Leandra would have politely interrupted , but she liked the idea of respect for even the boy's endless chatter.

Hojiam dropped onto the bench beside Leandra.

"I'll be driving tonight."

"Do you want to get a feel for her?" Leandra passed Hojiam the reins. They took them with a bright smile.

Leandra spent her time watching for wildlife. Now that she wasn't thinking about the path, many animals became clear. At least this part of the desert was full of life.

The sun set, sending their shadows far across the flat area they drove across. The cloud was a lot closer, looming high in the eastern sky, as beautiful as it was ominous.

"Xianju will keep your kitten safe, but if you have a cloth, get it ready."

"It's in my bag under the seat. A red shawl." Leandra didn't look away from the path. There were patches of soft ground she needed to avoid.

"It is beautiful." Hojiam wrapped it around their head, then pulled it off, looking ashamed.

"No shame in seeing beauty." Leandra glanced at Hojiam.

"I'm zuthi." Hojiam ran their fingers across the fabric.

"My kitten was asking about that," Leandra said.

"I heard. The young are inquisitive. You gave wise answers."

"I only spoke my heart."

"Is that not where wisdom begins?" Hojiam laughed musically. "When I became an adult, I chose to be zuthi. It gives me certain advantages, but it comes with a cost. I must stay balanced, not leaning one way or another, or the elders will ask me to choose again, and I will not be allowed to choose zuthi."

"A difficult situation."

"Perilous too. Most do not survive their second choosing."

"If it is allowed, I would like to learn more about this choosing."

Hojiam put the shawl on Leandra's legs.

"This is not the time."

They rode in silence until Leandra couldn't see well enough to drive. She handed the reins to Hojiam then wrapped the shawl around her head and face and leaned back and closed her eyes. Every Rehego learned how to sleep on the driving bench.

The storm began as a fitful breeze, slapping loose parts of the shawl against Leandra's face. The wind grew stronger and steadier until she could lean against it. Dust filled the air, finding its way under the shawl to fill her nose and get under her eyelids. The sand was a relief until it scraped her hands raw. Leandra tucked them under her arms. It abraded the fabric of her clothes and then her skin.

If she'd thought of it earlier, she might have put a rune on the wagon, but it would have sapped her energy quickly. Hojiam sat like a statue beside her, guiding the ox.

I should have put a cloth on the ox. Too late now. Leandra concentrating on not whimpering from the increasing discomfort. She'd experienced worse pain, but this gave her no respite.

Leandra realized Hojiam was in trouble when she felt the zuthi shaking, then holding onto Leandra to stay upright. She couldn't do anything about the dust or sand, but Hojiam was a different matter. Leandra drew a rune on the zuthi's leg, and strength flowed from her to Hojiam, strength the zuthi needed to withstand the storm.

She huddled into a ball and kept one thought central in her mind: Hojiam needed her.

When the wind cut off, Leandra gasped. The ox lowed mournfully as the weight of the wagon pushed against it. Leandra leaned on the brake to take some of the burden from the beast. Her arms shook by the time the road levelled out.

Lights appeared ahead and resolved into torches as they approached. Hojiam drove the cart into a stone courtyard. The ox went to its knees, then fell on her side. Hojiam slumped against Leandra, letting the reins fall from their hands.

CHAPTER 8

MORE THAN ONE KIND OF TROUBLE

They rolled into Coshport, rain pouring from the sky and wind driving it almost horizontally across the road. Everything Prenny could see was grey. The houses, the sky, the rock, the sea. She fingered the gentle yellow travelling dress she wore. What would the people in this grey village think?

A man in a flapping coat waved them into the largest building in the village. The coach fit with a hand's span between the side and the frame of the door. The rattle of rain on the coach stopped, but the howl of the wind echoed in the building.

The driver opened the door, and Yurgens clambered out. He offered Prenny a hand down. She accepted it gratefully and concentrated on not slipping on the wet steps. Once on the floor, she glanced around. Racks lined the walls and cracks in the walls let in both light and rain. An overwhelming stench of fish hit her nostrils almost making her eyes water. With iron determination, she kept her hands at her side instead of holding her nose.

Yennet stepped beside Prenny and gave her a slight nudge. Prenny's face heated, she was being rude.

The man in the cloak knelt. A woman knelt beside him in a similar cloak, also soaked and dripping.

"My lady," the woman's voice quavered, "we didn't know you were coming. We'd've welcomed you proper."

Prenny stepped forward and lifted the couple's hands so they rose to their feet. They stared at her wide-eyed. Prenny had seen the same look when Chancy ranted at the bandits.

"I am dry," Prenny said, "and thankful for it. I am Lady Prenny, heir to Lady Joan, Duchess of the North. The council has asked me to accompany Yurgens this season to see how we may aid you."

The woman stood open-mouthed as the man's colour returned.

"Lady Joan! She's t' one that defeated a company of mercs?"

"Not all by herself." Prenny grinned. "I will tell you the story later. At this moment I would love something hot to drink."

As she'd hoped, the hint of something practical to do brought the couple out of their daze. They led Yurgens, Prenny and Yennet to a door in one wall.

"After the first audit, we built this guest house onto the fish shed." The man waved his hand at the room. A curtain hid one wall. Heavy wood furniture gave places to sit, and a table and chairs could double as a desk. The best thing was the stove in the centre throwing out welcome warmth.

Prenny ran her hand along the table.

"This is beautiful work. I haven't seen this wood before."

The man beamed and came over to her side. Clattering noises suggested tea was being prepared. He showed her the peg construction and then a piece of firewood to let her feel the bark.

"T' trees come from up the shore. We work wit' Sham's Harbour 'n Seal's Bight to cut them 'n lumber. During t' winter, when we're stuck inside, we make t' furniture and carve. Master Yurgens likes t' plain work, so there's little we c'n show you."

"Later then. I'd love to see how your work is different from our woodsmen's." Prenny took the wrap she'd worn in the coach off, and Yennet lifted it out of her hand and hung it on a hook near the stove to drive the damp out. The two cloaks from her greeters hung nearby. Prenny ran her hand down the cloaks. "I've never felt anything like this."

"My lady, they are made from fish skin." The man reddened and ducked his head.

"It is beautiful and light too." Prenny smiled at the man, then put her hand up to her mouth. "My apologies for my rudeness. I haven't asked your names."

"My lady?" The man blinked at her. "Why'd you want t' know my name? I'm a fisherman."

"I once lived in a forest with bandits." Prenny raised her eyebrow. "God loves us all the same whatever we do."

"I'm called Moz, and t' woman is my bride, Mali." The man wiped at his eyes. "Come sit, Mali has your tea ready."

Prenny followed him to the table where rough plates had been laid out. The cups were carved from wood. Hers had tiny fish swimming on the outside, and the handle looked like vines.

"Moz can't carve nothing without decoratin' it." Mali put a black teapot on a flat stone on the table. A platter had slices of bread and dishes held jams. Another platter held fish fillets.

"Tis plain fare." Mali's hands twisted the sweater she wore.

"Plain fare is just what I need after that journey. The inns served me like a lady, and I went to bed hungry as often as not." She waved Yurgens to a seat. Moz was putting his cloak on.

"I'll let the rest know you're here." He bobbed his head then left back out into the fish shed.

The jams were tart, cutting through the nutty flavoured bread. The fish had a subtle smoky flavour. Before she realized it, Prenny and Yurgens had all but cleared the table.

"Yennet, you must be as hungry as I am. Have the last bit of bread and fish. I haven't left you any jam."

"Thank you, my lady." Yennet curtsied, then helped herself.

Prenny moved from the table to a rocking chair closer to the stove.

"Mali, come sit with me and tell me more about your home."

The woman pulled a chair over and perched on the edge.

"We fish when the weather's fine. It's not much of a living. In the fall, the women pick berries and the men hunt, or we'd starve. Like Moz said, in the winter the men carve, and the women knit." She ran a hand over her sweater.

Now that she could get a closer look, Prenny saw complex designs covering it - cables, flowers, balls.

Moz returned with some other people. They drew instruments from under their cloaks and played tunes which had Prenny tapping her toes.

They took Yurgens away, leaving Yennet and Prenny alone in the guest house. Mali stayed to keep the fire burning.

***

Yennet woke Prenny in the morning and helped her dress. Though she wore her heaviest wool, she still shivered until Mali stirred up the fire for breakfast.

"Mali, I would like to buy one of your sweaters. It will keep me warmer in the coach than my cloak."

"My girl's taking one off t' needles should fit you. She'd be glad to give it to you."

"Mali," Prenny started to argue, but Yennet shook her head from behind the woman. "I would be delighted to accept your gift. But I would be a poor guest if I took advantage of your kindness. Allow me to purchase other goods from you." Mali turned pink but nodded.

Yurgens returned with a sour-faced man who sat at the table with him.

"Vrank here owns the store." Yurgens introduced the man, who frowned at Prenny.

"What do we need with girls telling us how to live?"

"This is the Lady Prenny, heir to the North." Yennet stepped in front of Vrank and caught his gaze. Though she made no movement, he paled then turned to bow to Prenny.

"My apologies, Lady Prenny." Prenny nodded, not trusting her voice to conceal the instant dislike she'd taken to the man. Her opinion didn't improve as the man complained about the shiftiness and laziness of the folk of the village, how they didn't pay their debts on time.

When he finally left, Prenny had a headache from holding her tongue.

"My pardon, good folks, but I would like to consult with

Master Yurgens in private. Perhaps you could return at supper time." The men who had stood in stolid silence while Vrank had insulted them bowed and filed out. As the door closed behind them, Prenny couldn't hold her disgust in any longer. "Is he always like this?" She paced through the room.

"He is the only merchant in town. As such the villagers need to trade with him for any goods which come from the outside."

"I bet he overcharges for the goods, then interest on top of that."

"You wouldn't be wrong." Yurgens organized his papers. "But they would be much worse off without him. It is easier for one person to bring in all that is needed. If they were to try to order each on their own, they'd likely pay as much or more."

"You understand these things better than I do, I'm sure." Prenny took a breath. "But it feels like he's set himself up like a noble in the village but without any of the responsibility. What is good for him is not good for the rest of the people. We're here because these folks are so poor, they can't pay even the minimum tax. Does the merchant pay any tax on what he makes?"

"I don't believe so." Yurgen's eyes widened. He looked through his notes. "You are correct, my lady."

"If he was a noble, with the income he makes, what would he pay in tax?"

"Interesting question, and not one with an easy answer. Of course, he isn't a noble, but leaving that aside, there is still the matter of what responsibility he has to the crown and to the village. However, it is a matter which may be worth discussing with the council."

"Thank you, Yurgens. I will write my conclusions, and I'd like you to note your own. Let's give the council as much information as we can to help them in their discussion."

Prenny bought several carvings, a second sweater, two of the fishskin cloaks and would have bought more if Yurgens hadn't reminded her this was only the first village. She reluctantly agreed but hoped the little she purchased would help.

The next two villages were remarkably similar to Coshport, and Prenny bought more from each one. The merchant in Sham's Harbour was a cheerful man, but his books didn't look much different than the one in Coshport. In Seal's Bight, a woman ran the store and made the first two look generous in comparison.

Prenny took notes, and ideas began forming in her head. When the driver complained at how much Prenny was buying, she informed him they formed part of her report, then bought a sweater and fish cloak for him to stay warm and dry on the journey.

They spent two days on the road to reach the next village. Tasnent's Arm looked more prosperous than the first three. No one came to meet them, and they had to run through the ever-present rain to a squat building that grandly proclaimed itself to be the Inn on the Arm.

The food in the inn was as bland as the cooking at the other villages had been delicious. It was all imported from the city and not cooked well. Rough laughter came from the common room.

"I would like a bath," Prenny said. "The common room sounds like more than I could handle."

"I will inform the innkeeper." Yennet curtsied. She vanished into the noisy room.

A young boy appeared and bowed.

"Bat's ready, milady"

"I will have a drink before bed." Yurgens stretched. "Enjoy your bath."

The boy led Prenny to the back of the inn. He opened a door and waved her in. A chill breeze came through the door, and Prenny didn't see any sign of a bath. Her stomach clenched. This wasn't right. She turned to go back to the front of the inn, but strong arms wrapped around her and a bag came down over her head. Before she had a chance to scream, she'd been carried into the cold room and lowered through the floor. The trapdoor closed quietly, then scraping sounded as furniture moved above her.

Her abductors carried her away. Water dripping on stone was the only sound aside from the slap of feet. Hinges creaked, then Prenny was set on her feet and roughly pushed forward. The hinges squeaked as a door thudded into place. The bang of a bar rang like a seal of doom.

CHAPTER 9

LANDING

"There is Getthelm." Laef pointed into the distance. He'd appointed himself Lydia's caretaker and language instructor. She'd picked up enough to know that Getthelm was trouble. Red gave strict instructions to his crew to keep double watch, and no one was to travel alone on the streets.

Lydia closed her eyes at the thought of surviving on streets that made these wolf-ship sailors nervous.

I hope I end up in the right place. She'd given up on hearing a reply. God spoke to her only when needed. That silence meant she travelled the right track was scant comfort, yet it was all she had.

The shore grew closer and she could pick out individual ships, mostly what she thought of as wolf-ships but some like the one they'd taken her from. As they slid up to an empty place on the wharf, men in mail with swords at their hip stalked up to the ship.

"Red." One of them frowned while the other scanned the ship. "Didn't you find enough trouble the last time you were here?"

"I have a passenger who paid well for transport here. Let the thane know I will pay my debt."

The men stepped back, and other men shoved a ramp out to drop on the wharf.

"Off, girl, I'm done with you." Red pointed at the wharf.

Lydia handed the fur cloak to Laef and wrapped her arms around herself in an attempt to keep the cold wind from freezing her.

"A slave will not pay your bill." One of the men on the wharf glared at Red.

"Not a slave, a freewoman passenger," Lydia spoke as firmly as possible through her already chattering teeth.

"Throw her a cloak. She's no use dead."

"She leaves with what she brought onboard." Red crossed his arms belligerently.

"Very well, leave before the harbourmaster learns you're here and claims your boat."

"I have business here."

"Not unless I say you do."

The men glared at each other, neither budging until Lydia half expected them to draw swords and attack each other.

"Laef." Red didn't turn away. The young man carried the cloak and wrapped it around Lydia. When he returned to the ship, Red backhanded him, sending him to the deck.

Laef stood and met Red's contemptuous eyes.

"I've sailed from shore to shore. I will take what I am due here."

"Like hell you will." Red's hand dropped to his sword.

"Red," another sailor said. "It is the law; he has the right."

"I'll not pay—"

"If you set yourself above the law, I'll not sail with you." The man stood and towered over Red. Half the rest of the men also stood. The grinding of Red's teeth carried over the slap of the waves on the wharf.

"Pay him." Red snarled and pointed at Laef. "If we meet again, there will be bloodshed."

"As you will." Laef picked up a pack and waited as the oldest man in the crew counted out his share. Men piled skins, fabrics and more on the dock. "The gold, Red."

"That was paid to me." Red drew his sword.

"Did you row the boat yourself? Did you give up your share of the food to feed her?"

Red charged at Laef, and Lydia winced, thinking she was about to see his murder.

Laef whipped out his sword and kicked up the shield that leaned against his leg. Red's sword screeched as it slid off the shield. Laef slammed the shield into Red's face, but the older man didn't step back. He slashed again, and Laef caught the blow on the shield. This time he cut back, and most of Red's beard floated to the deck.

"Next one takes your head."

"Go." Red spat at the younger man. "If I see you again, you will die."

"One of us will." Laef sheathed his sword and picked up his bag. He walked to the old man and put out his hand. The old man dropped several coins into Laef's palm. Red screamed and ran at Laef with his sword held up.

Lydia shouted, but the big man gripped Red's arm.

"Stop, you shame us."

Red punched the big man, who shrugged and then lifted Red off the deck to slam him down across his knee. The crack of Red's back breaking echoed off the buildings behind Lydia. The sword clattered to the deck, then the big man tossed Red over the side. He sank into the water.

"Do you want the sword?" The big man asked Laef.

"Mine is good enough."

No one else on the crew wanted it, so it followed Red into the harbour.

"His gear apart from his share in the voyage?"

"Give it to the passenger. Red shamed the *Red Wolf* by barely keeping the least of his word." Laef nodded at her.

The rest of the crew nodded, and a bag like Laef's only much larger soon lay on the dock beside Lydia. She handed Laef his cloak and put on the much finer one belonging to Red. This one had a hood lined with fur, which she pulled up. Lydia stood straighter now that she wasn't shivering in the icy wind.

"Let the thane know the *Red Wolf* will pay the debt," the big man said.

"I will." The warrior picked up the large bag beside Lydia. "The thane will want to meet you."

The road wound up a hill to a level field. Lydia expected something like the palace in Belandria, perhaps smaller, but the building that greeted them looked like a wolf-ship flipped over and put on walls. They led her to double doors standing open to the cold. A couple of men were gambling off to one side.

"Guards?" Lydia pulled her cloak tighter around her. If anything, the wind was colder up here.

"Thane's too proud to have guards, but there's always men gambling there."

Heat struck like a blow as they passed through the door. The smell of men, dogs and food followed after. They wound past empty tables with dogs sleeping beneath. A couple of women in grey dresses swept the wooden floor. Fires burned in stone fireplaces along both long walls.

At the far end, a man lounged on a chair with cup in his hand. He glanced up when they came in and straightened in the chair. He held the cup out and a young boy darted forward to fill it from a skin. By the time Lydia and her escort reached the man, the boy held another cup.

"Who is this?" The thane had iron-grey hair, and his beard was more white than grey, but he didn't look soft. Despite the cup in his hand, his eyes were clear and sharp.

"A passenger the *Red Wolf* brought to our docks." The man who had done all the talking spoke. The other put the bag down beside Lydia, then left without a glance at the Thane.

"The *Red Wolf*?" The thane banged the arm of his chair. "I'll have his skin."

"Ogre sends a message. 'The *Red Wolf* will pay his debt.'"

"And why is the Ogre sending such a message?"

"He has taken the ship. Red Wolf is back-broken at the bottom of the harbour."

"Pity, I would like to have done him in myself." The thane looked over Lydia. "Take that cloak off and let me see you properly." He addressed Lydia in Imperial.

"My thane," Lydia curtsied, "I am a freewoman. I paid my

passage to your shore with the gold the Red will use to pay his debt." She pushed her hood back and met the thane's eyes.

"How can I be your thane if I've never seen you?" Something that might have been a smile curled his lips.

"I travelled to this shore to serve you as a freewoman."

"And what skills would I need from this freewoman?"

"I read and write in the Imperial language and the Belandria dialect. I have been trained in numbers and have some small skills in healing."

"And for this I'm supposed to do what? Keep you in gold and furs?"

"What I have is more than enough." Lydia slid her cloak from her shoulders. "You see, no gold, no fur, other than what the Red Wolf owed for his pitiful word."

"Why should I not take you and your goods?"

"Because a thane should be more honourable than the Red Wolf. He thought to cheat me by twisting the bargain we'd made, but God used his greed to bring me where I needed to be."

"Your god?" The thane leaned back. "I have no place for the weak southern god. We worship warriors, those who fight the hunger, cold, and dark."

"And so you should," Lydia said. "I am not one to claim only I am right in how I see the world. I will not insult you nor your gods." She smiled slightly. "But you may find God is not as weak as you think."

"Your God is no warrior."

"God is not mine; I am God's."

"I think I might like you, woman. What is your name?"

"I am called Lydia."

"Well, Lydia, have a drink to seal our deal." He waved the young boy forward, and she took the cup from him. He frowned at her. "Why don't you drink? Do you think I would poison you?"

"You wish me to drink to seal a deal. I must know the nature of our agreement before I can agree."

The thane roared with laughter.

"I've caught more than one captain, but you slip of a girl, you have courage. I will take you as a member of my household. No one will dare harm you as long as you follow the law. You eat and drink at my table. In return, you use your skills as I direct."

"I agree." Lydia sipped at the cup. It wasn't the wine she expected but a sweet drink that made her think of summer.

"Let me see what you've brought me." The thane pointed at the bag. The warrior dumped it out on the floor. Knives and arrowheads clattered among jewellery. Stones with runes cut in them rolled across the floor. Leather gloves and other bits of clothing tumbled in a heap.

The thane stood up, walked to the pile, and pushed things about with his toe. He picked out a couple of the pieces of gold jewellery and one of the knives. The arrowheads and the runes he swept aside. The clothing he pushed into a separate pile.

"Lydia, keep the rest of the jewellery. I'll not have people say I can't keep my house. You'll need a knife if you don't already have one, to eat if nothing else." He picked up the bag and gave it a shake, then reached in to pull out a scroll. He handed it to Lydia. "Boy, put the clothes in the bag. Your family can have them." The boy eagerly did as he was bid, carefully placing a ring to one side when it clattered out of a shirt. "Now, the arrowheads and stones, go throw them from the cliff's edge. I'll not have them weaken my house." The boy bowed and gathered up the things and ran from the hall.

Lydia picked up the ring and handed it to the thane.

"Loyalty and honesty should be rewarded. When you free the boy, give him this ring."

"What makes you think I would do such a thing?"

"I think you are more generous than you let the world believe."

The thane put the ring on his smallest finger and returned to his seat.

"Take a seat and tell me of your journey." He flicked a hand at the warrior, dismissing him. The boy returned, blowing on his fingers to warm them. He took a seat on a stool against the wall behind the thane.

Lydia told of how she was wakened from a deep sleep to be sent across the ocean. The thane roared with laughter when she told how she'd held the gold over the ocean to force the Red to give his word.

"I wish I'd been there to see his face."

"He was not pleased, but the reaction of his crew if he lost the gold was more worrisome. The gold still cost him his crew and his life."

"Are you going to tell me how gold is evil and will corrupt me unless I give it to your God?"

"My thane, you are not so foolish as to value gold over your life or honour."

"You are the strangest God's woman I have met. Even my own priests are always wanting a portion of my goods."

"Free offerings are true gifts, but how can a god be god if they must extort gold from their people? It is a human weakness that does such, and the humans who serve God's church are as weak as any other."

"I knew I was going to like you."

CHAPTER 10

A DARK PLACE

Prenny rolled into a sitting position and shrugged her way out of the bag they'd carried her in. After feeling her way to the wall, she folded the sack and sat on it hoping it would insulate her from the cold floor.

It didn't work. She stood up and steadied herself on the wall. The same rough stone formed the walls as made the floor, at least as far as her fingers could tell. The darkness was absolute. It made no difference if her eyes were open or closed. For something to do, Prenny felt her away around the room. She had three paces across and four in from the door.

Everything was rock except for the door. The wood of the door pushed in slightly. Not oak, but some lighter wood, maybe the same stuff the other villages used for carving. If she had a knife.

The men had pushed her into the room without searching her. Fury's bracelet still wrapped around her wrist. After some fumbling to find the right spot, she had the tiny knife in her hand.

With nothing else to do while time passed, Prenny dug away

at the wood next to the stone. It carved more easily than she expected, but she needed to widen the hole several times to reach in to cut deeper.

Her fingers ached, and she was sure blisters covered them, but it kept her occupied. When a pinpoint of light shone through the door, it took a moment for her to figure out that she'd made it through the door. With renewed energy, Prenny hacked away at the door, holding the knife in a death grip so she wouldn't drop it. When she thought the hole was big enough for her hand to fit, she reached through. The tips of her fingers brushed the bar just above the hole.

After more work, she could lift the bar slightly but not enough to move it away from the door. Tears leaked from her eyes, and she almost kicked the door.

"Think, girl." Prenny paced the room, but all she could come up with was to make the hole bigger. In her hurry, the knife slipped from her hand and clattered to the stone outside the door. She wanted to scream in frustration. Instead, she reached through the hole.

Once again, she could lift the bar but not enough to dislodge it. Then when she tried pushing up to try to throw the bar over the hooks, it moved to the left a finger's breadth. She repeated the action.

Her arms and legs cramped. The bar hit the tips of her fingers, bruising them. Yet bit by bit, it slid to the left. The sudden weight of the bar on her hand pushed her wrist into the jagged wood on the bottom of the hole. Then it skidded to the right leaving splinters in her fingers before the other end fell from the hook, the bar crashing to the floor with such a noise, she feared they'd hear it in the inn.

She didn't plan on waiting to find out. Prenny pushed the door open, snatched up her knife and returned it to her bracelet. If they heard anything, they would come from uphill. A lantern hung on a peg across the hall. After wrapping the bag around her hand, she lifted the lantern from the peg and headed down the slope.

Crashing waves sounded ahead, then she reached the end of the tunnel. A ladder led down into the waves. There was no way out that direction. Swimming in a river was a far cry from fighting the wildness of this ocean.

Prenny headed back up the tunnel, then spotted an opening to her right, missed earlier because she was too intent on the open air at the end of the tunnel. She slipped into it to explore. It opened into a space the size of the fish shed in Coshport. Boxes and bins were stacked haphazardly in the space. Crates held bottles of wine; others held bolts of fabric. A table in the corner had a stale loaf of bread and dried-up cheese. Prenny munched on them as she explored. The room was a treasure trove holding things she hadn't imagined finding this far north.

Then shouting came from up the tunnel. The men were back. Prenny searched for a hiding place, but nothing satisfied her. The men would find her. She backed up against the wall and knobs of stone poked into her back.

Before she could lose her nerve, Prenny blew out the lantern, then holding it in her teeth, she started climbing the wall. Even Fury couldn't climb like Prenny; it didn't matter if it was rocks, walls or trees.

Her reaching hand felt a ledge, more of a crack in the wall. Prenny squirmed her way into the tiny space only to find it stretched back further than she expected. Lying still as a mouse, she watched light play across the bit of ceiling in her view.

" 'oo knew she had a knife on 'er."

"She's a nob, t'ey all have blades."

" 'ow come she didn't fight then?"

"You gonna fight wit' a bag over ye'r head?"

"Enough, she didn't go up the tunnel. The only way out that direction is through the inn, and the table hadn't moved."

Prenny knew that voice. Anger warmed her. The traitor. But it made sense. Someone had to transport the smuggled goods to the city for sale. The poor people here wouldn't be paying for it.

"If she went in t' drink, we're scuppered."

"Search the room, every box and crate. Find her. Drowned in the ocean, she's no risk. Alive, she'll see we all hang."

Banging and clattering came from below along with cursing when a bottle smashed.

"Right, you two stay here. Move from this spot I'll slit your throats myself."

Prenny cursed silently, and her elbow knocked the lantern

making it scrape against the rock.

"You 'ear that?"

"She's here, right as rain."

"You go fetch t' boss. I'll stay to keep t' mouse cornered."

Prenny inched back trying to keep as much rock as possible between her and the room. Her feet slid off rock into open space. She clutched at the sides of the crack to hold herself still.

Cold air chilled her ankles, and rain soaked the hem of her dress. There was a way out, if it didn't kill her. Gritting her teeth with the effort, Prenny pulled herself back up the slope enough to brace her body with her feet. Using the knife, she cut away her skirt above her knees and immediately shivered as the cold air hit her legs.

The knife clicked back into the bracelet, and Prenny planned her next move. The best thing would be to go headfirst, but the space was too tight to turn. She squirmed onto her back and felt the roof. It was much rougher than the floor, giving her solid handholds.

Inch by inch, she lowered herself down the slope. Just as her knees left solid rock, her feet hit something. Prenny rested until her hands stopped shaking, then kicked off her shoes. From there, it was a matter of inching along until her feet started finding cracks and knobs to take her weight. She braced her back against one side of the crevice, her feet on the other, then started up.

Fortunately, the climb was only twice her height.

Once at the top, she could see the lights of the inn. Prenny ran from rock to rock until she came to the first house, then crept along the walls. No one was out in the icy rain. She darted across to where the coach was parked under a roof. She crept up and opened the back compartment of the coach and pulled out a dry pair of pants, a sweater and a fishskin cloak. Changing took seconds and the dry clothes let her warm up. They'd be down searching again, maybe finding the crack. They might think she'd fallen, but they might not.

She couldn't trust anyone in the inn, not the driver, only Yennet. How to get a message to her maid? Prenny followed the wall of the inn until she found a door. It opened into the room where they'd snatched her. The table had been pushed aside.

No sound came through the door. *How long have I been gone?* Prenny had no idea. When she cracked the door open, a buzz of voices came from the common room. Dared she try to find Yennet? Could they all be enemies?

She crawled along the hall, wincing at every loud laugh. A hand reached out of a doorway and yanked her in. Cold steel lay against her throat.

"What have you done with Lady Prenny?" Yennet's hiss was colder than the rain.

Prenny held up her wrist with the bracelet. "It's me, Yennet."

The steel vanished, and Yennet's strong arms held her tight. "We must let Master Yurgens know you're safe. He's frantic with worry."

"I'll bet." Prenny pushed herself up. "He'll be even more frantic when he learns I've escaped."

Yennet went still.

"Who do we trust?"

"I don't know, not the driver for sure. The tunnel starts in the inn. Everyone could be in on the smuggling."

"It's a stretch from smuggling to abduction," Yennet growled. "We deal with this ourselves."

"There are two men - they have different accents so maybe from different villages - and Yurgens." Prenny counted on her fingers." Someone made sure I ended up where they wanted me. What did they tell you?"

"A maid said you were relaxing in the bath and had asked to be left alone while you soaked."

"Mother made the mercenaries think she was weak until they were close enough to hit."

"What do you have in mind?"

"We jam the trapdoor. The only way out is into the ocean or the way I got out, and I'm certain they won't be able to fit."

"That keeps three of them out of trouble until low tide."

"Low tide?"

"There is probably a beach at the base of that ladder and maybe another path up the cliff."

"So we don't have any time to waste." Prenny stood up and brushed herself off. "I need to change. You have my dress in our room?”

Yennet led her to the room and helped Prenny change.

“Watch to see who reacts when I stroll into the common room. We order them held. The people have the choice of obeying my order or committing treason. They may be smugglers, but I doubt they are all killers.”

“And if you’re wrong?”

“We go down fighting.”

“My lady.” Yennet curtsied but had a predatory smile on her face. “What you see is a secret.” She opened Prenny’s trunk, then pulled out the lining of the lid. Behind were knives, a folding bow, arrows and more.

“Nice.” Prenny lifted out the bow and set it up and gave an experimental pull. “It would be a good squirrel bow.” She picked up the arrows. “If you give me my wrap, I can hide these beneath it.”

“Don’t hesitate.” Yennet stowed a surprising number of knives in her maid’s livery. “I’ll take care of the trap door and be right behind you.” Yennet loped out of the room.

Prenny walked down the stairs breathing slowly, pasting a smile on her face. She hardened herself and walked into the common room.

The driver turned pasty white, then bolted for the door. As he reached forward, Prenny’s arrow pinned his hand to the wood.

“If anyone else has a mind to commit treason.” Prenny held the bow with an arrow fitted loosely.

“Drop the bow unless you want to see your maid die.”

Prenny spun and put an arrow into the innkeeper’s eye, continued around to point her next arrow at a big fisherman who backpedalled into a table, tipping it over and sending drink cascading onto him.

“Treason is punishable by death.” Prenny scanned the room. “If you aid me, I will recommend mercy. If I fail to return, the king’s soldiers will raze this village. Choose now.”

One by one, the people in the room went to their knees.

“We didn’t wan’ nothin’ to do with Yurgens’ plan, but his men would kill us without a thought.” A woman Prenny guessed to be the innkeeper’s wife had tears running down her face.

"We will deal with them. How many are in the village?"

"I'm Garr'son my Lady. There's two aside from the innkeeper," the man who had fallen into the table said. "The rest are on a ship due tomorrow night."

"Then this is what you're going to do." Prenny pointed at the driver, still staring in shock at his hand. "You will bind him securely. Deal with his hand. I want him alive to face the king's justice. Then you will go to your homes and stay there. Anyone I see outside I will assume is a traitor, and they will die."

The people in the room pulled the driver away from the door and tied him up. They carried him out into the night. Others carried away the innkeeper. Prenny recovered her arrows.

"If we charge in without a plan, we'll be in trouble." Yennet leaned against a wall. "Are you sure there were no other exits?"

"Yurgens said as much when they were looking for me. There is the open water, but that would likely be as fatal as my arrows."

"Do we open the trapdoor and go down and fetch them out?"

"Not quite." Prenny sat at a table she focused on the problem to keep from thinking about the blood on her arrows. "They could hole up in the storeroom. There are weapons in there. It would be a nuisance if they were still free when the ship arrives. I will climb back down and get into the room. From the ledge, I can cover most of the room. You come down the tunnel in silence. Use your best judgement from there. I'll need some time to get in position." She stood up and looked at her clothes. "I'll change into something more suitable."

CHAPTER 11

THE KING'S JUSTICE

Getting back into the crack was easier than getting out. Prenny shivered. She'd regretfully left the heavy sweater in the room. It would have been in the way.

She peeked over the edge to check where the men were. Their angry voices covered any noise she made.

"You idiots can't even keep one little girl in check."

"Told ye, I heard somethin' up t'ere." The man pointed up at Prenny then choked as he tried to shout. Yurgens looked up and saw Prenny.

"Like a mouse in a hole." He shoved one of the men toward a crate. "There's crossbows there. Climb up and shoot her."

Prenny put an arrow into the man's leg just above the knee. The man squealed and fell to the floor. The other man ran out of the room. Yurgens ducked behind the crate holding the crossbows. The complaint of the wood being torn apart sounded over the wounded man's whining.

"You aren't the only one who can shoot," Yurgens said. "I

grew up hunting. Killed deer from fifty paces." He loaded a crossbow, then two more. "You might get lucky once, but not twice."

The first bolt slammed into the rock above Prenny, sparking before it jammed into her side. She gasped, but it was the broken end of the bolt that scraped her. The spark gave her an idea. The lantern stood to the side of the opening. She lifted the glass and slammed the bolt into the rock. After a few tries, one caught, and she turned up the wick.

"Come on, it's your turn!" Yurgens called up to her.

Prenny threw the lantern toward his voice, hoping to keep his attention until Yennet arrived. She was rewarded by cursing. Scuttling forward, she had her bow drawn before she got to the edge. In the brief second she had to aim, he lifted the crossbow. The fire had missed him, landing on a pile of fabric. Too late to go back. Prenny fired her shot and dove forward out of the crack, the bolt drawing a line of pain along her back as she curled to land on her feet. The stone floor hit hard, sending pain up her left leg. The bow clattered away as she rolled to give him a harder target, but no crossbow snapped, no bolt pinned her to the floor.

"With a bit more training, you'd be scary." Yennet offered her hand to lift Prenny up. "I doubt I could have made that shot." She nodded to where Yurgens lay on the floor. One of Yennet's knives stuck out of his neck, and Prenny's arrow pierced his heart. Yennet tied up the man with Prenny's arrow in his leg, then roughly bound the wound.

"I'll send someone down to haul him up to the inn." They dragged him into the tunnel where he wouldn't choke on smoke from the burning fabric.

Yennet put her arm around Prenny and helped her back to the inn.

***

"The ship will stand off away from the rocks." Garr'son drew lines on the table with his finger. Apparently almost being killed by Prenny had caused something of a religious conversion. He was determined to help them put an end to the smugglers. "They'll come in two boats with the goods. There's not much time to land, unload, and get off safely."

70

"What's the signal to bring them in?" Yennet played with one of the cups. As far as the villagers knew, Prenny had taken the three men alone, but Yennet kept a close eye on them.

"Lantern hung on the ladder. It guides them in, too."

"How many men?"

"Eight, four in each boat. They'll expect as many on the beach to help unload."

Prenny frowned. "I need them to surrender immediately. A fight will only get more people hurt."

"Cove was chosen to make it hard to ambush. Only way in is by sea or that ladder. Can't be seen from above."

"Fishing boats." Prenny tapped the table. "Wait out of sight until the boats have passed, then close in behind them. Put a couple of crossbows on each. I need a stronger bow and hunting arrows. I'll be at the top of the ladder. The men on the beach will have white paint on their backs so I know who to shoot. They get one warning shot, then they surrender or die."

***

The smugglers surrendered after the first shot from the fishing boats behind them. They were tied and put in the room where Prenny had been held. She left them a lantern. Garr'son stood guard outside the room. The men yelled threats through the door.

"We have a problem." Prenny sat in their room with Yennet. "From the threats the captives have been yelling, they expect the ship to return to rescue them. They still think it's a double-cross by the village. The smugglers are short eight men, but we don't know how many are on the ship. I don't want to leave the village vulnerable to retribution nor do I want them to free the men and bribe the smugglers to leave them alone."

"Make the smugglers think there is nothing left to attack," Yennet said. "You're going to need to make it convincing."

***

"The ship's in a cove up the shore. It isn't a good landing, but it will do in a pinch." Garr'son ran into the inn common room. "Looks like twenty of them getting ready to come down the coast to the village. They have swords and bows."

"Very well," Prenny sighed. "Let the women and children know to stay back in the hills to the north. No tracks, no sound.

Light the fires, then take your position. No heroics." She watched the big man leave. The last handful of men in the village followed him away, keeping out of sight.

"We need to get to our place." Prenny stood and led the way out the back door of the inn. The coach had been moved up onto the hill where the road overlooked the town.

They'd built a crude stockade across the hill. Gallows lined the hill. The closest to the village held the men who had died fighting Prenny. The others held dummies. Smoke poured from a few of the houses. Yennet lit the oil on the floor of the inn as they left. By the time they reached the coach, the village looked like a war zone. The men of the village moved around behind the stockade. Garr'son yelled random orders.

The line of twenty men swaggered into sight, then stopped in a bunch. Hands pointed up to the stockade and the gallows. An argument broke out with men shouting at each other. Some of them didn't wait for their leaders to make up their minds; soon even those arguing followed. An hour later, Garr'son reported the ship had sailed to the east.

They spent the rest of the day fighting the fires. Three of the houses were a total loss along with the inn.

"Hold the men until the king's soldiers arrive. If you follow my instructions exactly, I will ask King Harald to grant you pardons. I expect you will be put under rule from the capital at least until you have proven your loyalty to Belandria."

"My Lady Prenny," the innkeeper's wife stepped forward, then knelt. "I pledge loyalty to the king and Belandria and will accept whatever punishment is given us." The rest of the people knelt, many with tears running down their faces.

Prenny climbed up on the seat of the coach. She'd had some opportunity to drive teams before she came south to give her oath and learn about her duties as heir. With any luck, the coach wouldn't be too much different.

Yennet jumped up beside her.

"Let's go."

Prenny snapped the reins and they set off. She refused to look back at the columns of smoke still rising from the village.

***

The Council stared at Prenny with open mouths, while the king held hands over his face. Lady Marriette looked to be struggling with a fit of giggles.

Prenny sat straight in the dress Yennet had insisted she wear. Prenny hadn't been aware she owned such an elegant garment but gave thanks for it. Since she'd officially been sent by the council, her report was to them. She'd sent a capsule report to King Harald giving only the highlights.

King Harald straightened and took a deep breath.

"We have a few questions."

Prenny's hands clenched on the table.

"Leaving aside the question of Yurgens' treachery, that is easily checked now we know to look for it. The burning of a village—"

"Only part," Prenny lifted her head. "Three houses and the inn. No one will be without shelter this winter."

"Thank you, Lady Prenny." King Harald's glance should have turned her to ash on the spot. "The burning of three houses and an inn is not something allowed to nobles, never mind heirs who are representatives of council to *free*-towns."

She kept her gaze on the king.

"Your Majesty." A man in uniform leaned forward. "If I may?"

"General Huston, I invited you here for your input."

"If we leave aside the legality of Lady Prenny's actions, she repelled a large force with minimal loss to property and no loss of life. The situation arose through actions of the people of the village. Listening behind Prenny's words, I suspect the people were fully in support of her plan. They did outnumber her if they wished to do something different. If she were my subordinate, I would be commending Lady Prenny on her quick thinking and tactical brilliance."

"Lady Prenny, did the villagers agree to your actions?"

She closed her eyes. It would be so easy to just nod her head.

"I didn't ask, Your Majesty," Prenny sighed. "They had been engaged in activities that had nearly cost my life and which I saw as treachery. They had the choice of doing what I said or dealing with the smugglers on their own."

"If they had said no, what would you have done?" Lady Marriette leaned back in her chair.

"I would have taken Yennet and left the village, then sent a message at the earliest opportunity for soldiers to respond to protect the other villages which the smugglers might have decided to attack."

"You seriously considered the other villages to be at risk?"

"Once they successfully burn one village, what is to stop pirates from attacking the others?" duSarche rubbed his neck. "We had pirate troubles in your father's day, Your Majesty. Don't know where they came from, but we fortified the port and abandoned the rest until the pirates decided there was nothing left worth taking. Took years to rebuild." He shook his head. "I've already sent a message to my son. We'll have ships flying the Belandrian flag on that coast within the week."

"What would you need to build a proper navy?" General Huston asked.

"We have ships we could repurpose, so most of the work would be training. There are a few refugees from the empire who were navy. They'd be worth recruiting."

"We will leave the development of a navy in your capable hands, Lord duSarche. Bring a request for resources to council. This is something we should have been working on years ago." King Harald rubbed his eyes. "Given General Huston's comments, we will leave the question of the village. The skirmishers have been sent north. They will report and, if needed, we will pick up the issue again with that report in hand."

"You suggest leaving the merchants in place even though they conspired with Yurgens?" Raspin deLanguiers made a note on his paper. "Why?"

"There are a few reasons, my lord." Prenny gathered her thoughts. "First, there is no one else. Removing the merchants would cause great hardship to those villages. They are the only ones with the money and connections to bring goods to those remote locations. Even if we were to start today to replace them, it would take considerable time to earn the trust of the villagers and to learn what they need. Secondly, the crime of bribing a government official is nowhere near treachery. Yurgens recorded the bribes paid, but he did not say whether he demanded the money or if it was offered. What is certain is that the arrangement goes back at least to the creation of the villages as free-towns."

She bit back hasty words and breathed slowly until Raspin began tapping the table impatiently.

"The last reason is the merchants filled a void. I did some research when I got home. It didn't take long to learn they never wanted to be free villages. The count who held that coast under Lord duSarche abandoned them as too poor to be worth his time. Even prior to that, he paid minimal attention to the needs of his people. Five years ago, he was removed for being a fringe part of the treachery which injured Lady Joan. No one but Yurgens has given those people the slightest thought since."

"duSarche?" King Harald raised an eyebrow.

"I confess, I do not know, which strongly suggests Lady Prenny is correct." The old man lowered his head. "I must admit to struggling with my duties the last few years. I had planned to ask permission for my son to be installed as duke in my stead."

Murmurs went around the table.

"We will miss your sage advice, yet we do not wish to hold you to work which discomfits you. We will speak further in private." The king frowned. "Is there someone you can appoint to the northern shore?"

"To be honest, Your Majesty, no one who would do the job properly."

"Your Majesty, perhaps we might have a word in private," Lady Marriette lifted a hand, "and invite Lord duSarche to join us."

"Very well. We will take a break." King Harald stood and the council along with him.

They sat when the door closed behind Lord duSarche. Prenny slumped in her seat, her hands shaking.

"When you are ready." Lord Torrance placed a glass in front of Prenny. She sipped at it, discovering it to be a pleasantly sweet wine. "I would like to hear more of your suggested remedies for the situation."

Prenny sipped at the wine until the shaking stopped.

"I've been reading on the duties and responsibilities of the nobility and about the free-towns as part of my training to be heir."

"Your situation is unusual." Lence smiled at her. "I had tutors since I was a child, and my place as a noble was drummed into me. I had to change a lot of my thinking. It would be a challenge to need to consciously think of not only what is legal but acceptable to custom."

"It is," Prenny groaned. "I'm always afraid I'll do something wrong and all this will be taken away."

"Being heir is that important to you?" Lord Raspin leaned forward and steepled his fingers.

"How else can I help my people?" Prenny drank more of the wine. *I should put it aside.* "The whole point of being Duchess is to make life better for as many people as I can. There would be nothing worse than failing at that."

The council stared at her, some with their eyes wide, others with open mouths.

"Did I say something wrong?" Prenny fought back tears. *I'll never fit in. There's no place for me anywhere.* She reached for the wine, then changed her mind and pushed it aside.

"Far from it." Lord Torrance stood and bowed to her. "We are just unused to being reminded of our place in the world by someone so young." The rest of the council nodded.

Now the tears did find their way down her cheeks. Raspin handed her a kerchief which she used to dry her eyes, then twisted into a ball.

"We forget, Lady Prenny, that you are young. Not that it makes you less competent, but you haven't developed the thick skin of your older peers. That sensitivity is what makes you exactly the person we need at this time."

Prenny hiccupped and blushed.

"My lord Raspin—"

"Please call me Raspin. We are equals at this table." He smiled. "Perhaps if we turn the discussion to your interesting suggestions, it will make things easier for you."

Prenny closed her eyes and dabbed at them again.

"To begin with, the system in place is what the villages are used to, going back at least two generations. If we overturn it all at once, we will cause more trouble than we prevent. The villagers live by the barter system among themselves. The merchants hold accounts that are paid in goods, not coin. People are actually uncomfortable with using coin. I learned that when I bought from them. They would have been happier if I had something to trade or if I'd allowed them to simply give me things.

"I talked it over with Yennet on the drive home, and the conclusion I reached was that the healthiest thing to do would be to broaden the base of their bartering until they naturally felt the need for currency. It was that decision which led to the suggestion we ask the Rehego to trade with the villages. At the same time reminding the merchants of their responsibility to the community, thus the question of taxes on their profits. That they paid bribes to keep the extent of the profits a secret reveals they believe not only that the crown has the right to tax them but should."

"But you go further and recommend the merchants collect tax from the people in the village. Surely that isn't fair to the people you've already said are too poor to pay tax." Lence frowned.

"That is acknowledgement of what is already happening. By making it official, it allows us to monitor and control it, but it also allows the villagers the dignity of paying their share."

"They want to pay taxes?" Lence shook his head, "None of my people like them."

"It's about participation in their community. They won't be happy if they think we're treating them as people with no power to guide their own lives."

The door to the king's chamber opened and they all stood.

The king stood until Lady Marriette and duSarche were beside their chairs. "Please sit."

"We have a suggestion for council which will resolve the issues raised by Lady Prenny." King Harald looked at her with a twinkle in his eye. It made her more nervous, not less. "Lady Joan is the Duchess of the North. Lord duSarche agrees it makes sense to add the north shore to her responsibility. We are aware that she is presently in negotiations with the mountain tribes, and we do not wish to take time away from that vital work. Lady Marriette has given us a very interesting idea. We believe there is precedent."

Prenny's stomach filled with butterflies. She crushed Raspin's kerchief to keep her hands still. Lady Marriette smiled like a cat who'd eaten the canary.

"Thus we appoint Lady Prenny as Countess of the North Shore. She will be accountable to the crown through her mother, Lady Joan. The people already know and trust her."

"Oh no." Prenny moaned, and the council laughed.

CHAPTER 12

AMONGST STRANGERS

Leandra woke to the noise of strange birds outside the window. Raphael leaned against the windowsill, staring raptly at the scene.

"Mama, the birds are all colours. Why don't we have birds like this at home?"

"They live here. This is where their food and their friends are."

"Pretty."

"They are." Leandra pulled him away from the window long enough to change his clothes, then changed hers. Thoughts of Cameto twinged her heart, but she set them aside until there was time to reflect properly.

"Let's see if we can find our friends and some food." Leandra took his hand, and they walked out of the room. She followed the sound of conversation downstairs to a large room. People sat at tables laughing and sharing platters piled high with fruit.

"There they are!" Raphael shouted and ran to where Xianju and the others sat. A ripple of quiet ran through the room as people looked over at Raphael, then people returned to their conversations.

"Welcome." Vazee hugged the exuberant Raphael and smiled

at Leandra. She nudged Mahaloun who made space for Leandra. Vazee sat with Raphael on her lap and encouraged him to try each different fruit while he talked about the birds he'd seen.

Leandra tried the fruit and an odd hot drink, bitter but satisfying. No one interrupted, though people walked past with curious looks.

"Come." Xianju stood. "Vazee will watch over your kitten. I would introduce you to the elders."

Leandra kissed Raphael and told him to behave, then followed Xianju, Hojiam behind her.

They climbed a spiral staircase that disappeared into the stone ceiling. Tiny slits gave a view over the verdant jungle which flowed around and through the city. *Why do they need arrow slots in the oasis?*

The stairs ended at a polished wood floor. Windows stretched from floor to ceiling. Iron fretwork was the only thing separating the room from the drop. From here, the dark rock walls were visible on every side. *Hard to defend, but difficult to attack too. Enough. Rodrigo is having a bad influence on you.*

Five people descended a staircase to where Leandra and Xianju waited. They wore masks and long robes that covered them from neck to floor. Only the glint of eyes through holes in the masks proved them human. Each wore a stylized cat, but where Xianju and the others she'd met looked cat-like in an unassuming way, these had prominent snarls showing sharp teeth.

They formed a semi-circle and stood silently. Leandra stayed relaxed and waited. She was the outsider. They needed to welcome or turn her away before her words had value.

The silence stretched, but she refused to allow her heart to race or breath to become shallow. This was a test of these people. If they failed, Leandra was mistaken to think an understanding was possible.

"She may remain." The voice behind the spotted mask might have been alto or tenor. As impersonal as a stone, it gave no clue to the speaker. The five turned and left, leaving Leandra shaking.

"Fear not, you are safe." Xianju led her back to the stairs down.

Leandra didn't explain it wasn't fear making her shake.

***

After a week, Leandra had been shown through most of the city. It was very much like any other city, but the people wore drab robes and decorated their bodies. Leandra was a curiosity with her flamboyant Rehego clothes and unpainted face. Raphael unabashedly blended the two, refusing robes but continuing to wear the kitten facepaint.

Everyone was welcome to eat in the great hall. There was no cost, and she never saw anyone paying the slightest attention to who came or went. Leandra took the opportunity to get to know more of the Nekkest.

The oasis was very pleasant, but Leandra missed Cameto and fought frustration at the complete lack of anything like discussion of an agreement between the Rehego and Nekkest.

She and Raphael looked through the market for something to occupy his attention. All his toys were in the caravan. It was a testament to his fascination with the Nekkest that he'd waited almost a month before begging for a toy he'd seen a Nekkest child playing with.

They found a booth easily enough in the market, but Leandra didn't have much to bargain with. They sat on a bench while they played a game where they each decided who they thought would get the better deal. Raphael won more bets than she did. He wasn't held back by a desire to understand.

In the end, Leandra used a Rehego flute to bargain. When Raphael demonstrated the instrument, she wondered if the Nekkest would give him the entire shop.

After settling on the puzzle game Raphael wanted in the beginning, the Nekkest insisted on giving Leandra a deck of cards. She accepted graciously. They'd be fun to look through later.

A chill ran down her back. Leandra dropped the cards in her pouch and looked around for the source of the threat.

A Nekkest in a black robe stood on the far side of the market staring at her. The people had pulled back giving him a wide berth, even moving away from his line of sight. Raphael played with his new toy, unbothered.

The Nekkest strolled toward them. Something told Leandra this was a zuthi, but much stronger than Hojiam. They stopped several paces away and bared their fangs. Leandra couldn't call it a smile. The teeth were pointed, like Vazee's. Hojiam's weren't. *Is it a sign of power?* Bragging of power was foreign to the Rehego, but Leandra had seen enough to understand its uses.

"Huangoki." The Nekkest trilled the word as if they were imitating the birds and not a cat.

A different tribe?

"I am called Leandra."

"A worthless name, unearned." The Nekkest sneered in contempt and raised a hand. Leandra matched his gesture and held his gaze. The Nekkest turned and walked away.

"It's all right, Mama. I won't let him hurt you." Raphael planted himself in front of Leandra.

Xianju waited outside their room when they returned.

"The elders have called for you. Hojiam will escort you. I will stay with the kitten."

"Show Xianju your new toy." Leandra ruffled Raphael's hair, then followed Hojiam toward the hall and the stairs.

"Is there a significance to the pointed teeth?" Leandra hoped a blunt question would give her an answer though she cringed at the rudeness.

"It is the sign of a thakgoki." Hojiam didn't look at Leandra. "There are two schools of thakgoki. Both are dangerous." They said nothing else until they reached the room with the windows and polished floor.

"Do not be tempted to anger. Think on windows." They left, footsteps fading down the spiral.

Windows?

The elders filed down the stairs to stare at her. Leandra settled herself for another long wait, but Spotted Mask spoke immediately.

"You will be tested."

"Why?" Leandra responded. She could do terse as well as any.

"Huangoki," Black Mask trilled, and she shivered.

"I am Rehego, not Nekkest." Leandra stilled herself. "I am here to speak of peace and trade between our people. Nothing more."

"You will leave."

"Then you will suffer." Leandra met the thakgoki's gaze. "Your people are raiding because you need food. You will not get it without negotiating."

"We will take what we will."

Leandra laughed, and all but the black mask stepped back.

Behind her, a clang sounded and a wind sprung up, pushing her toward the edge. She formed the *knife* rune and the wind split to pass on either side of her.

The floor of the room twisted and tilted, the polished surface threatening to let her slip. Leandra formed *rock* and stood with her arms crossed.

My turn. She formed *fear* and sent the feel of the ghosts of Fassvin Dolmens to tap the elders on the shoulder.

"Stop!" Spotted Mask shouted. The wind died and the floor settled. The iron grate behind her squeaked as it rocked.

Black Mask's eyes glittered with hate. He stalked away up the stairs leaving the other elders to scramble after him.

Leandra started the climb down the stairs.

***

She sat at the window trying to decipher Hojiam's advice. Raphael played in the corner. *What are windows for? What do they have to do with the elders' games?*

The air shivered behind her. Leandra turned to see Raphael draw the rune *reveal.* He rolled his eyes and manipulated the puzzle.

"Come here a moment." Leandra left the question of windows for one of much greater urgency. Raphael brought the toy over with him and climbed into Leandra's lap.

"How long have you been using the runes?" Leandra drew *reveal* in the air.

"I practiced on the way here on the wagon. There wasn't much to do. The white lady showed me."

"Runes aren't for making life easier." Leandra vowed to have a pointed dialogue with Vazee. "They can be dangerous."

Raphael's face fell and he hung his head.

"Runes aren't bad nor are they good." Raphael stared at her with a wrinkled forehead. "They are like fire." She tried to remember how her mother taught her, but she had been older than

Raphael. "In the fire pit, it is welcome, food, fellowship. In the caravan, it is disaster and pain."

"Papa told me. He showed me how to make a good fire so I wouldn't start a bad one."

"Well, Mama is going to teach you the runes, so you use them well." Leandra drew a sign in the air. Faint light followed her finger. "This is the sign for a blessing…"

***

It became a new game. Raphael had to look for the runes around him, then guess how they could be used. Leandra let him practice a few safe runes and watched him fall asleep as he expended the energy in him.

"Just like we have to put wood in the fire, we need to feed the runes." Leandra held him on the window seat. "What do you think we feed the runes?"

"Sleep?" Raphael guessed.

"Close." Leandra gave him a squeeze. "We give them our energy, what keeps us awake. When you use too much, you fall asleep."

"What if I used a lot, a lot too much?"

"Then you might die. Your body wouldn't have enough energy left to keep your heart beating. Always listen to your heart. If it slows and weakens, you must stop immediately."

"I will, Mama." Raphael squirmed out of her lap and ran to the door and opened it. Vazee stood with her hand raised to knock.

"How did you know I was here, kitten?"

"The air wobbles funny around you."

"You are a clever kitten." She patted his head. Raphael grinned broadly.

"Mama is teaching me to rune."

"I felt it, kitten."

"Did the air wobble?"

"Something like that." Vazee came over to sit beside Leandra. "I owe you an apology." She nodded her head and frowned. "Even in the wagon, I could tell he was picking up things, like when Xianju was thirsty or Hojiam needed sleep. Unfocused, he would be in danger in Nekkest."

"The thakgoki would love a sensitive." Leandra threw the words at Vazee.

"There are two schools of thakgoki." Vazee looked over at Raphael as he played. "I belong to the group which believes the only right use of thakgoki is with the permission and understanding of the person. It goes beyond to how much we use, but that is the essence. The other group argues that since they have the power, they are allowed to use it as they wish."

"I've met people like that."

"I felt the ripples. You are subtle. That is good." Vazee sighed and hung her head, looking tired for the first time since Leandra met her.

"To protect the kitten, I put a shield on him, using what I learned of your runes. Not as subtle as I'd like, but the unfamiliarity of the runes works in our favour. Xianju, Hojiam and Mahaloun all consented, but I've taken the largest share of the burden, as I should. Teaching him the runes kept his reserves lower which helped."

"Burden?" Leandra's heart skipped.

"The kitten has been under attack since the day you arrived. As you said, he is irresistible to some of the thakgoki."

"You aren't going to last much longer." Leandra hugged the woman. Vazee stiffened, then relaxed.

"I take it I am forgiven."

"Very much so," Leandra said as she turned to Raphael. "Come here, darling." She looked for the shield on her son. It was almost undetectable even when she knew it was there. Switching a few of the runes and drawing new connections shifted the focus from shunting the attack to Vazee to making the attacks ineffective.

"That one's cold." Raphael giggled then climbed into Vazee's lap.

"The white lady is tired."

"She is, kitten." Vazee ran her fingers through his hair. "I think I'm going to go have a nice long nap."

"Mama makes me take naps."

"I'm sure she does."

Raphael jumped down. "Bye, White Lady."

At the door, Vazee leaned over to whisper in Leandra's ear. "I would die for your little kitten. All of us would."

Leandra closed the door, more confused than ever.

CHAPTER 13

CHANCE MEETING

Rodrigo stood on the hill, holding his daughter's hand as they watched the smoke rise from the village.

"I am tired of burnt homes and people with empty eyes!" Aimee shouted. "Why did we stop the Sword if these people were going to destroy themselves anyway?"

"With the Sword, it would be worse."

"How? How could it be worse?"

Milene pointed toward the village. "There are people moving."

"It's still stupid." Aimee crossed her arms and kicked a stone down the slope.

"I agree." Rodrigo squeezed her hand. "The Sword only took what was already in us and magnified it."

"Well, we need to magnify something different." Aimee stomped her foot. "Being human sucks."

"It does at times." Milene wrapped her arms around Aimee. The girl squirmed her hand loose, then buried her face in her mother's chest and sobbed.

Rodrigo's heart twisted. A part of him wanted to wail along with Aimee. The Balance felt shattered. He was no Grandmother to know how to restore it.

"Let's go." Milene took his arm and kept her hand on Aimee's shoulder.

"Papa, you're crying!" Aimee stopped to stare at him.

"It hurts so much." Rodrigo fell to his knees. "I don't know what to do."

Aimee clutched Rodrigo. Her love warmed his darkness, eased the raw wounds on his soul. Milene held both of them. He closed his eyes, and for a while, he basked in the golden light of his family's love.

He opened his eyes to meet the gaze of an old woman holding the hand of a young boy. Tears streamed down both their faces.

"I was taking Danald and we were going to jump from the bluff," the woman sobbed and hugged Danald to her. "Then something called us here."

"Love called you." Aimee stood and walked to the pair and put a hand on their shoulders. "My name is Aimee - ancient love. Take your love and share it make it grow. It is the only hope for your people."

The grandmother and Danald headed down the hill, heads high, still holding hands.

"Wise words." Rodrigo put his hand on Aimee's head.

"It's time I started acting my age."

"Thirteen?"

"Four thousand." Aimee watched the spot where the pair had vanished around a curve.

"Four thousand and thirteen." Milene stood beside them. "Love is messy. We hurt, we cry, but if we stop feeling, then love loses its meaning."

Aimee hugged Rodrigo and pulled Milene over.

"Then we will hurt and cry and feel together." Her words came muffled. "But what can we *do?*"

"We help the next person and the next. Remind them love is still possible." Milene whispered. "We can't save the world, but we can help one at a time."

"Then let's get going." Aimee gripped Rodrigo's hand. He

hooked his arm through Milene's.

***

As they walked into the village, Rodrigo didn't know if it was his hand or Aimee's shaking. Milene was solid as a rock beside him.

"Oh no." Milene pointed at the church steeple, still towering over the town. "This is Siana's home." They plodded along the road until Rodrigo recognized the inn, more rubble than building now.

"Tam." He called out to the man pushing rubble aside in a search. Tam turned and stared at Rodrigo.

"Who are you, and what do you want?"

"I bought a knife from you years ago." Rodrigo held up the claw knife.

Tam frowned and clambered down to take the blade from Rodrigo and examine it closely.

"It's my mark. Only made two of them." He handed the knife back and shrugged. "So what?"

"We're friends of Siana." Milene hesitated before the name, and Rodrigo prayed it wasn't Siana's body Tam was seeking.

"She and the young'un are at the church. More people live there than in their own homes now." Tam dusted his hands off on his pants. "Come on."

They walked through the ash-coloured village. Even the people were grey. A few poured water on smouldering piles; others poked through the rubble. No one looked up. The courtyard at the church bulged with humanity. Babies cried. Mothers hushed their children. There weren't many men.

"Anyone doesn't hide fast enough, they end up fighting for whatever army comes through." Tam didn't slow down. People moved back. Some stared and pointed at the newcomers.

He led them into the church. People crouched beside figures on blankets. Some of the forms had their faces covered, and weeping rose in discordant waves. Rodrigo's heart ached. He'd striven to save the Rehego, but what had he done for these folk?

Siana knelt beside a blanket where a little boy lay, his chest barely moving. A bandage wrapped around his head.

"Sia, friends of yours." Tam folded beside his wife and put a gentle hand up to the boy's cheek. "Any change?"

"Nothing good." Her voice came toneless and flat.

"Mama, Papa." Aimee knelt beside the boy and put her hand on his face. Rodrigo knelt behind her with his hook on her shoulder. Milene had the other shoulder. Their free hands intertwined.

"What are you doing?" Siana reached out to slap Aimee's hand away. Tam caught her hand.

"Look, Sia," Tam spoke hoarsely. The grey of the boy's face took on a golden hue as Aimee glowed softly. He put their joined hands up to the boy's face. "Come on, Deddrick, come back to your ma and pa. We're lost without you. I miss your laugh, your endless questions."

Aimee spoke quietly in a language Rodrigo didn't know, but the meaning of the words flowed through him.

Her glow brightened. Like a bubble, it filled the church and then vanished through the stone walls.

Deddrick opened his eyes. "Ma, I'm thirsty."

Siana picked him up, laughing and crying together with Tam. Aimee sighed and stood up. Rodrigo helped Milene up, though he probably needed the help more.

Every eye in the church was fixed on Aimee.

"This building is dedicated to love." Her words echoed musically. "Speak about your love, of hope. In the end, even death fails before love."

The people turned to those on the blankets, and whispering arose.

Aimee collapsed into Rodrigo's arms. He carried her out into the sun.

"I can't tell you how amazing that was. You blessed me by letting me help you." Rodrigo rocked her gently. "I never got to hold you when you were a babe. Didn't get to teach you to walk or to play the tin whistle. You leapt into my life as a wise-ass child and made me more complete than I'd ever dreamed possible."

Milene sat and leaned against him, muttering her own litany.

Aimee opened her eyes and sighed before putting her arms around him and holding him.

"How did you know what I needed?"

"You told us." Milene ran her hand through Aimee's golden hair. "Your hair is still glowing."

"The more I access the power of the cup, the more that will

happen." She sighed. "I know now why I came as your daughter. Without your love, I wouldn't be strong enough."

"We need you too." Milene began braiding Aimee's hair.

"I don't need braids." Aimee peered up at her. "Oh, go ahead, I'll live with it." She grinned at Rodrigo. "I'm still your wise-ass daughter. I'm not going soft on you."

"I wouldn't have it any other way."

Siana and Tam came out, each holding one of Deddrick's hands.

"Whatever I can do for you, ask." Tam shed unabashed tears.

"People need a place to find hope." Rodrigo paused to feel Aimee's heart beating. "But no place is safe in the Empire." He passed Aimee to Milene and fished paper out of his pouch. He held a pencil awkwardly in his left hand and wrote a brief note and handed it to Tam. Tam looked at it and frowned.

"I can't read it."

"You don't need to." Rodrigo found another scrap. "What it says is that I will pay passage for you and anyone with you over the ocean to Belandria."

"Passage for me, Siana and Deddrick?" Tam looked at the paper like it had turned to gold in his hand.

"Them and anyone else with you. Take the whole village if you want."

"Who are you to make such promises?" Tam glared at him.

"I have made very successful trades over the years. As a result, I have more money than I can spend. Whoever you give that note to can exchange it for however many people you tell them. You'll need to go to the moneylender with the captain." Rodrigo wrote on the other paper and handed it to Tam as well. "Take this with you."

"But what will you do for money?"

"Make more if I need it." Rodrigo grinned up at Tam. "That's the fun part."

"Thank you, thank you." Tam bowed like Rodrigo was the emperor. "I have a forge hidden in the forest. I can make you a knife, a sword, whatever you need."

"I need a hand." Rodrigo raised his hook, and Aimee jabbed him with her toe. "Rather, a fitting which will allow me to grip things like cups and pencils.”

"I have some drawings." Aimee crawled out of Milene's arms and fished in her bag. "Here." She pushed a pile of paper into Tam's hand, then gave him the ring. "Whatever you make, it must have a ring this exact size and shape on the end."

Rodrigo took the hook off and showed it to Tam. He nodded.

"Go, we'll be fine now." Siana kissed Tam on the cheek, then watched him walk away. "I wouldn't have him if it weren't for you and Milene."

Deddrick tottered over to Aimee who picked him up and tickled him.

"What happened to your hand?" Siana blushed, the mark on her face getting darker yet.

"I cut it off to get rid of a cursed sword." Rodrigo shrugged.

"Come on, you're teasing me aga…" Siana stopped staring wide-eyed at Milene's serious face. "You aren't teasing." She shuddered. "I can't imagine doing that."

"You would to save the world," Aimee said.

"Save the world?" Siana sat down and shook herself. "You really are a spy."

"I used to be." Rodrigo nodded. "It was safer for you not to know."

"You told me the truth and I didn't believe it, and you planned that."

"He's like that," Aimee said. "His mind is really twisted. In a good way."

"Thank you for that," Rodrigo said.

"Tell me all about this cursed sword."

"Let me." Aimee waved a hand. "It will be funnier."

By the time she finished the telling of the tale, there was a crowd gathered around and the evening sun coloured the courtyard gold.

***

"It's perfect." Rodrigo fit the new device, which Aimee called 'the claw', in place. With a bit of effort, he had it holding the pencil and wrote another note. He passed that one to Siana.

"When you get to Belandria, be sure to visit the palace and ask for Harald. Tell the guards Rodrigo sent you. Show them the note."

"Harald works in the palace?"

"He does," Rodrigo said. "I'm sure he'll be delighted to see you."

Siana hugged Rodrigo, then Milene. She whispered something in Aimee's ear that made his daughter blush.

"Look me up when you get back to Belandria."

"I will." Rodrigo shook Tam's hand. The couple picked up their bags. Accompanied by a small crowd of others, they headed along the road toward the coast.

"Will they find a ship to take them?" Milene put an arm around his waist.

"For what I promised, any captain will take them."

"I didn't know you had that much money, Papa." Aimee poked him.

"Sorry, it didn't seem important." Rodrigo shrugged apologetically. "I had Milene and you. What did I need with a pile of money?"

"Shouldn't you have told her Harald is the king of Belandria?"

"It's more fun this way."

Milene and Aimee both rolled their eyes.

CHAPTER 14

CHANGE IN THE WIND

Lydia put the final touches on the thane's document. He could read but didn't care to, and most of the captains had the same attitude. Yet the piece of paper with signatures in blood became as powerful as an oath to the gods.

Even if they had a ready source of ink, the northmen would still have used blood. They just thought that way.

"Lydia," Tomak Thaneson pushed through the curtain to her tiny office. "The weather is clear. Come skating with me."

"I have neither the skill nor the skates." Lydia stretched and her bones popped. *When did I get so lazy?* "But I'm sure you will be able to remedy both problems."

Tomak's face froze in half disbelief and half delight. She'd always been polite but probably came across as cold. Life would be much easier if she weren't so shy.

He took her hand and pulled her out of the office into the hall and along to the doors still wide open to the freezing air. Tomak helped her into her cloak and boots. She pulled on the hat and mitts. It should take a good while for her to freeze.

Instead of walking down the hill, Tomak commandeered a sleigh and drove them down to the harbour.

She never expected any part of the ocean to freeze solid, but teams of horses pulled wood, stone and other goods across the ice.

The sleigh stopped in front of a small hut. Tomak picked up his skate blades, then led her inside. He checked several pairs of blades before he found ones he liked. Her stomach felt strange as he knelt to fasten them on her boots. He put his own on much more quickly.

"Hold onto my arm, and I'll help you down to the ice."

Lydia teetered on the blades. She felt strange to be suddenly so much taller. She gratefully clung to Tomak as he guided her down wood steps to the ice.

"We'll start easy. Hold onto my hands, and I'll pull you along." He helped her onto a cleared path with snow on either side.

Lydia started stiff as if already frozen but relaxed when Tomak kept his speed down and others gave them a wide berth. She watched his feet. There was a rhythm, like dancing.

"Let me try on my own."

"How about I hold one hand while you try?" Tomak let go of her left hand.

She tried to move her feet like Tomak, but her feet just slid back and forth.

"Turn your foot slightly so the blade bites into the ice, then push."

Lydia tried and glided forward. She copied the action with the other foot. Little by little she found a feel for the ice and let go of Tomak's hand. She revelled in the wind blowing past ruffling her cloak. Her effort kept her warm. A curve in the path approached. Tomak shouted something, but her knees shook. She didn't know how to turn or stop.

When she hit the bank, she expected hard blocks, but the snow burst up into a cloud around her, then cushioned her when she fell. She rolled onto her back and roared with laughter. *When did I ever laugh like this?*

Tomak arrived and helped her up, a panicked expression on his face.

"That was fun, but maybe you should teach me to stop."

They skated until Tomak insisted she return to the hut to warm up.

"You feel warm, but the temperature is dropping. I don't want you freezing your skin."

"That can happen?" Lydia leaned back against the wall and sighed. "It was worth coming here, just for this."

"Why did you come?" Tomak glanced over at her.

"That's right, you came back from voyage after I arrived." She tried to count how long she'd been in Getthelm. When the time came, God would move her to the next step. "God sent me here."

"Why would your god do that?"

"God doesn't explain things. I trust there is a reason."

"Father didn't tell me you were so brave."

"Brave?" Lydia scrunched her face as if she were tasting something new. "I'm not sure it's brave. It's always been that way."

"If my father told me to go to a strange place and wait without any reason, I'd be nervous and worried."

"Would you go?"

"He's my father, but also my thane. It isn't my place to question. At least not out loud." Tomak grinned. "Maybe we should head back up to the hall."

"Can we come back tomorrow?"

***

Work in the morning, skating in the afternoon became her new routine. Tomak introduced her to his friends, and she discovered herself part of a large group of young men and women. They took her skiing and on an overnight trip north to see the reindeer pass in their thousands.

They celebrated holidays she'd never heard of. Tomak gave her a pair of skate blades of her own. She gave him a drawing of him skating.

One of the warriors took to making lewd comments when she walked past him. His words tied her stomach in knots and set her face to burning. He took that as encouragement to become even more forward.

One day Tomak must have been standing just in the hall when Lydia returned from meeting with the thane's storemaster. He came through the door into the hall with his sword drawn and backed the man against the wall.

"How long has this been going on?" Tomak's words were cold and curt.

"Too long." Lydia's face burned hotter and she had to fight against tears and a shake in her voice. *Why is he angry at me?*

"Henric, you know my father's views on men harassing women servants, and Lady Lydia is a free member of the household under the thane's protection."

Henric had a stubborn look on his face, and he opened his mouth.

"Before you speak," Tomak held up his hand, "if you so much as suggest an insult to Lady Lydia's honour, I will meet you in the training ground." He dropped his hand. "Now what were you going to say?"

"My apologies, Lady Lydia."

Lydia didn't see Henric again. At odd times, the thought would strike her that Tomak was ready to fight a duel for her. She couldn't decide how she felt about that.

The thane sent a servant for her. She put on a light cloak. Even with the roaring fires, the hall was cold in the depths of winter.

"Lydia." The thane waved to a chair sent on the platform beside him. "Are you enjoying life in my hall?"

"I am," Lydia said in surprise.

"You didn't expect your God to worry about your happiness?"

"I never thought about it." Lydia blushed. "I was always concerned with God's happiness."

"As a father, my greatest happiness is the happiness of my children."

"You are right." Lydia laughed in delight. "Thank you for teaching me that."

"Speaking of my children's happiness." The thane studied her, head tilted. "Tomak has asked permission to court you."

"Court me?" Lydia's mind went blank.

"Since we know nothing of your father, he decided to ask me."

"I don't know who my father was." Lydia studied her hands.

"But then I lived with a man who treated me as his daughter, another who welcomed me and gave me a place in his household, and as you said, God." She looked up at the thane. "The first is far away and would be delighted at the idea. God," she shrugged. "I will assume God agrees until he says otherwise. If you wish to give him permission, I would be happy."

"Then I will inform him he has my blessing." The thane leaned over to her. "Don't make it too easy for him." He leaned back with a faraway gaze in his eyes. "His mother was a warrior. I had to beat her in three contests of her choosing before she'd take my hand. I'm sure she let me win, but not easily."

***

"Father said he talked to you." Tomak stepped into the tiny office. "Did he tell you about my mother?"

"He did." Lydia nodded and put down her pen to face him. "He must miss her terribly."

"He does, but he dotes on my youngest sister who lived when Mother died. Mother told him it was her battle and she won the important part, then made him swear to love the babe."

"How many brothers and sisters do you have?" Lydia looked him. "You don't talk about them much."

"I have two younger brothers. They live with my mother's brothers learning to be warriors. A younger sister who chose a husband and travelled to his home last year, and then my baby sister. I will introduce you. Did you have a large family? I mean with the man who adopted you."

"He has a daughter. You'd like her. She's as fierce a warrior as anyone I know. Everyone calls her Fury. She's eleven now. There are the twin boys, Alfaric and Diene, who are six and full of mischief. There is a boy, Fury's friend Nikay, who I think was around as much as he was home."

"I'd like to meet them someday."

"Perhaps you will."

"So what horrible tasks will you set for me?" Tomak put his hand on her cheek. "Father won't be satisfied with anything but the most challenging."

"It is an interesting tradition." Lydia grinned wickedly. "I expect it to be a lot of fun."

"So, out with it, and you can make the official announcement at dinner."

"I think I will wait until dinner, but I will give you a hint. You've already completed one task."

***

Lydia had never seen the hall so packed. The thane must have given a hint to the people.

Tomak sat on the far side of the thane. A young girl sat between Lydia and the thane.

"Are you the thane's daughter?" Lydia asked. She needed something to distract her from the ravenous butterflies in her stomach.

"Frija." The girl turned to Lydia. Her face was contorted. One eye was blank white, the other a piercing grey. Intelligence shone from the grey eye.

"I'm Lydia."

"Sister." Frija reached out with a shaking hand. Lydia took it and held it gently.

"Sister."

Frija's face lit up in a smile, and Lydia returned it. Her heart went out to this girl. In that instant, the nerves vanished and warmth filled her.

"Tomak?" The girl waved down the table and raised an eyebrow.

Lydia's face burned, and Frija made a strange barking noise which Lydia realized was laughter.

The meal was exquisite, but it could have been stale bread and she wouldn't have noticed. After the platters were cleared, Tomak jumped over the table and came to stand in front of Lydia.

"I have come to ask you to be my wife." Tomak stammered out the words. Lydia's mouth went dry.

"Sister." Frija croaked, and Lydia imagined her rolling her grey eye.

Lydia stood and looked at Tomak. It hit her at that moment how much she cared about him. She closed her mouth on the 'yes' she wanted to shout out.

"To be my husband, you must prove yourself." The hall shook with the cheers of the people. "I will set you three tasks. The first you've completed. To teach me something I didn't know. To prove this, we will race around the skate track." Cups banging on the table sounded like thunder. "The second is about the mind. You must ask me a riddle I can't answer." The thunder boomed louder yet. "The third, you must tell me the name of the bravest person in Getthelm and their deepest desire."

Tomak's mouth dropped open as the thunder grew so loud Lydia wondered if any cups would remain after this night. When the noise dropped, Tomak gave her a crooked grin.

"The answer to the third wouldn't happen to be you, Lydia, my love, and your desire to be my wife?"

The crowd laughed and clapped.

"Sadly, no," Lydia said, "there is one braver than I. But your answer wins you a kiss for luck." People hooted as Tomak leaned over the table to claim his kiss.

The touch of his lips set off a fire in Lydia she knew wouldn't be quenched until he completed the third task.

CHAPTER 15

COUNTESS OF THE NORTH SHORE

Prenny climbed out of the coach and ran to the door. Catrin opened it and swept her into a hug and swung her around.

"Oof. You've been doing some growing while you were gone."

"Fury had me training with the staff and all kinds of things." They moved aside to let the coachman carry in Prenny's trunk.

"That's all you brought for the winter? I doubt your old clothes will fit you."

Prenny pulled the letter out of her coat, where she'd kept it safe the whole trip. "That's something I need to talk to you and mother about."

"Come on in," Catrin waved her through the door. "Don't know what I was thinking, keeping you standing on the doorstep." She dabbed at her eyes. Prenny ran to the parlour where her mother was usually to be found talking to someone from the village. It was empty.

"She's upstairs." Catrin put a hand on Prenny's shoulder.

"Don't make a fuss; it makes her cranky."

Prenny dashed up the stairs and into her mother and Catrin's bedroom. Her mother sat in bed with a quilt around her shoulders. She had a ledger on her lap with a finger placed as if she'd fallen asleep in the middle of reading.

"Mother?" Prenny knelt beside the bed and took her mother's hand.

"Sorry, I dozed off." Joan smiled broadly at Prenny. "It's so good to see you. Stand up and let me see how you've grown."

Prenny stood and spun in place.

"You are beautiful."

"How long this time?" Prenny pulled a chair over.

"Three months," Catrin said from the doorway. "It's getting worse."

"From the moment that poison dart hit me, I've been living on borrowed time." Joan tried to sit up straighter, and Catrin came to fuss with the pillows.

"Isn't there something we can do?" Prenny had asked the question before, but maybe they'd found something new.

"Nothing's changed." Joan patted Prenny's hand. "Fury's fire saved my life, but it ravaged my body." She held up a hand. "Don't you dare tell Thuria. Her life will be hard enough without feeling guilty for how she healed me."

"She asks after you." Prenny wiped at her eyes. "I think she knows."

"I will write her a letter." Joan sighed. "You can take it back for me."

"Won't it be faster to send it by messenger?" Catrin frowned. "Prenny just got here."

"I am just here for a visit." Prenny put the letter on the bed. Joan picked it up and read it through. "I'm so proud of you." She passed the letter to Catrin. "I had hoped spending the year at the palace would help you grow. It has, and more than just your dress size."

"I don't recall an heir as young as you sitting on council, and now a countess in your own right." Catrin put her hand over Joan's. "We've always loved you and were certain you'd do great things."

"I had the best teachers, and I'm not talking about the ones at the palace." She shook herself. "I only have a week, and I'm not spending it moping about. Catrin, do you think Mother can get down the stairs? I'd like to host a tea and see the people. I'll go visit Suze, then let folks know."

"Anytime tomorrow." Catrin looked at Joan and caressed her cheek. "She's getting stronger."

Prenny left her mother and Catrin alone and ran down the stairs. She didn't want to take the time to change. Outside she slowed to a walk. The dress might trip her. Townspeople waved at her. Prenny left the town on the faint path which led her to the graveyard.

She knelt by the stone and pulled a few weeds.

"Aunt Suze, they've gone and made me Countess of the North Shore. I don't know anything about fishing, and I've already made a mess of things. But I fought a battle, or rather, I didn't. You always told me the best way to win a battle was not to fight." Prenny put her head against the stone and sobbed. "I had to kill people, Aunt Suze. I didn't even feel sorry until later when everything calmed down. I swear Yennet held me half the way home."

She laughed. "If I were like Mother and Catrin, she'd be the one. You always teased me about the boys, but you made sure I knew what I needed to know. If I find someone, it will be because of you." Leaning back, Prenny looked into the darkening blue of the evening sky. "Watch over Mother. I'm not ready yet. At least she's comfortable and doesn't seem at all afraid. Catrin, I don't know how she'll take it."

Prenny stood and brushed the grass from her dress before setting out back to the house.

***

Prenny rode into Redemption, now vastly different from the bandit camp where she'd been a child.

"Take all the time you want." Tanim came up beside her. "I'm going to find Linnet."

"Why don't you just ask her to marry you?"

"I want the time to be right - a field of my own, a house just for ourselves."

"Tanim." Prenny closed her eyes. "The perfect time will

never come. There will always be something. Let her share your dreams or stop leading her on."

He stared at her, then rode off without a word.

"Wonderful, another good job, Prenny." She tied her horse in front of the community office, then walked in. "Hey, Kat."

The former bandit ran around the desk to embrace Prenny.

"How many people have told you how much you've grown?"

"Everybody." Prenny rolled her eyes. "How are the foresters doing?"

"Hance still writes to Somphin for advice, but he's been right on the mark for the last year. There's a tree he's out scouting now, says it will pay double our tax for the year."

"That's great." Prenny went over to put her finger on the map showing Redemption and where they'd cut trees. "What other sources of income do the people have?"

"Some sell what they harvest, nuts and mushrooms. But most everything is tied up in the forest."

"I'm going to be working with some people, fishermen. They knit amazing sweaters and carve every piece of wood they get their hands on. Looks like there'll be a market for the stuff in the capital. People have more money to spend."

"And you're suggesting we find something similar." Kat rubbed her chin. "It's a good notion. Never know what people will buy. Linnet got one of the men to build a kiln, and she's working on those pots of hers. I'll bring it to the council."

"Working with fishermen?" Kat leaned against the wall and crossed her arms. "I smell a story. Out with it."

By the time she'd finished, including the parts she'd left out for her mother and Catrin, Tanim was sitting on the porch, tapping his toes impatiently.

"Looks like Linnet's busy today." Prenny sighed. "Time to head home anyway, and at least I don't have to drag him away."

"He's a good man."

"He is." Prenny looked out at him. "I can't remember the last time I had to belt him."

"You were good for him, taught him the world wasn't his on a platter." Kat hugged Prenny again. "Write letters when you can, dear."

"I will."

She pushed open the door and nodded at Tanim before mounting her horse. He jumped into his saddle, and his horse danced as she picked up his agitation.

"Calm down, or she'll throw you." Prenny glared at him. "And I don't want to have to lift you up on her back, again."

"That was years ago," Tanim protested but leaned over to pat his horse and talk quietly to her.

They'd almost made the main road through the forest when he coughed.

"About what you said to me." Tanim's voice sounded strange from behind her.

"Sorry, it's none of my business." Prenny shook her head. *Figures he'd start this when I can't look at him.*

"She said 'yes'."

"What?" Prenny turned onto the road and waited for him to catch up. "What are you talking about?"

"Linnet said 'yes.'" Tanim grinned broadly and his eyes sparkled. "We're getting married in the spring. Her ma and pa were delighted."

"You asked her today?" Prenny's head spun.

"You told me to." Tanim laughed and leaned back to stare up at the leaves. "She said 'yes'!"

"Congratulations." Prenny grinned back at him. "She's a lucky woman."

"Really?" Tanim looked over at her.

"You were an awful nuisance when we were kids, but the last few years, you've grown up and got serious."

"Thank you, Lady Prenny." Tanim half-bowed in the saddle. "From you, that is high praise indeed. Maybe you can wait until after the wedding before you go back to the city."

"I'm not staying the winter. I'm leaving tomorrow morning." Prenny blinked away tears. She'd barely said hello, and she was leaving again. "If it is possible, I will come for the wedding, but I can't promise. King Harald made me Countess of the North Shore, so I'll be working hard." She found herself telling him about the people in the villages, so poor yet welcoming and generous. "I want to make their lives better without making them different."

"If anyone can do it, you can," Tanim said. "You're the smartest person I know."

"Linnet's about my size, right?" Prenny smiled. "I'll tell Catrin that Linnet can have her choice of any dress in my closet."

"She'll be honoured to wear one of your dresses. Linnet admires you."

"Linnet can keep the dress, Tanim. It will be my gift to her."

"I can't wait to tell her. She'll be so happy."

He spent the rest of the ride telling her all the plans they'd made in the course of the afternoon. She handed him the reins at the door of their house.

"Be blessed, Tanim. Be happy." She waved and went into the house. Up in her room, she opened her trunk, then hung most of the dresses in the closet. They were restrained for the city, but here they were an extravagant luxury. On the table, she put a stack of silver coins and wrote a note to Tanim and put it beneath them.

None of her favourite clothes fit. She'd get more pants and shirts in the city. Sometimes they were best, and propriety could hang. Books filled the space left by the clothes. She added a few other things to remind her of home.

"Take a couple of quilts." Catrin came in.

"I have some at my room in the palace."

"Take more. I don't want you to be cold."

"I will then. You choose them for me."

"Do you want your bow?"

"Oh yes." The sight of the innkeeper with her arrow in his arm flashed into her mind, and she put her hands over her face.

"It isn't my place," Catrin pulled Prenny close, "but sometimes life forces us to do terrible things. You won't ever forget, and you shouldn't, but don't let it haunt you."

"Catrin, I love you." Prenny put her head on Catrin's shoulder. "Isn't it horrible, I can't remember if I've ever told you that before. You're my mother as much as Mother. You know what I mean."

"You been my daughter since the day you ran in and chose this room. You were so full of light, and it's only grown brighter."

"I'm scared, Catrin. I'm scared of making a mistake and hurting people. I'm scared I'm not good enough. I'm scared of

106

losing Mother."

"It's all right to be scared." Catrin squeezed her tight. "It's all right because you won't let your fear stop you from doing your best."

***

The coach rolled through the falling snow into Coshport. Moz waved them into the fish shed.

"The king's messengers come a while back." Moz opened the door to the guest house. "We wanted a proper place for our Countess."

Prenny stood in shock. Yennet put a hand on Prenny's back.

"If it isn't good enough, you can have another house. Our house isn't very nice but…" Moz clutched his hands together.

"It's beautiful." Prenny walked through the room running her fingers over the carving. Fish danced, whales sang, animals played. The table, the chairs, the beams. Rugs lay on the floor in rainbow colours. The stove was lit and warming the room. Where the curtain had been were two doors.

The door on the left opened into a bedroom, which like the other room was fantastically decorated. A wool blanket covered the bed. An afghan crocheted in the crest of the North Shore lay on the foot of the bed.

Mali looked up and smiled.

"Welcome, my lady. I hope you like it."

"I adore it." Prenny turned in a circle. "It's so alive."

Mali opened the trunk at the foot of the bed. "We put together the clothes you'll need to stay warm through the winter."

Furs and sweaters overflowed. Prenny picked up a hat and tried it on.

"Tis winter fox, that one. They turn white when the snow comes."

Prenny flopped on the bed and sighed.

"I'm home."

"My lady," Yennet put her head in the room. "Would you like tea?"

"I'd love some." Prenny jumped up and continued exploring. The second door opened into a back room. Another door led outside, and stairs climbed to a second level where she found another bedroom and an office.

"Mali," Prenny said as she sat at the table. "I would like to invite everyone to drop in for tea tomorrow. We can set up in the fish shed. I brought a few treats with me."

***

She stopped at a looming grey house on a hill away from any of the villages. Leaves rustled under her feet as she walked the halls. She felt colder than she had outside. It reminded her of the remains of the estate house outside the village where she'd grown up.

"Remind me to tell the people they can scavenge anything useful from this place, take the stones from the wall if they want. I don't plan on ever living here."

Prenny led the way back to the coach and never looked back.

In each village, the people had prepared a home for her. They were each unique and amazing. She held a tea and talked to her people.

When she arrived in Tansent's Arm, Prenny's gut hurt. A crowd gathered around the coach. They'd rebuilt the inn, and she saw some other new houses too. When she stepped out of the coach, the crowd cheered.

"My lady." The innkeeper's wife stepped forward. "My name is Leohl, and I welcome you on behalf of all."

They led her into the inn, only it wasn't an inn. They'd turned it into a house for her. The layout was the same as the inn, with the common room and kitchen on the first floor. Upstairs her room took up half the floor. The remainder was guest rooms and a room for a bath. They'd even made an alcove for Yennet in her room.

The last thing they showed her was the room with the trap door. Stairs led down to the tunnel; lanterns waited on a table. Leohl lit one and guided her down the tunnel.

"This room," she opened the door where Prenny had been held prisoner, "we made into a secure place to store whatever you wish." They went farther down the tunnel to where the opening to the ocean had been closed with a wall and a door. In the cave where all the smuggled goods had been kept, shelves were built. "More storage, if nothing else you will be able to store what you collect for taxes here."

"This is incredible, but why?" Prenny looked up to the ledge which led to escape.

"This is our pledge, my lady. We are done with smuggling."

"Let's go back upstairs and invite everyone in for a party." Prenny smiled. "I feel like celebrating."

CHAPTER 16

EVEN KITTENS HAVE CLAWS

Raphael ran down the steps to meet his new friends. They dashed about the Hall in a mob. The adults looked on with either amusement or annoyance. One of the mob spotted a bright coloured bird outside.

He paused a second at the door. Mama had told him to stay in the Hall, but the bird was sitting on a branch, laughing at the children. It wasn't far. Raphael dashed out to join the crowd.

The bird sidled back and forth on the branch, then swooped to the next tree. Raphael followed, giggling, like the bird was the Pied Piper. The door of the Hall disappeared as they sprinted around a corner.

The chase became a game. The bird doubled back and cackled from behind them as if it had transported without flying. Raphael's chest puffed as he stayed with the leaders as older children dropped out or lost track of the crowd.

Finally, the bird flew deeper into the jungle. Raphael climbed over or crawled under fallen trees. Vines reached out to tangle him, but he dodged and wove until he stood panting in a tiny clearing.

His clothes were soaked with sweat and water dripping from above.

The bird, bright blue and gold and red, gave one last defiant call then flew up into the canopy and vanished.

The game was over. Raphael had won. He danced in celebration, then turned to go back to the Hall. There was no path. Something snarled behind him. He picked up a stick and glared at the big cat. It stared at him, its tail snapping from side to side.

"Bad kitty." Raphael hefted his stick as the black and gold striped cat crouched and bared its teeth. "Mama." The cat blurred through his tears.

***

Mama. Leandra lifted her head. Raphael had called her.

"Sorry, Hojiam, I must go. Raphael has gotten himself in a pinch."

"I will come with you." Hojiam stood and loped after Leandra.

Leandra went down to the Hall.

"Did you see my kitten? He's dressed like me."

A couple pointed to the door.

"He went out with a mob of children. They'll be back soon enough."

"You must teach your child more respect," an old woman stomped over and berated Leandra.

"Take it up with the elders." Hojiam stepped forward. The woman's face grew more sour.

"I see where –"

Hojiam bared her teeth. "Do you really want to challenge me?"

The woman went grey and stumbled back. Hojiam pushed Leandra to the door.

"I smell magic." Hojiam turned in a circle sniffing.

Leandra drew a rune. "He's this way." She sprinted away, not slowing as the path led her into the jungle. Branches clawed at her. The ground slipped away under her feet.

Hojiam grabbed her hand and pulled her to stop.

"Only an elder has such power."

"I don't care." Leandra's heart burned within her, and she pulled free of Hojiam's grip.

A cat roared and Raphael's high-pitched screech echoed through the jungle. Leandra formed *knife* and slashed her way through the jungle. Hojiam shouted behind her, but the words were lost in Leandra's panic.

She broke into a clearing, already seeing Raphael's body torn and bloody. The reality struck like a blow of hope and despair combined.

A tiger lay crumpled against a tree. Raphael glowed with power. The elder with the black mask stood across the clearing. She couldn't see his face, but his satisfaction radiated from him.

"He has broken the law."

"One with no name cannot break the law." Hojiam moved in front of Leandra as Raphael dropped his stick and ran to bury his face in Leandra's skirt.

"Who knows what blasphemies these strangers commit?"

"You would use a child as a pawn in your game? You planned this. Which is more likely, a nameless child wielding such power or an elder?" Hojiam stalked forward. "You are a disgrace, a snivelling coward, a liar." With each accusation, she pointed at the elder.

The elder in the black mask snarled and threw a hand forward. Hojiam rocked slightly, then sneered.

"Strange that an elder has so little power. Almost like he sent all his power elsewhere."

Black Mask raised both hands.

"Enough." Spotted Mask stepped out of the foliage. "You know the law. The jungle is sacred."

A sharp point poked Leandra in the back.

"Resist and you die." The eyes behind the mask looked cold and dead.

"Raphael," Leandra whispered. "Remember the rune I told you never to use? Use it now."

The black-masked elder shouted and reached out, but Raphael disappeared, leaving only a rustle of leaves to mark his passing.

"Kill her." Black Mask pointed at Leandra

"There is no bloodshed in the jungle." A gravelly voice said from behind her.

"Then take her somewhere else and kill her there."

"Elder, how many laws have you broken here?" Hojiam didn't look around as the man with the gravelly voice began to drag Leandra away. "I will meet you in the arena unless you care to break that law too."

***

Fighting with the man did no good, but Leandra didn't expect to escape. She wanted answers, and since her friends didn't have them, she'd ask her enemies.

As she wrestled, she drew runes on the man. Aisa had taught her and she'd refused to use them in the years since, but for Raphael, she'd pay the price.

"Take me somewhere private." Leandra walked quietly as they approached the city.

"I will kill you when we reach the city." The man's knife didn't move from her back.

"I would prefer to die in private, and the elders wouldn't like you making a fuss."

"I know a place." He dragged her to the left. Leandra drew the runes again, adding power to them. Even if they worked, they might kill her.

They reached a gate. The man froze as if the gate was too much for him to deal with.

"Give me the knife, and we'll go through the gate."

The pain of the knife in her back increased. The man grunted strangely.

"We are not in the city until we go past the gate." Leandra fought to keep her voice calm, reasonable. The knife withdrew. The man pushed her into the gate. Wrought iron leaves dug into her face.

"Fool, you can't open the gate holding a knife." Vazee stood on the other side of the gate.

The man handed the knife to Vazee, and she unlatched the gate. Mahaloun tackled the man and held a blade to his throat.

"Don't kill him." Leandra held up a hand and Mahaloun froze. She heaved a sigh. "Stand him up to face me."

"Wait a moment." Vazee stared at the man, then nodded to Mahaloun. She examined the man again. "Sloppy, but the circumstances weren't ideal. This will turn him and you into vegetables." Vazee slashed at the runes erasing bits and pieces. Once she stopped and had Leandra draw a new rune.

"I don't think I've seen such a construction before." Leandra studied the result. "Erasing to change the runes." Possibilities blossomed in her mind.

"We can talk about it later." Vazee touched Leandra's face. "Sleep."

***

Leandra woke with Raphael cuddled up against her. Voices sounded in her head.

"Four coppers, on a six showing."

"That's a coward's bet."

"It's safe."

"That's what I just said."

Leandra pushed them into the background.

"Your little kitten appeared in front of us, announced that you were in trouble, then collapsed." Xianju sat in a chair sipping on a cup of what they called coffee.

"I could use a cup of that." Leandra fought the fog in her head. Xianju poured one and put it in her hands. The warmth helped to push back the fog.

"Astonishing that a child his age could use speed and not die from it." Xianju looked at Raphael fondly. "Lichou must have had him almost on fire with power."

"Lichou?"

"The elder with the black mask. His control over the elders is almost complete now that Oghsun is dead. Yuchiva, the one in the spotted mask, is holding out, but the other two are puppets."

"Why are you only telling me now?" Leandra's gut knotted as she ran her hand through Raphael's hair. How close had she come to losing him?

"We weren't sure, and it is dangerous knowledge. Lichou is a master at reading people, and as you have learned, he has no hesitation about killing."

"He wants my kitten for something and was willing to expend an enormous amount of power to capture him."

"Your kitten is a natural sensitive as well as being able to hold an astonishing amount of power. The combination is rare, and one few thakgoki could resist." Xianju closed his eyes looking exhausted. "Lichou wants to restore the Nekkest to our former glory. For him, that means ruling over all the south. We are warriors. For centuries we formed the protective wall around the golden emperor, then an emperor died without an heir. All sides in the ensuing war tried to control us, knowing we were the key to the throne.

"Just as our country was divided, so were we. For the first time in our written history, Nekkest fought Nekkest. A few, distraught over the betrayal of our law and custom, gathered their families and goods and set out to cross the desert. The legend is that a huge black jaguar guided them to this oasis, then ordered them to live in honour until the time came that the world needed them."

"The black claw you gave my kitten." Leandra blinked. "The legend isn't just a story."

"No." Xianju handed Leandra the claw. "My family has passed the claw down from generation to generation. The story says a young boy told the black jaguar he didn't want to kill people. Nekhaize, the jaguar, gave the boy her claw and his name and promised to return. She told him to train for peace as the rest trained for war."

"My kitten and the claw…" Leandra swallowed bile as the implication hit her. "Lichou thinks he can use them to bring Nekhaize back and control her. I very nearly made a similar mistake, and even so, it almost destroyed our people."

"You were wise to send the thing of power away with Cameto. We should have told you to send your kitten too, but we hoped…"

"I understand your hope, and my kitten would too."

"This is why we have been a shield between you and Lichou as long as we could."

Vazee ran into the room. "Hojiam is to face Lichou in the arena."

Xianju paled. "Do what you can, but you know it is their choice."

"I'll come with you. Loan me one of your robes, and I'll paint something on my face."

"The designs we wear are not something we take casually." Xianju put a hand on Leandra's shoulder.

"I understand." Leandra forced her impatience aside and put her hands over her face. "The robe will be enough."

Vazee led Leandra into the street, followed by Mahaloun. Streams of people walked in the same direction.

"The arena is a place of power and testing," Vazee's voice whispered in Leandra's ear. "Normally it is a matter of an agreed-upon test to determine the victor. Lichou will be out to destroy Hojiam."

They entered a gate and walked up a spiral that let out on several levels. Vazee led them to the top level.

Far below, two figures in black faced each other across a circle perhaps a hundred paces wide.

One of them raised their hands, and the gathering power made the hair on Leandra's neck stand on end.

CHAPTER 17

THREE TASKS

Lydia wished she'd considered the length of the track before she'd named it as the course for their race. She rounded the third corner of the track which snaked around the harbour. Tomak didn't look to be breathing hard at all. At least the weather was fine. The people crowding the sides of the track cheered them on. They didn't care who won as long as they got a show.

She crouched low and pushed a little harder on the long straight stretch. The crowd blurred past, their roar barely audible over her rasping breath. A small shape wandered onto the track, then a larger one. A toddler and her mother. Neither had any traction on the ice. The mother grasped the child but fell. She screamed as Lydia flew toward them.

Can't stop in time, can't go around. Lydia jumped at the last second and tucked up into a ball to keep her skates clear of the people. To her shock, she landed on her blades and then almost forgot to slow for the next turn, a tight one which sent her back in the direction she'd just come from.

As she reached the last straight stretch, black spots filled her vision. Tomak was somewhere behind her. *Shouldn't I lose this race?* Her legs refused to slow, as if they had to go full out or stop completely.

A dozen strides from the finish line, Tomak swept her up in his arms and they crossed the line together. The thane welcomed them with mulled wine. Frija had a broad grin on her face. Tomak knelt to get a hug from his sister in her chair. Lydia tried to copy him, but only his strong arm kept her from falling on her face.

"My heart just about stopped when you jumped over those people on the track." Tomak put his arm around her and helped her up.

"Your heart almost stopped? No one was more surprised than me when I landed on my feet."

"I wasn't. Scared they'd try to stand, but you move much more gracefully than you think. Why do you think I stayed behind for the whole race?" He gave her a lecherous look, and Lydia laughed and put her head on his shoulder.

"Tomorrow, the hard part begins." Lydia sighed enjoying his warmth. "Don't take too long to find the riddle.

***

"Would that I had now
what I had yesterday,
find out what that was;
mankind it mars,
speech it hinders,
yet speech it will inspire.
This riddle ponder,
    O, my love!"

Tomak stood in front of her at supper. There wasn't nearly the size of crowd as there had been for his declaration of love, but they made a loud enough racket.

"My dear Tomak." Lydia couldn't keep her lips straight. "The answer might be harder if there weren't a river of it flowing through the hall." She leaned over to swipe the thane's cup. "The answer is ale. The solution to every problem when you're drinking it, and the bane of thought in the morning."

The people loved it.

He proposed riddles whose answers were rivers, hammers, spiders and more. Lydia began to despair.

As she worked on her accounts for the thane, she plotted. Should she answer wrong on purpose? But that would be cheating and Tomak took the contest as seriously as a sworn vow. She'd not insult him.

If he were smart, he'd be asking for help. Frija would have an impossible riddle for sure. Her laughs grew louder with each riddle and answer.

A storm blew in and kept people inside for a week. Lydia grew desperate to see something other than the walls around her. Looking for a distraction, she went through her office and came upon the scroll from Red's bag.

Lines crossed and re-crossed the parchment, some straight, some crooked. Oddly familiar lines dotted the sheet. She turned it around trying to decide which way was up.

"Looking at an old map?" Tomak slipped into her office with a tankard of mulled wine. She put the parchment on the table and stepped back. It did look like a map.

"Where is Getthelm on this?" She traced the line she was certain formed the coast. "It would have to be here somewhere." She drew a circle with her finger.

Tomak laughed and almost spilled his wine on the map. He pointed to the center of the circle. "Here, though it wasn't Getthelm then, but Hecklasfurd. The legend is that the thane went on a raid to the south, planning to steal gold from the empire itself. Only one man returned, and him mad as they come. That was at least four generations back."

"Why would Red have a map from a madman from how many years ago?"

"The survivor didn't return for ten years, in that time Hecklasfurd became Getthelm. Instead of settling here, he went to a cousin's holding, which happens to be not far from where Red crawled out from under his rock."

"Why would he have the map with him?"

"Who knows? Maybe he thought to raid the empire himself. Now's the time to do it while it is consuming itself like a starving wolf."

Lydia put the map away, but it haunted the back of her mind for the rest of the week. The storm broke and the hall filled as the people celebrated getting out of their homes.

"The ocean fed me
over me was the sea;
waves covered me,
close to the ground.
Footless I often,
when the flood came,
opened my mouth.
Now men do eagerly
desire my meat;
with a sharp knife
they cut my skin,
discard my hide,
before they swiftly
swallow my flesh:
they eat me uncooked,
then hang my tormentor
around their neck."

Tomak recited the riddle and tilted his head at Lydia. Her mind went blank. As the silence lengthened, her heart beat eagerly. She smiled.

"I have to admit I am lost." She didn't feel lost, more like jumping up and shouting in triumph.

"The answer," Tomak turned around with his arms out wide, "the answer is the lowly oyster, who lives in the sea and is eaten eagerly, and…" He pulled something out of his pouch, "holds the pearls women love to wear." He handed Lydia a necklace. The chain was exquisitely wrought; but compared to the pearl held in a gold filigree cage, it might have been string.

Tomak came around the table to fasten the necklace. Lydia captured his head and gave him another kiss. The look Tomak gave her melted her insides. Frija snorted so her face had to be as naked as Tomak's. She didn't care.

"The second test is complete!" the thane shouted, since Lydia was still caught in Tomak's eyes.

Lydia worked on the map to keep thoughts of Tomak at bay. Dreams had her waking flushed, both embarrassed and disappointed. She found old records written in ancient script, which looked more like lines carved on a rock than letters. Comparing letters written in the runic script and the more modern, she gradually worked out the meaning of the words on the map.

Hjoenr travelled the edges of the world to come upon the empire unexpectedly. I, Rauorfel, recorded this journey. It might have been better had we besieged the gates of Hel.

Lydia's heart ran cold. For reasons beyond her comprehension, this map was key to her presence in Getthelm. She pulled out a blank paper and copied the map down to the finest detail, then on the back wrote the translation of the runic writing. She put the original in a leather pouch and hid it in her desk.

"Sister," Frija greeted her. A boy who might have been the twin of the thane's cup boy placed Frija's chair beside Lydia. The man who carried Frija put her in the chair. Then both bowed and backed out of the office. The boy's eyes carried such devotion it brought tears to Lydia's eyes.

Frija's grey eye glanced at the hall, and Lydia was sure it glistened. It was so impossible as to be painful. Frija looked at Lydia and gave the slightest of shrugs.

"Sister." Frija pointed at the pearl hanging from its chain.

"I knew you'd come up with something."

Lydia showed Frija her office and her work. The girl looked to be younger than Fury, though with her palsy, it was only a guess. Frija pointed at the map, so Lydia held it to help Frija see better.

"Ring." The young girl pointed.

Lydia looked at the ring she'd worn since leaving her foster-parents' palace. The markings on the ring matched a word on the map.

Hjoenr

"How did Hjoenr's ring end up in my foster-mother's homeland?"

Frija tilted her head.

"Mother came from a country to the south and east of Lusia, a few weeks' journey from the Holy City."

"Map." Frija slapped the paper.

"You're saying he made it south? Or at least one of them did."

"Hjoenr."

"You're right, he's the only one who makes sense. But why would Rauorfel say it was a journey into Hel?

Frija shrugged.

"Right, maybe I'll write and ask if Mother knows."

Frija called her servants, and Lydia gave the boy the copy of the map.

"Keep it safe for Frija to study." He bowed and carried it like it was treasure.

That night at supper a guest sat in Frija's seat.

"Frija doesn't like him." Tomak leaned over to whisper. Ogre sat in the seat Tomak usually occupied.

The guest looked both heavily muscled and soft. He drank a lot and made unsubtle advances. "I am Thane Kristif. I could be good to you."

Lydia grit her teeth and stayed coldly polite.

She was debating whether to stab the man or herself by the end of the meal.

"Thane, do you still have that squirrel. Maybe she can come out and perform." He pointed down to Frija. "There she is. Say something squirrel."

"Fool." Frija spat the word at him. "Coward. Die squatting."

Kristif shrieked in rage and tried to climb over the table, tipping it and himself off the dais. He fought to untangle himself.

Lydia spotted a servant going about their endless sweeping of the hall and ran to snatch the woman's broom. The visiting thane stood up and staggered toward Frija with his knife out.

Tomak pulled his own knife and picked his way over the destruction of the table as Ogre stepped in his path and shook his head.

Frija's boy servant stepped in front of her as the guest stabbed at the girl.

Lydia spun the broom in the moves Fury had taught her for years. The handle connected with the Kristif's knife hand, making the knife grind across the boy's ribs instead of piercing his heart.

Another spin and the straw smacked the drunkard in the face.

He staggered back and she tripped him. She tossed the broom aside and landed on his chest with her knife all but touching his eye.

"You are worse than a fool or a coward. You dare insult the sister of my heart! Hear this then. If you or any of your family, Thane Kristif, step foot in Getthelm unless it is to beg forgiveness on your knees, every one of your blood will die in a foreign land to feed the crows."

The echoes came back to her, and Lydia heard the echoes of God's voice speaking.

Ogre loomed over her.

"Princess."

Lydia stepped back, knuckles white on her knife. Ogre slung Kristif over his shoulder.

"We sail tonight," he bellowed. "If any man isn't onboard, I'll leave 'm behind." Ogre left the hall, followed closely by his men.

Lydia dropped her knife and ran to where Frija wailed over the boy lying on the floor.

"His heart beats." Lydia put her hand on Frija's knee. "I need needle and thread." She pointed at the jug on the table. "Pass it here." She used the wine to wash the wound and made sure there was no cloth in it. Tomak put a threaded needle in her hand, and she sewed up the wound.

"Holy God, heal this boy, keep the fever from him." Lydia drew a cross on the boy's forehead, and it glowed briefly. She didn't have to look to know the wound had stopped bleeding and would heal with only a scar to brag about.

Tomak lifted Lydia to her feet.

"Only one person dared face the man. Frija is the bravest among us, who refused to let politics rule her." He smiled crookedly at where Frija sat on the floor, brushing the boy's hair with her hand. "I would say she is with the desire of her heart."

"I agree," Lydia said. "That's the third task."

"We'll have a big party later, but I plan on spending some time with my wife." Tomak swept her up and carried her from the hall.

CHAPTER 18

THE STORM

The wind shook the inn, making Prenny shiver even though the stove radiated enough heat to cause the air around it to waver.

"Tis the first bad storm of the winter." Leohl picked up an afghan and wrapped it around Prenny's shoulder.

"The first?" Prenny walked over to peer out the window. She couldn't see the house across the road.

"Aye, milady, though it isn't so bad once the snow's down."

"Just how much snow do you get here?" Yennet looked up from where she sat sewing on one of Prenny's dresses.

"Usually three or four fathoms." Leohl poured tea and laid out biscuits and jam.

"Fathoms?" Prenny closed her eyes. They'd think her a dunce if she kept repeating words like this.

"Aye, forgot as how you grew up away from t' water. A fathom is the span of a man's arms." Leohl put her arms up to demonstrate.

"That would be enough to bury the inn!" Prenny took a breath. "Obviously the houses are built for this weather, but I can't imagine."

"The snow'll settle some. But I expect we'll be using the winter door after this one."

"That would be the door which opens on the second floor."

"Most houses have'm." Leohl pulled a chair out and Prenny sat down to eat.

"No wonder Yennet keeps needing to let my dresses out." She reached for her favourite jam, a bright orange, very tart spread.

"That's not the part that's growing." Yennet gave her a wicked smile and Prenny's face burned. It didn't stop her from enjoying the snack.

The storm blew itself out after a few days and Prenny followed Leohl out to a changed landscape. White covered the world except for the grey shake roofs of the village. People were out and about. They wore a rainbow of coats.

"How wonderful!" Prenny grinned. She found that her feet remembered how to walk on snowshoes, though the ones here were more egg-shaped and not as long. The villagers waved cheerfully and asked her how she'd come through the storm. The inn would stand a lot more than that.

Prenny didn't mind that they called her residence 'The Inn' out of habit. She kept the common room open for any to drop in, and if Leohl wasn't cooking enough to feed the entire village, other women were bringing by bread or game meat.

The ocean stayed grey, even with the bright blue sky, but she never failed to be fascinated by its everchanging mood.

The gathering at the inn was exuberant. The few young people Prenny's age convinced her to try dancing, and soon the inn resounded with music and laughter.

The knock on the winter door froze everyone in place. No one knocked on the door. Visitors were expected to open the door and walk in and call out. If no one were home, they could leave or make tea and wait for them to come.

"Yennet." Prenny pointed upstairs.

"Yes, my lady." Yennet slipped upstairs, seconds later she poked her head around the corner of the stairs. "I could use the help of a couple men."

Prenny stood to follow them, but Yennet gave the slightest of headshakes. *Caution is needed.*

"Let's start the music again. I think I'm beginning to get the steps." Prenny smiled at the musicians. They shrugged and took up the tune. Late in the night, the last villager left, and Prenny went to find Yennet.

Her maid sat in a room with a man lying still on the bed. His skin was bronze and hair raven black. His breathing rasped.

"He's got a fever, milady." Leohl changed the cloth on his forehead.

"Help, people," the man muttered, then slid into a language unlike anything she'd heard. She knew Imperial and Belandrian dialect and the northmen language Suze taught her when Prenny lived in Joanslet with her mother and Catrin.

"Says his family is sick wit t' fever. Were caught by t' storm on t' way to t' medicine elder."

"How far away?" Prenny leaned forward.

"Can't be too far given his condition."

"We must go to help them." Prenny stood. "Leohl, I'll need you to come with me. The Paal boys are likely still up; they just left. Yennet, please stay here and do what you can."

"It's better if we don't interfere wit' t' wild'uns."

"He came here and asked." Prenny stood.

"He's delirious."

"Leohl." Prenny turned in the door. "I'm not asking."

Leohl bundled Prenny up in a ridiculous amount of clothing. It felt inadequate as soon as she stepped onto the snow. They tromped over to the house down toward the shore with lights still on.

"A wild'un come to the inn. Sick like. The lady wants us to find his family and bring 'em here. They's all fevered."

One brother stood and threw on a coat. "I'll fetch Garr'son. We'll want more'n one sled. He talks the lingo best, goes huntin' wit' 'em sometimes."

In a short time, Prenny rode on one dogsled and Leohl on the other. She wanted to demand to be treated equally and walk with the others, but it would mean leaving the warmth of the quilts. Between Garr'son's lantern and the quarter moon's light on the snow, they were able to follow the trail easily enough.

" 'old up 'ere.'" Garr'son held up a hand. "The tribe c'n be tetchy about strangers."

They waited while he walked forward a bit and called out in the same language the sick man had used. He waited a bit, then called out again, then a third time. This time a weak reply came.

"They will accept our help." Garr'son called and waved them forward.

The family lay on furs in a snow shelter. Even in the cold, the smell hit Prenny like a hammer. She remembered it from the days in the forest.

"Leohl, do you have willow around here?"

"Willow?" She shook her head.

"Y'll find it not far from 'ere." Garr'son pointed.

"I know what ye mean." One of the Paal brothers strode into the darkness. They loaded the two women in Leohl's sled. A young boy they wrapped up and put with Prenny. A tiny body lay in the corner of the shelter.

"We can't leave it for the animals." Garr'son gently picked it up and wrapped it in cloth before handing it to Prenny. "Treat 'er gentle."

"I will." Prenny fixed the wrap and tried to push back tears.

The ride back to the inn lasted much longer than the ride out. The cold form in her arms broke Prenny's heart. She stopped trying to hold back her tears. They froze on her cheek, but she didn't move her hand from the toddler to wipe them away.

The lights of the inn were a welcome sight. When they pulled up, Garr'son took the toddler from Prenny.

"We 'ave a place t' keep 'er safe, milady."

"Thank you, Garr'son."

He nodded and walked away.

Prenny hauled herself out of the sled, then picked up the boy, only a little older than his sister.

"Milady!" Leohl rushed over. "You'll get yourself sick."

"It's all right." Prenny shook her head. "I've had it. We all did, and most of us lived. T'ain't a big deal."

She handed the boy to Leohl to shed her outdoor clothes, then carried him back to the room where the two women and the man lay. She put the boy beside his mother.

Leohl brought up hot water, and Prenny made tea from the bark off the sticks the Paal brother brought. Nobody could tell which brother was which, and the brothers didn't care either.

"Let it steep some yet," Prenny said. "When they c'n stand it, give the adults a cup, the boy a quarter cup. We'll need water in a few hours to make a new batch. Wake me if anything changes."

Yennet nodded from where she sat. Leohl put her arm around Prenny and guided her to her room.

"Where did you grow up, milady?"

"I lived with bandits in a forest. My mother adopted me 'bout six years back and made me her heir. T' king said it was fine by him, so here I am."

"I won't tell anyone." Leohl looked at her wide-eyed.

"It isn't a secret, Leohl. When I git real tired, I fergit to talk noble." Prenny fell onto her bed and was asleep before Leohl covered her with a quilt.

***

Prenny woke to the sound of wailing. She climbed out of bed and wrapped herself in her robe.

"My lady, you should get dressed." Yennet came over with a simple gown.

Prenny sighed. "You are right. It will be more respectful."

Dressed and her hair braided, Prenny stood by the door, her hand shaking.

"It's all right if you don't go to her."

"No, Yennet, it's not all right." Prenny leaned her head on the door. "The night my folks died, I had the fevers, same as them. Three days passed 'for I knew they was gone. It never felt right. I didn't get to say goodbye, never got to cry on any shoulders. No one to tell me the world is a terrible, unfair place, but we have to make the best of it."

Yennet wrapped her arms around Prenny.

"You are so young. I keep forgetting how strong you are."

"I don't feel strong, Yennet."

"Don't know that many of us do."

Prenny put her arms over Yennet's.

"I don't know what I'd do without you."

"You'd run about with your hair askew, but all the important things, you'd do just fine."

Prenny laughed and wiped her eyes. "Well then, on to the important things."

The woman sat rocking and wailing as she held her son. For a horrible moment, Prenny thought he'd died too but then saw his shoulders shake with his sorrow. The older woman lay with her face covered. The man sat beside her.

Prenny had no idea what to do, so she sat in the chair and did nothing. Time passed. Leohl came in with tea and bread. She got them to eat, then bullied Prenny into eating too.

"Daughter, *niskiic?*" The woman spoke to Prenny.

"She's in a safe place," Prenny said. "They are taking care of her."

"Things we must do."

"I understand." Prenny stood. "Come with me."

The man and woman had a quick conversation, then the man took the young boy. The woman went with Prenny.

Outside Leohl guided them toward a hut with a trapdoor in the roof instead of a door off the second story. One of the young men stomped over and poked a finger into Prenny's chest.

"What're ye doing letting them wild'uns here? They're dirty and wi—"

Prenny's fist connected with his gut, cutting off his tirade. Her left hand crunched into his nose. Then she kicked him to the snow and stared down at him.

"The punishment for assaulting a noble is severe, Petan."

"You ain't any noble, just some brat pretending to be important."

"Stand up, boy." Prenny shook with rage.

"I ain't no bo—"

"STAND UP!" Prenny shouted with the voice she used on the other brats in the forest. Petan lurched to his feet.

"Now hit me." Prenny stood with her hands on her hips.

"I can't hit ye; ye'z a girl."

"Are you afraid to hit me? I just whipped your ass, and I'm going to whip it again."

Petan swung a reluctant haymaker at her. Prenny stepped out of the way, then landed a punch in his ribs under his arm before she kicked out the back of his leg and sent him to the snow again. She landed on him and twisted his collar. He tried to hit her with his knee, and she drove the point of her elbow into it.

"Stop, stop." Petan put his hands over his face.

"Who am I?"

"Lady Prenny," Petan babbled.

"That's right, but I grew up a bandit's brat, had t' fight for my life. You ever fought for your life, Petan?"

"Wit' the ocean." He lowered his hands.

"First time I was here, you remember that?"

"My da made me sit at home."

"So you won't remember that I had to kill people, people who didn't care about you or your da. I shot an arrow into a man I thought was a friend. Do you know why I did that?"

"They were bad people?"

"No, Petan, because they were bad people who threatened my people. You, your da, Leohl. That is what it means to be noble, Petan. Not what kind of bed you were born in."

She stood up, then held up a hand. He took it reluctantly, and she hoisted him up.

"Go put some snow on that nose. And next time you take into your head to insult my guests, I'll get really angry, and I won't be so gentle with you."

She turned to the woman.

"My apologies for his rudeness."

Leohl translated for her, and the woman said something back.

"Not sure how t' say that," Leohl said. "Better get Garr'son t' give it a listen.

In the hut, the toddler lay in a tiny wood box, sprigs of green around her. Garr'son stood and spoke to the woman. She responded, then sat beside the toddler and ran a finger across her cheek.

"Let's give 'er time alone."

They climbed out of the hut and walked back to the inn.

"She said something to Leohl that she didn't understand."

"The woman's name is H'eenicha. Her brother is Kel'aaka. Their mother was T'iinisc.

"H'eenicha called her daughter Niskiic."

"That's right. Her son is H'lanics."

"What happened to H'eenicha's husband?"

"He died in a raid by the R'arhed. The red-bearded devils. They live up where the mountains come out of the ocean, and a meaner lot you'll never find."

"You have the opposite problem to mine." Prenny looked at Garr'son. "I forget to talk like a noble on occasion. You forget to talk like a villager."

"What are you going to do about it?" Garr'son glared at her.

"Nothing. You've been nothing but helpful. When you're ready to talk, you will."

"Thank you."

Prenny led him into the inn.

"I'd like you to teach me the language of H'eenicha's people."

"They call themselves the De'e'tcha, people of the forest."

"Nice." She hung her coat and hat up, switched her boots for leather slippers.

"The villagers don't like the De'e'tcha much."

"I noticed, but that isn't going to stop me from talking to them."

"Why do you care? It isn't like they are a problem."

"Tell me, why don't the coast villagers like their neighbours?"

"Don't know, story is Hildasport to the north was abandoned to them."

Prenny sat at a table in the common room and waved him to a seat.

"I'll bet you the nobles, when they bothered to come up here, sneered at the De'e'tcha, probably afraid they were going to encroach on the estate. I don't think the De'e'tcha are the problem. I think it is very likely that we are."

CHAPTER 19

TIL DEATH DO US PART

Lydia cuddled up to Tomak. Only a week and she had a hard time imagining sleeping alone again. Now she understood the looks Harald and Sara exchanged at times, just before they disappeared for a while.

She ran her hand along Tomak's side feeling the scars. Her fingers were fascinated by the textures of his skin. If she wasn't careful, she'd be waking him up. From the last week, she didn't think he'd mind. Her lips curled into a smile. Definitely, he needed to wake up.

A rough hand covered Lydia's mouth and cold steel touched her throat.

"Come without a fuss and I let him live. So much as a squeak and I slit his throat." She recognized Henric who had disappeared after Tomak had chastened him.

Lydia bit her tongue and clenched her hands. She wouldn't put Tomak at risk. Her head nodded, and he pulled her from the bed. The light sleeping robe gave no more warmth than if she was unclothed. She felt naked, exposed to this attacker.

"Let me take my cloak." She pointed to the lightweight one from Belandria.

Henric snatched it and threw it at her, then dragged her along, one hand again over her mouth, another grabbing at her body.

"You aren't any lady. No lady would ride Red's ship. Now you're going to treat me right, but first,"

He pushed her into the office. "Kristif wants Red's map. He says it's a treasure map."

"He's as much a fool as you." Lydia dug out the satchel with the map. Henric backhanded her to the floor. As she struggled to her feet, she dropped Hjoenr's ring.

Henric wrenched her arm behind her back. "No games."

The slap of feet on the floor made Lydia's heart soar. Henric dragged her into the hall.

Tomak shouted in rage and charged in. He was naked but carried a sword in his hand. Lydia grabbed at the traitor's arms trying to slow him. He slammed the hilt of his dagger into her face, and she dropped to the floor. She'd never experienced pain like this. Her eye screamed, and she couldn't see out of it.

Henric knocked Tomak's slash down so it hit his armour. At the same time, he ran Tomak through the chest, slamming his hilt into where Lydia's husband's heart beat.

Tomak dropped like a stone and Lydia tried to scream. Shouts came from all around. Henric threw Lydia over his shoulder and sprinted through the hall.

He didn't go through the main door, but a smaller one that led to the stables. A horse waited, saddled and ready.

The world swam around her as he mounted the horse and put her across his knees.

Lydia couldn't find her voice, but she screamed inside at God.

How could you do this to me? I was happy!

I am familiar with grief, my child.

No matter what else she said, God didn't answer.

If you aren't going to explain, then I'm done. You can find another person to be your Holy Mother. I will die before I serve you again.

They arrived at the winter docks, close to the ocean where

the currents kept the water from freezing.

The wolf-ships were burning. The flickering light making her head hurt worse.

Ogre was waiting on the dock with a rowboat bobbing in the waves behind him. A sailor kept it in place, carefully not hitting the dock.

"She was to be unharmed."

"The witch fought me; I had no choice. We need to go, now."

Horns blew in the city, multiplying by the second.

"I'll not have a traitor on my ship." Ogre pulled Henric off the horse and broke his neck, taking the satchel from his waist. He lifted Lydia with surprising gentleness and jumped into the boat.

"Go, I would rather not be within bowshot when they arrive."

The other man pulled at the oars. Ogre placed her in the stern, then unshipped another pair of oars. They flew across the water to the wolf-ship. Voices shouted in the distance, but Lydia let go of consciousness and let her pain and grief carry her away.

***

Shouts of rage and grief woke Frija. She poked the boy lying next to her. He opened his eyes immediately and looked at Frija.

"Up."

He rolled out of the bed and pulled on his clothes before he dressed Frija.

"I know you're in a hurry, but you need to stay warm." He cupped her cheek for a moment, and Frija leaned into the touch. He and his father were the only people aside from the thane and Lydia who dared touch her. Everyone else feared catching her curse.

The father came in and picked her up, cradling her in his powerful arms.

"Lydia."

The man strode out of the room, the boy following with her chair. They found the crowd of people around Tomak on the floor. Her father slashed at the walls with his sword, but Frija saw the blood still flowed from Tomak's wound, slowed by the sword still piercing his chest.

"Help."

The man shook his head. The first time he'd ever refused her.

"I'll take her." The boy wasn't as strong as his father, so he carried her on his back. They went out of the back door of their home. A narrow path would lead them up the hill, but it was buried in snow. The boy waded into the snow. He slogged up the slope to a cave marked with three stones forming a doorway.

The boy gasped and shivered uncontrollably, but he carried her through the door without hesitation.

A sickly blue glow lit their way, and they went down endless stairs into the bowels of the hill. The temperature rose along with the stench of death. They entered a cave perfectly round, no more than two fathoms across. In the center, beside a crack in the floor, lay a stone knife.

"Tekate," Frija called out. *Fool, in such a rush you didn't think to bring a sacrifice.*

The boy set her down, then picked up the black stone knife and set it to his wrist.

"No."

"You need to be alive to talk to her. She won't listen to a nameless servant."

She shook her head.

"I would die for you. I love you, and I will wait for you in Hel."

"Name." She put her hand on his. "Heurfrij."

"Frija." The boy spoke her name for the first time. He leaned over and brushed her lips against hers, then slashed his arm from wrist to elbow and fell with his arm over the crack in the floor, his blood running down into it

Frija Arrisdotter, the voice in her head was colder than ice.

"I have come to offer my life in the place of Tomak Thaneson."

I know him not by that name.

"Tomak Ekirson"

He is dying. He'll be mine in a few dozen heartbeats.

"Let me die in his place."

What do I need with your death, Frija Arrisdotter? You won't long outlive your brother.

Tears ran down Frija's face.

"He can't die. Lydia loves him. My sister, I would not see her grieve."

She is far from here already. She belongs to another, and I cannot touch her. I have no use for your death. Will you give me your life?

"I will give whatever I must for my brother."

He lives and will be strong to do what he must. Now, Frija Deathsdotter, go and do what you must. I will call on you in time.

"Yes, Mother." Frija stood and looked at the boy, no, Heurfrij. "Thank you, my friend. With your name, your family will be free." She recalled the brush of lips on hers, and heat ran through her.

Death is not the enemy of life, though humans think so.

Frija picked up the knife and used the point to scratch the rune for death into her cheek. Then she laid it beside Heurfrij and walked away without looking back.

***

A life and a death have been given for you, Tomak Ekirson. Get up, you have a task to complete.

Tomak sat up, and the crowd of servants and warriors scrambled away from him. It would have been funny if he didn't hurt so much. The pain faded rapidly. He looked down to see the wound closed, a new scar added to his collection. A warrior wrapped a cloak around Tomak.

The thane stared at Tomak, looking caught between relief and fear.

"Don't be silly, Father." Frija walked up behind him. "Tomak is still very much human."

If the people had scrambled from Tomak, they fled from Frija. She wore a black robe, and death's rune glowed on her cheek. Only Tomak and his father held fast.

"Tomak has a task to accomplish, or the world will burn. A life and a death were given to purchase his life."

"I must go after Lydia. If they've harmed her..." Tomak scrambled to his feet.

"Lydia lives, but that is not your task. You could search all the world and not find her. Seek your destiny, and what you love will find you." She handed him Lydia's ring. "She left this in her office. They took the map Hjoenr used to travel to the empire."

"What have you done?" The thane reached out to Frija, hesitated, then touched her face.

"I have become Deathsdotter." The look of compassion on her face undid Tomak, and he strode over to embrace her.

"Frija or Deathsdotter, you will always be my beloved sister."

For all the coldness in her voice, she was warm to touch.

Deathsdotter laughed, and he realized it wasn't coldness, but fear of their reaction.

"Mistress?" Heurfrij's father stood with his head down. "I failed you, my life is forfeit."

"Your son, Heurfrij, has served me in life and in his death. You are a free man, Heurfotter."

Tomak's father roared with laughter.

"Heurfotter, fetch your other son here." The man ran off.

"My thane." A warrior knelt in front of him. "All the ships are aflame. The *Red Wolf* has escaped. Henric is dead of a broken neck on the dock."

"Ogre." Tomak spat the word out.

"He has his fate." Deathsdotter stepped back from Tomak. "But he is both more and less than you think."

"Are you always going to talk in riddles now?"

"Of course." Deathsdotter's lips might have twitched into a smile.

"Of course." Tomak sighed. "My ship was pulled up in the fall so my crew could work on it. Rouse them and tell them to meet me with North Flight at the winter docks."

The warrior saluted and left at a sprint, gathering others as he went.

Heurfotter returned with his son.

"Your brother gave his life for my daughter," Tomak's father glance defiantly over at her, and she rolled her eyes. "In return, she granted him a name. Your father is Heurfotter. What name would you have me give you?"

"You have always been kind to me, my thane." The boy knelt. "If I may be bold, I would like to be Thanescup."

"Thanescup, you are free. What do you choose to do?"

"If you allow, I will continue to serve as I have."

"Very well. I'm happy not to need to train another cupbearer." The thane pulled something from his pouch. "Lady Lydia left this with me to give to you when I freed you." He put it on Thanescup's thumb. "Wear it to remind yourself that you are free, responsible for your own actions and words from this time."

Heurfotter knelt. "With Deathsdotter's permission, I will continue to serve her as I can."

Deathsdotter nodded.

"Very well." The thane tilted his head in thought. "You now own everything which once belonged to Henric, with two portions in ten set aside as his debt to Lady Lydia for his treachery."

"You are generous beyond measure, my thane." Heurfotter saluted.

"Let's go see your new home and pack for the voyage." Deathsdotter pointed down the hall.

"I will bring a tent down to the ship, Deathsdotter. I will be honoured to have you onboard."

Deathsdotter nodded at him, then led Heurfotter away.

"Father, call Ekir home and make him your heir. I have my ship and my steading. I have what I need in this world. You don't want anyone thinking they can take Getthelm with one blow," Tomak said.

"I will, my son. May you have a fair wind in your sails."

Tomak spun and ran off to make ready. Each step carried him farther from Lydia.

I will see you again, even if I must defy death to do so.

CHAPTER 20

BATTLE OF THE WINDS

A blast of wind picked up sand and hurtled it across the arena toward one of the figures. Leandra guessed Hojiam since she was smaller than Lichou. It stopped like it hit a wall. Sand blew high in the air and to the sides. Grit reached them even at the highest point of the stands.

The wind didn't slow, and the visibility lowered further. Leandra briefly thought of using the runes to shield them, but no one else was using magic. They wrapped their faces and watched avidly.

As if the wall was eroding, it shrank until it became a dome, then that grew smaller until even Raphael wouldn't have been able to stand. When it collapsed like a bubble everyone gasped, including Leandra, but there was no body on the sand.

A column of wind and sand burst from the ground behind Lichou and rose in a high curve to slam down on him like a hammer. It spread to the side leaving him standing untouched.

Not quite untouched. He shook sand from the mask he wore. His anger showed in the violence of the circle he drew with his arm.

A storm erupted in the arena. Spectators ran away, and Leandra couldn't be sure that no one had been sucked into the vortex.

"If he hurts anyone but his opponent, the elders will award the match to Hojiam." Mahaloun spat out sand and wrapped his face cloth tighter.

"That is if there are any elders left. I have my doubts." Vazee's voice was muffled by her face coverings.

The sand lifted high enough to block the sun and plunge most of the arena into darkness.

Then it froze. There was no transition. One second Leandra couldn't hear over the roar of the storm, the next her ears popped in the silence. Walls of sand loomed over the arena

"Hojiam commented on my subtle use of magic. I take it subtle isn't her style."

"She's become a thakgoki. Every desertwalker must be donating. I've never seen such power."

"Get down." Leandra dragged Vazee to the floor, and Mahaloun dropped beside them. A wave of air rolled over them to crush the sand wall. It came from all directions, focused on a single point in the arena. Blocks of stone fell, shaking the arena. A crack ran through the floor beneath them.

"We have to get out of here!" Leandra shouted over the rumble.

"To do that we'd need to go down there." Mahaloun pointed to where people fought to escape the cataclysm.

Leandra drew runes on the floor. Blood from scrapes and cuts marked the stone.

"This will hold for a while"."

"Let me loan you power. You'll kill yourself."

"It's forbidden," Leandra waved her hand, "for this very reason. Trust me."

"I do." Vazee's hands were latched onto the stone, her fingers dug in as if it were soft clay.

The rumbling didn't die down; it increased.

"When the building falls, hold on to me." Leandra gritted her teeth and scribbled runes as fast as she could, then stroked through them to erase and change, building up the most complex rune she'd ever heard of.

The stones rolled in a circle, grinding until they returned to sand. The sand levelled out leaving the floor of the arena in pristine shape.

Lichou stood in the centre, as relaxed as if he'd been drinking tea, not fighting for his life. Beside him lay a crumpled form. Even from this distance, Leandra could see there wasn't an unbroken bone. Even more horrific, she could feel life in Hojiam.

"I have been vindicated, though Hojiam broke all the laws of the arena."

"We aren't safe yet," Vazee whispered.

"I'll see him burn." Mahaloun ground out the words.

The ground shook. The few people left moaned where they lay.

"Her co-conspirators try to take revenge." His shout echoed off the walls, the sound building until Leandra wanted to put her hands over her ears. Instead, she drew the last line in her rune.

The air solidified around them. Leandra grabbed at Vazee and Mahaloun, as the floor disappeared beneath them.

Vazee screamed as they fell, the walls of the arena coming down on top of them.

They didn't hit the floor. A ball of crystalized air held them as the building collapsed on them.

Leandra was shocked at how quickly it ended. She released the rune just before she gave in to unconsciousness.

***

Leandra walked through a market, the sun warm on her face. There were crowds around her, people of all kinds, speaking a symphony of languages. She tried to ask one where she was, but the woman didn't see her. A Rehego man argued with a wiry woman who didn't come up to his chest, but it was the man who was nervous.

A throng of children ran and played. They were of all colours and sizes, a couple of them with their faces painted like Raphael. One child ran right through Leandra, sending a chill down her spine.

She wandered looking for some purpose, some reason for her being in this place.

"You must go see the fortune teller," a man said, towering over her, black as basal, but with a warm smile.

"Where's the fortune teller?" Leandra reached out to catch the man's arm, but her hand passed through him, and he walked away.

"The fortune teller will help you."

Leandra spun to see a woman wearing a dress with layer upon layer of fabric, but she moved with the grace of a fox. The woman winked at Leandra, then morphed into a white fox and ran away. Leandra followed as well as she could. But now the people bumped her and blocked her way.

A wind came up and blew cold rain into her face. The people vanished as if they had been made of sugar. In the distance, a red tent had a flag on a pole in front.

The longer she walked, the further the tent moved away and the colder the rain became until she shivered uncontrollably. Leandra smacked her head and closed her eyes and reached out to push the door of the tent aside.

"Took you long enough." Her mother looked up from a table with tarot cards set out.

"Mother?" Leandra ran forward, and her mother's face saddened.

"Not really. We are avatars of the Grandmother." She became the woman who came to heal Rodrigo when they were young. "Grandmother is not a person but an idea. The one who imparts wisdom and holds the Balance." She shuffled the cards and handed the deck to Leandra. "Shuffle."

Leandra shuffled, wondering why she was in this place and what was happening to the others.

When she'd finished and handed the card back, the woman's face changed again.

"Right." The cards appeared in the Celtic cross.

Leandra sighed. It was a weak reading. The only outstanding thing was three aces implying success, but this reading was about love and marriage. The kind of reading women desired when they feared what the future truly held.

"Again." The face of the woman was tattooed, not like the Nekkest but in geometric patterns. Her grey hair hung in braids. Leandra shuffled and tried to focus on her purpose for the world.

This time the reading was stronger, three major arcana, but

instead of love, it showed business. Success, failure, change - it all hung in the balance. Leandra sighed. If she were making a deal, this would be a positive reading, but for saving the world, it wasn't much better than the first.

"Again." This time the face was a young girl, but the rune for death glowed on her cheek and the depths of her eyes sent Leandra's heart racing in panic.

Reluctantly, Leandra shuffled the cards again, thinking of the world and how it hung in the balance.

The reading made her gasp and try to push away from the table, but she was frozen in place.

It started with the world card, normally a sign of joy and arrival, but Leandra couldn't shake the idea this was a reading for the world itself. Only two cards were not major arcana. The chariot, sun and star surrounded the world, but ahead the devil promised fear, division and evil influences. The investment of the present was a sacrifice and a shift in values, the only path to spiritual fulfilment. The culmination was death. Whatever happened, the world would never be the same. Each person's acts would come home to roost.

"Is this what you desired?" the girl said, her voice sharp with sarcasm. "You should know better. What is the Balance but knowing that the world is always on the cusp?"

"Why me?" Leandra tried to stop the shaking in her hands.

The girl's laugh cut her like a knife.

"I am the avatar of the Balance." The girl spoke like Leandra was a child. She felt like one. "You are the avatar of the choice. You aren't alone, but each of you must decide on a path, and some paths leading to life are more painful than others."

The tent began to darken. The death rune glowed in the blackness briefly.

"You of all people should know death is not what you think it is."

***

Leandra coughed and spat out dust.

"Nice of you to join us." Vazee's worried expression warred with her flippant words. A ball of faint light floated over her head. "When you planned on burying us under the stones of the arena, did you consider how we were to get out?"

"I did." Leandra groaned. Every part of her hurt. "I figured you'd manage that part."

Vazee laughed and Mahaloun grunted.

"Let me see how deep we are." Leandra drew a rune for sight, and blinding pain struck her, but she pointed up at an angle. "The open air is about three paces that way." She rubbed her forehead.

"You overextended." Vazee brushed a hand across Leandra's temple. "Try to avoid using your power for a while."

"That would be easier if we didn't have three paces of solid rock to get through."

Mahaloun put his hands on the rock.

"Good thing it is solid, it is holding up everything above us."

"So blasting it out of the way is not a good idea." Vazee sighed. "Why aren't things ever easy?"

"When they are, we don't pay attention. No one complains about an easy road."

"Aren't you a bundle of joy." Vazee concentrated on the rock. "Maybe if we go around?"

"Might as well get started." Mahaloun carefully moved boulders to the side and scooped out dust and gravel.

Leandra and Vazee together struggled with chunks of stone that Mahaloun moved easily. They crawled through, hauling stone along a path wound between huge pieces of the arena. When Leandra's arms ached and her fingers bled, Vazee healed her enough to keep working.

"To do more would require you to accept power. I will not do that without your permission." Vazee shrugged. "The line between huangoki and thakgoki is a thin one, but it cannot be crossed twice."

A final grunt from Mahaloun and fresh air blew past them. He climbed up and out, then hoisted Leandra and Vazee up.

Leandra blinked in the light. People wandered aimlessly or dug in the rubble. The destruction took in neighbouring buildings. Mahaloun led the way through the fallen buildings to a clear road.

Leandra wanted to run to Raphael but couldn't force herself to do more than limp. They arrived at the elder's hall. It was full of Nekkest arguing about what to do next and who was at fault.

144

Probably a good thing we are grey with dust and look twice our age. Leandra didn't like how many people wanted to blame her for the disaster. They climbed the stairs to the guest level. Leandra lurched into an almost-run to Xianju's room. She needed to hold Raphael.

When she pushed the door open, she screamed in fear and rage and fell to her knees.

Xianju lay in the center of the room, bloody and still. Raphael was gone. She could feel no trace of him anywhere in the oasis.

Vazee knelt beside Xianju.

"He left a message for me." She brushed tears away. "Lichou has taken Raphael and Hojiam. He needs the Prodigy and the Cripple for the rite to call Nekhaize. The last piece for the rite is the stone altar. They will live, for now."

"We have to go after them." Leandra pushed herself up but staggered and fell to the floor again.

"We wouldn't be able to catch them, and if we did, could you face Lichou?"

"Then what do we do?" Leandra lay on the floor. "Raphael!" she wailed.

"There is only one place for him to complete the ritual." Mahaloun ground the words out. "We go there and stop him."

"That still leaves us facing Lichou." Vazee paced in the room, hitting her leg with her fist.

"Vazee." Leandra forced words past her fear and grief. "You need to heal me. I give you permission. For Raphael's sake, I will become thakgoki, though it means exile from my people." *Cameto, I'm sorry.*

Vazee sat at Leandra's head and lifted it into her lap. Mahaloun stood behind her, his hands on her head.

"Know that the line cannot be crossed twice. There is no going back."

"I understand." Leandra sobbed and Vazee stroked her hair.

"Do you swear to only use power freely given?"

"I will swear it. The world will not be made better by evil."

"Then accept my permission to use my power for good."

"Accept my permission to use my power for good," Mahaloun rumbled.

Power flowed into Leandra, filling gaps she didn't know were there. She could easily get drunk on it. Leandra gripped it and focused, taking only what was necessary, then severing the link.

"I'm impressed." Vazee widened her eyes. "It takes most months to learn that control."

"I don't have months." Leandra closed her eyes.

Mama is coming, my kitten.

CHAPTER 21

THE GATE OF DESPAIR AND HOPE

Lydia woke to someone pawing at her. She struck with her fist and connected solidly. Something in her hand cracked painfully.

"Bitch," the someone said.

She tried to force her eyes open without any luck.

"Touch her again and I toss you overboard," Ogre rumbled, and Lydia stopped panicking. Twice he had proved honourable.

"I'm leading the viiking."

"Yes, and I am the captain of this boat. On land, you command. Here, you touch her, you swim to shore."

Angry footsteps stomped to the other end of the *Red Wolf.*

"Laef."

"Aye, Ogre."

"I set you to guard the princess. Anything happens to her, you'll be swimming too."

"I'm not arguing, but why are you so determined to protect her?"

"Two reasons. First, she was on a ship from Belandria with a king's ransom, and she faced down Red, cool as ice. Second, she is Tomak Ekirson's bride. I have no interest in having that bunch as my enemies. Once she's done her job, I'll deliver her home, body and honour intact, pay a weregild for the abduction and never see her again."

Tomak is dead. The sight of the sword running through her husband made her sob.

"Laef. Water, cloth and food. Bring clothes while you're at it."

"Now, Princess, I know it's horrible to be torn from your new husband, but I'm a man of my word, and only took this viiking if it was clear you weren't to be hurt." Gentle hands washed her face, and she opened her eyes but could only see out of her right eye. "There's a start. Life is better with light in it. I have a daughter your age. She's a spear maid like her mother, can't beat either of them in the ring."

"If you want to see your daughter again in this life, don't step off this ship until you land on your shore." Lydia ground her teeth. *Stop that. I'm not yours anymore.*

"Are you a witch to be casting curses?" Ogre tilted his head, looking more curious than afraid.

"Worse." Lydia put a hand to her left eye and found a pit where her eyeball should have been. "Much worse." Pain shot through her head.

"Laef, shake a leg." Ogre's bellow made her start. "I should have left you on the wharf, but with the boats afire and the town running down to put them out, I wasn't thinking straight." He washed her hair the best he could. "What colour is your hair?"

"Boring brown." Lydia sat on her hands to keep them away from her eye.

"Not anymore." He held a lock of hair where she could see it. It was red as fresh blood.

What are you playing at? I am not yours.
Whatever you say, my child. I am with you.
"Great, I'll be Lydia the bloody one-eyed…" She ran down, her anger fleeting in the face of her grief.

"Princess." Laef returned with more water, as well as clothes and food.

Lydia, impatient with the blood-stiff fabric of her dress, cut it off with his knife, uncaring of modesty, then tossed it overboard. She pulled the pants, blouse and jerkin on over her small clothes. The legs were too long, she cut them shorter with the knife. A rope from Laef made a belt. A black silk cloth held a bandage over her left eye socket.

"I need a knife."

Ogre eyed her doubtfully, but Laef pulled one from his belt and handed it to her. She looked it over carefully, recalling what Rodrigo had said about knives the day he thought it would be amusing to teach Nikay and Fury how to throw them. Lydia tossed the knife a couple of times, then flipped it and threw it, to stick into the mast alongside similar marks.

"Thank you, it will do." Lydia staggered over to the mast to retrieve her blade. She spent the afternoon playing with the sheath and her rope belt to hold the knife where she had easy access but it wouldn't get in her way. Laef found a cloak to keep her from the cold.

In the mornings, she woke needing to shake frost or snow from the cloak.

***

"How about you teach me to sail?" Lydia walked up by where Ogre stood holding the steering oar.

"Why?"

"Why not?" Lydia looked ahead. "I'm bored, and I need to move around to get stronger. I could spend the time practicing my knife throwing."

Ogre laughed. "Hit the mast solid, and I'll teach you."

Lydia pulled the knife and threw it underhanded in one motion. It thunked into the mast.

"I would have thought missing an eye would cause you trouble." Laef pulled out the knife and brought it to her. "I knew a guy who lost an eye and he couldn't shoot the bow anymore. Never saw him throwing knives."

"Since you're here, show Princess around and teach her the ropes and knots."

Laef introduced her to the crew, but the men following Kristif ignored her. Kristif leered at her. The temptation to put her knife into his gut was tempered by the knowledge that he and the rest of his men wore mail.

She worked keeping the ropes tidy and swept snow from the deck. The activity kept her warm and free of ever-spinning thoughts of Tomak and his death.

When she discovered a skill for sharpening blades, the men and women of the ship's crew kept her busy. Laef set up a tiny tent for her to sleep and work.

Lydia woke one morning looking forward to the day. She felt guilty but could almost hear Tomak saying her happiness was his greatest desire.

"Ogre said since you're working on our personal gear, we needed to pay you." Laef brought her bread and meat along with a hot drink for warmth. Then he reached into his pouch and produced the tiniest knife Lydia had ever seen.

"Won this in a game of bones." Laef drew the blade, and Lydia saw it had a ring with a place for the thumb on the back of the blade and a 'tail' sticking out the other side of the ring to keep it from spinning.

The leather sheath was the right size for an eyepatch. From the front, no one would know it held a knife. Lydia cut leather thongs and braided them, then used them to put the patch on. Laef told her to keep the black silk, so she put it in a pocket of her cloak.

Her fingers brushed against the book Harald had given her. She didn't want the book anymore, but Fury's necklace lay in her box under the bed. Sara's ring lay on the floor of her office. The book was the only gift left from her family.

"That a book?" One of the women peered at it. Lydia handed it to her. The woman held it nervously. "You can read this?" She gave it back.

"I can." She opened it and read a passage out loud. *"In all things trust in God, for the purposes of God are far beyond mortal understanding."* Lydia rolled her eye and closed the book.

"Thank you, Hoárr." The woman paled and looked like she wished to take back her words.

"One-eyed." Lydia sighed. "At least it isn't Dreyra Hár."

"Haptabeiðir has only one eye. He traded the other for wisdom." The woman leaned in to whisper, "Hoárr is one of his

150

names. It is said he sees the mortal realm with one eye and the immortal world with the other which is hanging on the world tree."

"And the crew wonder if I am *that* Hoárr?" Lydia laughed, but the woman didn't join her.

"It is well known he gets bored in the immortal world where nothing changes and walks the world as a one-eyed man with a red moustache…" The woman looked down.

"Right, and since I'm a woman and a moustache would look odd, my hair is red."

"If you are – him – forgive us."

"You are forgiven." Lydia's voice echoed making the crew stare at her and the woman to crawl away.

"It would have been nice if you had *asked,"* Lydia said.

I couldn't chance your saying no.

And what about God?

Since you are fighting, he's not likely to interfere. Besides, he has a hand in this too. Hjoenr thought he was travelling to find treasure, and he did find a precious pearl, but what he didn't know was that his job was to leave his ring in what was Hecadem then. It came down through the generations to the daughter who would carry on his purpose."

I don't have the ring. I'm not Hjoenr's daughter through all those generations either.

The god's laughter rang in her head, making her wince.

And you are sure you know better than a god, your God, whose you are? And this, after you found a boat to bring you to Getthelm, inherited an old map from that rascal Red, then were made a member of the thane's household.

And what about Tomak? What purpose is there in us being married only for him to die?

You haven't sufficient humility to hear that truth. The voice carried undertones of sorrow.

I'm still mad at you.

Your anger won't break me.

Enough playing at being Haptabeiðir.

Who's playing? The voice lashed her soul. *The fate of the world hangs on your shoulders.*

I didn't ask for this.

None of us did.

The sudden emptiness in Lydia made her lonely. All her life, God had been a constant. She'd never thought much about the reason. Haptabeiðir was right; she did lack humility.

***

Lydia spent her time reading the book and thinking, or perhaps it was praying. She wasn't sure anymore. Was she really Hjoenr's descendant? Then why did Sara have the ring? More importantly, what was she trying to prove by her rejection of God? Not one person in the stories she read in the book didn't experience loss.

She lay awake looking up at the stars. The holy book said God knew their number and names.

"How many are there?"

More than there are grains of sand in the world.

"I'm sorry." Grief rose like a tide in Lydia. "I'm sorry, but I miss him every day."

Lydia, you have been crafted to be who you need to be. You are forgiven, my child.

"But I have nothing to remember him by."

You do have something, more precious than pearls or gold.

Why does Haptabeiðir explain things, and I get riddles from you?

Haptabeiðir loves his riddles. Don't think that all he told you was all that he told you.

Lydia sobbed and curled into a ball. *It is good having you back, but it only makes me miss Tomak more.*

My child, I have never left you.

***

They sailed east, occasionally seeing land like a cloud on the horizon. Lydia dove into the holy book but also took time to talk to the crew and learn their names. Just as she felt they would sail forever, Ogre turned the *Red Wolf* to the south.

The storm hit like a hammer, pushing them north. The men took turns rowing while the women tended to injuries and kept the brazier fire burning for hot drinks.

Ice coated the *Red Wolf* and made her heavy in the water. Lydia helped the women break ice from the ship and throw it over the side. They suffered through being wet and cold, their clothes freezing stiff and chaffing their skin.

Not one of them looked worried. At the oars, they sang bawdy songs to keep time. When they had time away from rowing, they huddled in corners to gamble with runes.

Lydia sat in her tent, slightly drier than outside, and cast her mind over the stories she'd read in the holy book. She had no desire to allow the elements to ruin it.

"Hoárr, pack what you are taking." Laef crouched outside her tent. "We'll be making landfall before the moon is up."

She didn't have much to pack. Everything she owned, she carried in her clothes. When he returned, Laef helped Lydia wrap the thin mattress he'd found her, using the tent as pack and waterproofing.

The rough water ceased suddenly though the wind didn't slacken. Where they had been drenched in salt spray, now ice crystals slashed at any exposed skin. While trying to find a way to wrap her face with the black silk, Lydia discovered she could see through it.

Kristif's men looked askance at her, but the Ogre's crew cheered her and shouted blessings over the howl of the wind.

Laef shuttled Kristif's men ashore in the small boat. Lydia, he left to last.

"Listen, I can come with you and keep you safe."

"No, Laef, you'd die. Go back to the ship. When you get home, look to your left."

"Riddles?"

"They have their place, Laef. We're not meant to understand before we understand."

"No wonder they call you Hoárr, you tell riddles like him." He rowed into the white and vanished.

"Now you are mine." Kristif stood behind her.

"No, I am God's." Lydia turned to frown at him. "Do you truly think this an accident?" She tapped her eyepatch under the silk. "We must get on our way." She walked past the man, then stopped but didn't turn around. "There is but one path which will lead to your survival and riches you can't imagine. Walk carefully."

***

They slogged through the snow, at times up to their waist.

The storm blew out, but the temperature dropped, and the men had ice hanging from their beards and moustaches. Lydia left the silk wrapped around her face but for her nose and mouth. It cut the edge of the cold surprisingly well.

"Hey, your turn to break trail!" Kristif yelled. There was only one person he refused to call by name. Lydia pushed up to the front and headed off to the east.

"You're going the wrong way, idiot."

"How do you know?" Lydia didn't turn or raise her voice. "In fact, you were going the wrong way."

"The map shows south until we hit the river."

"I'm not following the map." She pointed ahead. "I'm going where we need to go."

Kristif yanked her cloak, sending her into the snow. Lydia rolled onto her back and watched the polite discussion between Kristif and his men. Polite since no one had drawn their knives yet.

"We're tired of you pushing our luck. Hoárr is god-touched. You keep beating on her and something bad will happen."

Kristif swung at the speaker, but another man grabbed his Kristif's arm and, with the help of a third man, held him back.

A fourth helped Lydia out of the snow and even brushed snow from her cloak.

"If we go Kristif's way, what will happen?"

"We all die before morning." Lydia shook herself, then started east again. The men followed her, leaving Kristif on his own yelling and cursing his men. He finally followed behind, still shouting.

A woman in furs and leather stepped out of the trees, an arrow held loosely on the string. She called out something Lydia didn't understand, but one of the men stepped forward and engaged in a long dialogue. The woman shrugged and walked away. Lydia followed the interpreter along the woman's track.

Two hours of walking brought them to a collection of skin tents, smoke wafting from the tops. The woman led Lydia into one tent, after pointing the men toward another.

Lydia unwrapped the silk and sat where the woman pointed.

The oldest person Lydia had ever seen sat wrapped in a thick fur. She opened her eyes, and Lydia gasped. They were white and sparkled like diamonds. The old woman could clearly see as she nodded at Lydia before going back to sleep.

The sudden heat of the tent made Lydia sleepy, so she wrapped up in her cloak and slept.

***

"I've been waiting for you. The white raven spirit told me to send my granddaughter's granddaughter west to meet you."

"I am Lydia, called Hoárr." Lydia looked around. The forest was bursting with colour and life. This had to be the old woman's dream.

"I am Vakate." She waved at her surroundings. "I always loved the spring. The land is so alive. I wish we had more time, but you are one who understands the working of the spirits."

"I know better than to argue with them." Lydia smiled and touched a flower, allowing a bee to crawl on her hand. "At least I do now. They appear to enjoy a good argument."

"That they do. It is why they walk this world. I have not met the one-eyed god, but we know of him."

Lydia let the bee fly away. Vakate put her hand over her left eye, and it didn't seem odd when she held out an eye made of diamond to Lydia. She took the eye and slipped it into place under the eyepatch.

"One-eye has taken you as far as he can, now Vakate, granddaughter's granddaughter, will guide you from here. Please take care of her. She is headstrong, but big-hearted and you will want a woman with you in the time to come."

"I will, Grandmother." Lydia nodded respectfully.

A burst of ecstasy so sharp as to be almost painful ran through Lydia, waking her.

Vakate sat beside her namesake and wailed. Lydia crawled over to hold her.

"Hush, child, you knew it was time. You must meet the King of the World. I have earned my rest."

King of the World?

You'll know in time.

Rest well in the eternal spring, Grandmother.

Vakate pulled the blanket over the old woman.

"We must go first thing in the morning," Vakate sighed.

"There is one who will not be happy to see my back." She ran her hand over Lydia's hair. "Why has your hair changed colour?"

"That spirit has returned to his people."

"What is your name?"

"I'm Lydia, but I'm called Hoárr,"

"Well met, Lydia. Now you should rest. The way is long."

Lydia lay down again, and this time there was no dream.

CHAPTER 22

A NEW ENEMY.

The De'e'tcha stayed a week. Petan appointed himself their guide and protector, though Prenny and Garr'son were with them constantly. They only spoke De'e'tcha. Prenny did her best to explain why she thought they should meet with King Harald.

"Why should we care?" Kel'aaka shook his hand and waved at the village around them. "How can he think he owns this when he isn't even here, Can he stop the tides or command the caribou?"

"As I understand it," Prenny wrapped her cloak tight as if the mention of the ocean made the air colder, "it isn't about ownership, though I'm sure there are those who'd disagree. It is about responsibility. I don't own this village or the others, the people or the land, but I am supposed to do what I can to help the people."

"I will think on it." Kel'aaka pointed south. "Who are those people on the road?"

"It looks like trouble." Garr'son frowned. "They are carrying too much to be visiting."

"I will collect my sister and nephew, and we will go."

"Peace go with you on the road," Prenny said. "We will meet

again, I hope."

Kel'aaka turned and loped back to the inn.

She led Garr'son and Petan to meet the people. Prenny recognized someone from Coshport. He leaned on a stick as he limped along the road.

"Petan, run to the inn. Tell Leohl to be ready and then rouse the village. Garr'son, set some lookouts, especially on the trail to the north landing."

The men ran off. Prenny ran toward the crowd.

Children came to meet her, mobbing around her, crying and all talking at once about bad people on a boat.

"Come, we can talk in the inn." Prenny picked up the smallest and took another by the hand. The adults nodded, and their pace increased slightly.

***

"They attacked without warning." Vrank had his hands curled around his mug. "Got as many out as we could. Distracted them from slaughter by yelling about my store. They came in t' front as I went out t' back. Almost didn't make it." He touched the bandage on his arm. "But they were more interested in loot than me."

"Twas awful, milady." A woman put her hand on Vrank's uninjured arm. "Bodies in the street, girls screaming. They burned the village. Smelled the smoke from the road."

"Is this all who escaped?"

"Them's we know about."

Prenny looked around the room counting heads, naming the people she knew. There were far too few. Mali and Moz were missing. The man who played fiddle to set her feet tapping. The woman who brought bread every morning Prenny was there but never said a word and blushed deep red if Prenny thanked her.

"What did the invaders look like?"

"Come on a ship, flew the Belandria standard. Rough looking. Shaggy, more like bears than people."

"Damn." Garr'son sat down and put his head in his hands. "They'll be taking prisoners for slaves. Woman of childbearing years, young men, older children. The weakest and the strongest they kill."

"You know these people." Prenny sat beside him. "Drink

your tea, then you can tell me about them in the coach." She stood up and looked around. "Petan, my bow and as many arrows as you can find. Put a couple of spare bows in. Then any men who can hold a gaff, you're going to lead us to Seal's Bight then Sham's Harbour. Bring them all here. They take what they can carry, no more. No heroics. If these scruffy devils have already shown up, hightail it back here."

"What if they come here next?"

"Set a watch. If you see a sail, any sail, everyone goes up to where you hid from the smugglers. I'd send you straight there, but it's too cold for the old folk."

"You sound like you're starting a war." Yennet frowned from where she leaned against the wall.

"The war has already started, Yennet. I have to keep as many people alive as I can until we can get to the king."

"Why not send someone now?" One of the Paal brothers asked.

"There will be men on the road to ambush anyone who tries." Prenny slowed her breathing. "It's what Chancy would have done. If it was only a raid, they'd hit here, but they took the southernmost village. They plan to bottleneck us here, then capture anyone they missed at the villages all at one go."

She stood up, then climbed onto the table.

"Attention! Leohl is in charge while I'm gone. Do not fight if you aren't absolutely forced to. None of us are a match for these brutes. If they come, torch the village to cover your tracks. Anyone with a bow, you're rearguard and will slow any attack."

"Milady, I can take m' dogs and cut west across country for help." The Paal brothers stood shoulder to shoulder.

Yennet coughed once.

"Go, now. Tell the king to be cautious. These men wouldn't attack if they didn't think they could hold off Belandria. They have at least one Belandrian ship. We don't know what else they have."

Two of Petan's younger friends caught Prenny on the way out of the inn.

"Let us ride w't ye, milady. T'will get the warning there faster."

"Good idea, but if we see smoke, you're staying in the

coach."

"Aye, milady." The boys bolted off.

"T' coach is almost ready." Taul came in and announced. He was the shortest man in the village but not one to anger. "I'll be driving ye."

"Good."

***

The coach, or more accurately the coach fitted with skis, rumbled and shook as they headed toward Seal's Bight.

"I was one of the Rau'ch's slaves. Took me off my father's ship. We'd come up to trade. They killed everyone else, then burned the ship. After ten years, they got careless. I killed the man guarding us working the garden. I tried to get everyone to come, but they were terrified, so I told them to run to the Rau'ch and tell them what had happened. They might've had a chance to live then." Garr'son shook, his face white. "I've been dreaming of them coming after me ever since. If I go to them, maybe they'll…" He trailed off and stared at his feet. "I'm a coward, milady. I should have told you, told the king, but," he pulled the neck of his sweater down to show a whitish callous around his neck, "I'd be a slave again."

"Belandria doesn't allow slaves. A couple of nobles got hung for trying."

"Didn't know that." Garr'son sighed and scrubbed his face with his hands. "I fight the best I can, but leave me behind—"

"The hell I will." Prenny put her finger into her chest. "I need someone who can talk to these people."

"They aren't ones for talking." Garr'son nodded at her bow in the corner. "That's the language they'll listen to."

"How can I dictate the terms of surrender if I can't talk to them?" Prenny frowned at him.

"Surrender?" Garr'son shook his head.

"Only cowards refuse to surrender." Yennet lifted her head from where she sharpened and checked her knives.

"You mean it the other way."

"Think about it." Prenny grinned at him. "It will keep you distracted, but before you do, how do I say 'throw down your weapons'?

***

They'd dropped young Bill at Seal's Bight, with a note sealed with her signet ring. Thoms jumped out at the junction to Sham's Harbour.

"Back in, Thoms," Taul shouted from the seat of the coach. "I can see smoke."

"Drive toward Coshport. Be ready to turn and run."

"Aye, milady."

When they got closer to the village, Prenny climbed up beside Taul, and Yennet handed up bow and arrows.

"Aim for the legs. They'll have armour and maybe shields. You don't need to kill them, just slow them."

They rounded the first bend to see villagers running while men with bloody axes and spears chased them. The men grinned as if it was a great sport.

Prenny strung her bow and fitted the first arrow to the string.

"Keep going until I say, then turn and wait for my command."

The villagers ran harder when they saw the coach. The invaders stopped smiling and put on a burst of speed.

Prenny drew the bow, pointing as much at the sky as at the invaders.

"Maybe this will slow them down." She released the arrow and had another on the string without looking where her first shot went.

An invader stumbled and went down. Prenny sent her second arrow, close enough to aim and not count on luck or divine intervention.

"Time to turn around." Prenny climbed up on the top of the coach. "Yennet, I'll need your help. Garr'son, climb up with Taul."

Three of the invading Rau'ch dropped to her arrows before the rest lifted the shields off their backs and spread into a line, ignoring the villagers.

"Thoms, take the villagers to Tansent's Arm. Listen to Leohl. Get them off the road. The more we force the enemy to split their forces, the more of us will survive."

The young man jumped out and ran to the villagers, encouraging them to follow. They didn't slow as they passed the coach.

"Taul, follow the villagers, but don't crowd them." Prenny didn't turn around. "Yennet, shoot high, I'll hit them low."

They ran through the arrows at a terrifying pace. A few more of the enemy dropped but not enough.

"I'll slow them some." Taul shouted and jumped from the coach, forestry ax in his hand. He rolled to his feet. Prenny cursed the fool.

"Don't slow, Garr'son. If you see anyone flanking us, put on the speed and get us out of here. Don't stop for anything."

The Rau'ch laughed when Taul charged at them. He would have come to shoulder height on the shortest of them.

One of the invaders made a show of using his shield to protect his ankles. Taul threw the ax and split the man's head. He picked up the shield and his ax before the others could react to their fellow's death.

"Tell me when we're down to six arrows, Yennet." Prenny used the distraction of the fight to good effect.

Then an arrow pinned her leg to the top of the coach.

"Drive!" she screamed and pushed Yennet toward the front. "We stop, we die, but make our speed uneven."

Arrows fell around her. Prenny spotted the archer and sent a cloud of arrows in his direction. More came from behind but fell short.

"Making the turn, hold on!" Garr'son yelled. Prenny clutched at the rack the coachmen could tie her luggage to if she had any. She snatched at the bow before it slid off the top of the coach. All but three of the arrows slid out of reach, the quiver jamming against the rail.

The coach slowed.

"Don't slow down."

"They have Thoms!" Garr'son yelled back and kept slowing.

"Yennet, run them down."

The coach leapt forward. Prenny snapped the arrow holding her to the roof, snatching up and firing the three remaining arrows at the men closest to Thoms. Now that her leg was free, she could slide over to pick up the quiver. A man with a bow sprinted toward her from behind. She shot two arrows at him. The first missed as he dodged to the side, the second cut the bowstring then drew a red line on the side of the man's neck.

Prenny spun around, staying low. The invader holding Thoms drew his knife across the boy's throat and red spilled over Thoms and the snow. The man heaved his ax at the horse. Yennet swerved. Prenny slid to the side. The coach bumped over Thom's body. She rolled back then put an arrow into the Rau'ch man's laughing mouth. The last few arrows she sent at the couple of Rau'ch who kept chasing them. One fell; the other stopped.

Thoms was a red spot growing smaller as they drove away. Prenny vomited over the side of the coach, then crawled to the back to watch for more enemy.

They passed the villagers from Sham's Harbour, then Seal's Bight, yelling encouragement but not stopping.

"Get to Tansent's Arm. Leohl will tell you what to do."

With the slower pace, Yennet came back and bandaged Prenny's leg, then swung her down into the coach.

"I will watch," Yennet said.

"Don't stop in Tansent's Arm. We're going up to Hildastown."

"It's deserted."

"Probably, but it is a place to start searching for the De'e'tcha. We need their help to survive."

Mother, I tried to think of what you would do, but you didn't tell me it was so hard.

CHAPTER 23

TIME TO CHOOSE

The hardest part of becoming a thakgoki was ignoring the runes demanding to be used. They whispered in her mind, *make this less heavy, that stronger, listen in on a conversation, create a circle of silence.*

In the end, she put on a pair of heavy gauntlets to make her fingers too clumsy. The runes became sullen and hard to work when she did want them. She didn't mind; the runes should be hard.

While she was healing and going through her negotiation with the runes, Vazee and Malahoun made arrangements with the desertwalkers to guide them to the Black Jaguar Temple.

They set out with no fanfare. The Nekkest cleared rubble and ignored the lack of government. Leandra approved. Governing should be about hints, not clubs to the head.

The desertwalkers were an eclectic group. Men, women, zuthi, the only requirement was they had to have made their first choosing. They were reticent, grieving and angry over what happen to Hojiam and guilty that the gift of their power had been turned against her. Leandra walked with Vazee and Mahaloun. They talked to pass the time and miles.

164

"The desertwalkers grant a place to people who cannot, or choose not to, be part of the Nekkest. They can return with a choosing."

"Hojiam said something about being forced to choose again, it being possibly fatal."

"The Nekkest made a compromise long ago. People got to choose their place and identity; all they need to do is prove they have the skill. At some point, gender and sexuality got mixed in and things became messier. There is no skill set for being a man or a woman other than being human, but some wanted to choose. Thus it is allowed for one to choose a new gender on occasion. The zuthi rose from a group who didn't want to deal with being either gender. Sadly, instead of leaving it at that, the elders of the time ruled the zuthi had to be neutral and not show characteristics of either male or female. Children, they said, could experiment with being a girl one day, a boy the next, but adults had to grow up and decide."

"What makes the choosing so dangerous?"

"It isn't the choosing. There is no trial or danger, only a simple declaration. The danger comes in the aftermath of being someone you don't wish to be. Slightly more than half of zuthi walk into the desert after their second choosing. The rest make themselves annoying by trying to get the rules changed. Xianju was a supporter and, as the peace elder, had significant influence with the people, though the elder council didn't like him. His death is a great loss. His child is not in a position to take up the study of peace. It has happened before, but it is always a troubling period until the position is restored."

"Hojiam is his strength, his child." Leandra put a hand to her head. "It would be hard to switch from the child's nickname to their choice name."

"For some, it is harder." Vazee glanced at Leandra. "I have noticed your kitten is still Raphael when you speak your own tongue. There was no need to adopt our customs."

"I'm not sure why I did, like giving Raphael the claw. It felt needed for the Balance."

"What is this Balance?"

"It's a Rehego thing, or rather, we Rehego talk about it in our own way. We accept our choices for good or evil. Some which look good turn out to be evil, often the worst kind of evil. When we talk about the Balance, it isn't about keeping equal amounts of anything. More that we walk a narrow path with consequences for every choice. We have one who holds the Balance. They give advice and strength to those making difficult decisions."

The desert wasn't dead, far from it. Leandra learned to check for scorpions in her clothing and boots in the morning, as much because they were a treat as the pain of their sting. Snakes hid under rocks, mice lived in burrows and far above vultures circled.

Scrubby bushes became more common, then a nuisance as they impeded travel. The desertwalkers refused to cut them down, so Leandra became adept at keeping her clothes from tangling in the sometimes-thorny branches. Her Rehego clothing of pants and blouse helped.

The bushes gave way to clumps of wiry trees, which in turn straightened and rose to the sky. The slope of the ground grew, and Leandra's legs ached each morning.

Vazee taught her much of the history of the Nekkest and where their customs came from. Once in a while, the white lady would instruct Leandra on the life of a thakgoki. The heavy gloves were in Leandra's pack, the runes placated.

Vazee talked about the magic as if it were a child to be entertained. She had a wide range of exercises for Leandra to use the magic but not for anything which needed doing by hand. Like the image of magic as a child, the exercises were amusing - such as holding different coloured light in various orders or creating illusions to illustrate a story. Leandra grew comfortable with her new relationship with the runes and magic.

One evening a group of people met them in a clearing. The leader, at least Leandra guessed she was, towered over the others, but the proportions were strange. She puzzled at it while one of the desertwalkers talked to the woman. The tall woman nodded, then strode off.

"Stilts." Leandra spoke to herself, but Vazee put a finger to her lips.

"They welcome us to their territory and wish to stand tall in our presence. It is polite to accept them as they present themselves just as they do for us."

"They will guide us to the temple. They have guarded the pathway as long as it has been here." The desertwalker came over to them. "We embark in the morning on the most dangerous part of the journey."

***

Before the sun came above the mountains, they were following a young man on stilts, not as tall as the woman of the previous evening but still head and shoulders above the tallest in their group. They wound up the side of the mountain, switchbacks letting them see the drop to the valley floor. An eagle flew beneath them, Leandra moved away from the edge. She'd never walked so high above the earth. It made her feel exalted and terrified.

The track grew narrower, and the occasional stone slipped over the edge to vanish swiftly. They had lunch in a small perfect grove where the abyss wasn't in sight. Tiny birds swooped down to snatch crumbs from the ground. Leandra scattered a few extra just to see them closer. At first glance they were grey, dull coloured creatures, but up close they showed flashes of colour on their throat and under their wings.

"They are hidden finches. I've only seen them in this grove." Their guide sat beside Leandra. He whistled a few notes, and one of the birds landed on his hand. Leandra held her breath. "Put out your hand."

Leandra held up a finger, and the finch hopped onto her finger. It tilted its head at her.

"You are beautiful."

The finch pecked at her finger, drawing blood and then sipping at it. Leandra watched, entranced. After a couple of minutes, the bird flew away, and Leandra sucked the blood off her finger.

"I've never seen anyone react that way." The guide stared at Leandra. "Most people shake them off at best. Many curse and try to kill the finch, though none has succeeded to my knowledge."

"Beauty has a price, and someone must pay it. I can spare a little blood."

"And if the whole flock came?"

"I would give what I could." Leandra smiled at him. "Your hearing must be extraordinary."

"Pardon?"

"You heard me say you walked on stilts. This is a subtle gift. Beauty and danger together. Perhaps a way of testing how I would use the knowledge." Leandra put her hand on the guide's shoulder. "You already walk tall here in the mountains. I've never seen anyone so graceful on stilts. I must admit I saw them and judged, wrongly I might add. They only help us see what is already there. Like you need a close look at the hidden finches to see their colour, a closer look at you reveals hidden depths." She waved her finger. "Such as feeding me to the bloodsucking finches." Leandra grinned. "I think I deserved it. Thank you."

"My name is Chgetke. I am named after the finches. I'm told I bit my father and drew blood when I was born."

"Mine is Leandra. I am the white queen of the Rehego, though it took seeing into the darkness of my soul to become the light."

Chgetke put his hand over Leandra's heart. "I would be friends with you, Leandra, white queen. Wherever you travel, you are welcome in these mountains."

"I am delighted to call myself your friend. You are always welcome at my fire."

They left the grove and returned to the narrow trails up the side of the mountain. Chgetke guided them into a cave before it began to grow dark.

"The trails are no place to be at night." He used wood stacked against the wall to light a fire.

***

Leandra woke to a brief cry. Chills ran along her spine. Calling light, she counted heads. One of the desertwalkers was missing. She jumped to her feet and drew the rune for finding and ran out after the missing member of their group.

Only after she'd started on the path up the mountain did Leandra consider whether running out into the night was wise. It wasn't usually her style. She was a queen - Rodrigo was more the heroic type. Something was wrong. Leandra dropped the light and cast a more difficult rune to let her see in the dark. One of the runes made a suggestion, and Leandra grinned. She put an illusion of herself three or four paces ahead, then crept forward.

The night stilled as if it knew what was coming and held its breath.

Ahead, a shadow crouched over a deeper shadow. Leandra slipped on a rock, and a pebble rolled across the trail. In the quiet, it sounded like a landslide.

The crouching figure's head snapped up, then it leaped through the illusion and bounded up to Leandra.

"Chgetke," Leandra spoke silently, but their guide acted like she'd slapped him.

"He was warned to stay in the cave." Chgetke spoke with a lisp.

"It is hard to hunt and stay aware of consequence." Leandra sat on a rock. "I have made the same mistake."

"He isn't dead." Chgetke looked down. "Quite."

"Like the finches, you hide behind layers of truth."

"I thought I could deal with the hunger." He hung his head.

"Are you alright for the moment?"

Chgetke stared at her eyes wide.

"If you need, ask." She walked over to the desertwalker.

"Don't save…" the zuthi rasped, "rather die."

"That's hard on the others."

"I desire…" they wept, and Leandra held them. She drew runes of healing as she let power trickle into the zuthi.

"How can you not?" Leandra ground the words out. "It is human to love, to desire, in one way or another."

"They will make me choose. I'd rather die."

"Who will make you choose? There are no living members of council who are not traitors to the Nekkest. Will the walkers drive you out?" She shook the zuthi gently. "It is always a risk to love, though you risk more.

"The guide…"

"The guide also fights his own nature. You came out to die. Is it his fault he almost killed you?"

"His fault he didn't finish." The zuthi staggered to their feet, then off the edge of the cliff. They screamed a name as they fell.

Leandra couldn't tell if it was a farewell or regret. Her heart ached.

"Leandra." Chgetke crouched at her feet. "Help."

She drew her knife and cut the back of her arm near her wrist and held it out to her friend.

"I trust you."

***

She wore one of her gauntlets the next day to keep the cut clean. Leandra had told the story of the night, leaving out only Chgetke's name and the true reason for her wound. When she told them the name the zuthi screamed, one ran out of the cave and Leandra's heart twisted with pain.

They started on their day's journey two short. The walker's heads were down, and more than one cheek glistened with tears.

"Are you sure it was wise?" Vazee pulled Leandra to the back of the line and kept her voice soft.

"No." Leandra looked up to where Chgetke led them. Something had gone out of his walk. "But it was right. We can't afford to lose our guide nor can we afford distrust. Maybe it is time for you to step out and name yourself. I don't wish to see any more die because love is forbidden them."

"You are right. Whatever happens, the Nekkest are changed for ever. We may as well try to make it for the better."

That evening, Vazee stood after the meal was complete.

"You know me through Hojiam. I am the nameless. If it weren't for Xianju's intervention, I would have faced exile for my defiance. What you don't know is that I refused another choice. I am neither woman nor man nor zuthi. As defiant as I was in the choice, I was meek in life, not stepping on toes. I was given charge of the finding of more supplies before Nekkest starves. Thus I met Leandra of the Rehego and began my redemption. This trip is the next step. I will stand between Nekkest and Lichou at the cost of my life. That means I will also stand between you and those who threaten you, even if it is Nekkest itself."

The walkers listened in silence. When she'd finished, they stood.

"We will witness."

Vazee shook until Leandra feared she'd fall.

"I choose to be a zuthi, but I refuse to renounce love and joy. For my name I will be called Rebel Joy, Xiuefa."

"Welcome, Xiuefa." The walkers said in chorus.

With everyone looking at Xiuefa, Leandra was the only one to see the tears on Mahaloun's cheeks.

In the morning, Mahaloun was even quieter than normal. Leandra was sure there were stones more talkative than him. She moved ahead to walk beside Mahaloun. He made a point of not acknowledging her, suddenly fascinated by the view.

Intent on avoiding Leandra, he stumbled on a rock and would have gone over the edge if she hadn't pulled him back

"Out with it." Leandra crossed her arms.

"What?" He growled more than spoke the word.

"Whatever you're moping about. It's just become a hazard to this mission."

"None of your business." Mahaloun pushed past her. Leandra grabbed his shoulder and slammed him against the cliff.

"My son is out there, his life depending on us. If you aren't focused, he could die. Not to mention Lichou getting god-like powers."

"I could push you off the edge."

"Try." Leandra held his gaze. When he didn't react, she slammed him against the rock again. He put his hands on her shoulders and pushed. She didn't shift a finger's breadth, and his shoulders cracked the rock behind him.

"You are going to deal with whatever is making you act like a child before you take one more step." He shoved her again, and the rock cracked more.

"Who made you leader?"

"I did, just now, because someone needs to keep us in line, and no one else is doing it."

He slumped his shoulders and shook his head.

"My kitten used to try my patience. He once stood from sunup to sundown rather than take a bath. If I can outwait the world's most stubborn four-year-old, I can outwait you."

"Why didn't you just throw him into the bath?" Mahaloun's hands played the seam of his pants.

"What would that teach him? Only that the bigger, stronger person is right, even if they aren't. I've been that bigger, stronger person; I won't be again. He got to think all day about his side of things and my side. If it took him the entire day to figure it out, so be it. Obedience is only healthy when tempered by thought."

"You sound like Xianju."

"I'm flattered."

"It wasn't a compliment. He was afraid. We could have taken down the council, and all this with Lichou would never have happened."

"I thought that about my brother for years. I'd challenged him to join me in changing the world, and his response was always 'then what?'"

Mahaloun looked at her, forehead like a plowed field.

"More of Xianju's words."

"Okay, so you attack the council. There are three possible outcomes: you win, you lose, or nobody wins. Let's start with you winning. You've kicked out the council, the Nekkest are free of their chains. Who's going to make sure the sewers get fixed?"

Mahaloun gaped at her.

"Overthrowing a government means you take over governing. All of it, from the people at the top to the people fixing the sewers. Do it wrong and you have another coup and another. Keep in mind that's if you win."

"If you lose, the bad guys stay in power and know they need to consolidate that power. Every person who ever spoke the slightest complaint will be at risk. It won't matter to you - your head would be decorating the hall as a reminder." Leandra shook him.

"But the worst case is a stalemate. You're balanced equally, but once you've started fighting, you can't stop. Civil war. Brother killing sister, neighbours betraying each other. Panic, famine, plague. If you're lucky, some outside force comes in and stomps on both sides."

Mahaloun turned green and slumped to sit on the path, head between his knees.

"I didn't know, I swear by the Black Jaguar."

"But Xianju did. He was courageous enough to be thought a coward. Rodrigo was the same. Eventually he convinced me to see the results of my desire, it made me a sick as you are now." She sat beside him. "Unfortunately, someone else set the fire. Hundreds of my people died. Thousands of the people of the Empire continue to die while armies crisscross the land and lay waste to it. Even if the fighting stopped like this," Leandra snapped her fingers, "it would take decades for the land to recover, centuries for the scars on people's heart to heal."

"Then why try?"

"The first thing to do is decide what you want. Do you want to rule the country? Would you know how if you had to? Probably not. What is your desired end? More freedom, allow the zuthi to be who they are, make the choosing a real choice, create more tolerance for those who don't fit in."

"That's what we want, but Lichou…"

"Lichou broke through the checks and balances of your system and subverted the council. He must be stopped, but you can't stop him by fighting those he's terrified into serving him. Think, why did he have to murder or break the minds of the other councillors? They would have tossed him out. What you want is the right people on the council. Xianju should have been there. Perhaps he stopped going because he knew he'd be the first to die, and he didn't wish to leave you without guidance."

"So we use the councillors?"

"Not use, educate. Show them the reality of the laws they support, suggest alternatives which won't end in chaos. Change comes through education, from the lowest to the highest."

"That would take a long time." Mahaloun sounded thoughtful rather than sullen.

"Belandria's been working on it for more than ten years, and we still have a way to go."

"You said you're Rehego."

"I am, but because of Belandria's hospitality and generosity, I am Belandrian too."

"The others are lucky to be visiting your home."

"I would like to think so."

"About what you wanted to talk about." Mahaloun dropped his voice to a whisper, a basso version of Raphael when he finally was ready to talk. "I'm in love with Xiuefa, but now she's a zuthi…" He took in a breath that was almost a sob.

"I believe it's time we had a proper talk." Xiuefa sat down on Mahaloun's other side. "If you would excuse us, Shi'iposu.

"Shi'iposu?" Leandra stood and stretched.

"Roughly, stone breaker."

"Right." Leandra walked along to where the desertwalkers waited in a group.

"Shi'iposu." They bowed.

"Why Shi'iposu?"

"Breaking rocks is hard work, and it has to be done right or you've wasted your time." The oldest of the desertwalkers said.

"I'm guessing you were a stonemason before desertwalker."

"Worked in a quarry, but I've been known to lay a stone or two in a wall." He straightened. "We decided that you are our leader. We didn't listen to Xianju, but the black jaguar is giving us a second chance."

Leandra scanned the group. They stood straighter than they had since they started. They looked like they had something to live for.

"Very well." She nodded at them. "You know my name; give me yours."

I should have let Cameto come here and taken the easy job for myself.

CHAPTER 24

LEARNING CIVILITY

Cameto swore as Teekja dragged Lupji into the wagon.

"What was it this time?"

"A young man who considered red hair amusing. He had friends."

"Of course he had friends. No one in their right mind goes into this part of the city without friends."

"Cowards, all of them," Lupji muttered.

"And you're a drunk."

The Nekkest jumped off the bed surprisingly quickly for someone just hauled in semi-conscious.

Cameto's fist connected with the Nekkest's gut and the man went down gurgling.

"If you're going to be sick, go outside."

The red-haired man crawled out the door.

"You're faster than the training master," Teekja said.

"He's too predictable and too easily goaded to the attack, and that's when he's sober, which isn't often."

"He misses Nekkest and the desert."

"I should send him back."

"It would shame him." Teekja pushed her black and white hair out of her face.

"And this doesn't?" Cameto pointed out the door where gagging noises told him Lupji was on the last stage of his night before sleeping. Tomorrow he would apologize so often it would make Cameto angrier than he was now. Cameto's father had drunk too much. The big man hadn't understood it then and didn't now.

"It might be easier if we were accomplishing something. Wandering in this wagon, however comfortable, is not achieving anything."

"Are you ready to represent the Nekkest on behalf of the council?" Cameto sighed again and put the kettle on for tea. "Is he?"

"You are right," Teekja said, "but it doesn't make it any easier."

Pounjou slipped into the caravan. "Lupji is asleep under the caravan. It is safe enough for now."

"Good." He set out cups for tea.

"I settled the matter of the wager. A young man will be by in the morning to collect. It was an unusual one. They insulted each other. The first one to get angry lost." Pounjou grinned. "Lupji never had a chance."

"Interesting wager, I wonder who came up with it."

"That would be me," a quiet voice spoke from outside. "I wanted to make sure the young man got home and wasn't injured."

"I'm more concerned about his opponents." Cameto walked to the door. The woman outside might have been twice his age.

"Bruises, scratches, they'll be fine." She shrugged. "Better than when they all carried knives and chips on their shoulders."

"Why don't you join us for tea. You're welcome at our fire."

"I am honoured." She climbed into the caravan. "It will be cold tonight. He'll need a blanket."

Pounjou slipped away, then returned with a quilt and went outside to wrap up his comrade. Teekja made the tea while Cameto cut bread and put out butter and jam.

"My name is Xynthia." The woman sat at the table. "Recently retired from the king's service."

176

"I am Cameto." He nodded toward the others. "They will introduce themselves when they are ready. Names are of particular importance to them."

Xynthia smiled. "As they should be. Are you the Cameto who is bonded to Leandra?"

"That would be me." He set out mugs before sitting.

Teekja brought the teapot over and sat. "You may call me Teek."

"Thank you, Teek." Xynthia accepted a mug of tea, then dosed it with sugar and cream. "Are you from the Confederacy? My grandfather told stories of fighting people with markings like yours. He always spoke of them with respect."

"They are…relatives, but we have been severed from the Confederacy for many generations."

"I understand." Xynthia smiled. "My great-grandfather came from Lusia. I would hate to be asked about the Empire on his behalf." She looked over at Cameto and raised a brow. "Cameto, if you don't mind advice from an old woman, go present your guests to the king. You don't want him needing to send a message to look for you."

"I'm not sure he hasn't already." Cameto examined his guest over his steaming cup. "You don't seem to be the usual kind of person in this district."

"Politics will do that to you. I live a little closer to the river, but when I ran for councillor, I didn't know it included this chaotic corner of the city. Since I'm in the position, I might as well try to make things less chaotic."

"It sounds like you were succeeding, at least until Lupe arrived. He is the impersonation of chaos."
Teekja sipped her tea, then added more sugar.

"You speak the Belandrian dialect very well," Xynthia said.

"Cameto won't let us speak Nekkest while we're here." Pounjou shrugged theatrically. "It has aided in our desire to learn."

"If you have an open area, you could try teaching…" Teekja frowned and tried to think of the word.
"I don't know what you'd call it here. It translates roughly as the Game."

"And what would this Game's rules be?"

"The rules are less important than the opportunity for the young men to flaunt their prowess for the young women who come to watch. Lupe can talk your ear off about the Game. In essence, one team tries to move a ball down the field while the other stops them. Causing injury is frowned upon, and imagination and elegance are celebrated." Pounjou sighed and shook his head. "I was never very good at it. Too concerned with keeping all my body parts. Lupe on the other hand…He may have hit his head a few too many times."

"Perhaps I will stop by early, before you leave for the palace. I'll bring breakfast in payment for the lesson on the Game."

***

"I still think we should have stayed longer." Lupji sighed and looked out the back window.

"You would have us there another year if Cameto hadn't threated to tie, gag and throw you into the caravan." Teekja nudged him with her elbow.

"Did he really need to bring out the rope?"

"Yes," Teekja and Pounjou said in unison, and the three of them laughed.

Some people looked up and then away, as if seeing the brightly painted caravan was bad luck. Others, especially children, would wave and shout greetings.

"That's not Belandrian," Teekja said to Cameto after one particularly loud greeting.

"It's Rehego. Some of the younger ones are learning the language. It's nice to hear it."

The streets grew wider and the buildings bigger. Lupji's eyes widened. Nekkest was his home, and he'd never thought much about the architecture. On their travels here over the weeks and months, most of what they'd seen had been wood, with the occasional stone hall or distant estate house. He'd taken to thinking the Belandrians weren't great builders. But here buildings soared up several stories. Bridged-over alleys connected them. Not only the height, but the decoration of different coloured brick and stone took his breath away. Nekkest was all the same off-white stone. Here red, grey, yellow, black formed patterns and even pictures.

The palace came into view, and Lupji forgot about the

colourful buildings. It was grey, its wall textured more than colourful, but it was huge. He wondered if they could fit all of Nekkest into the building.

"How many people live in there?"

"Don't know." Cameto shrugged. "Never thought about it."

"You can ask when we get there." Teekja reached out and took his hand. Pounjou took her other one. His friends were as nervous as he was.

***

Lupji's nerves only grew worse as they walked past guards at the doors and saw men and women in coloured uniforms bustling about.

"It's like a city within a city."

"True enough, young man." The man guiding them didn't come to Cameto's chest, but it didn't bother him. He wasn't arrogant. Lupji decided the man knew what he was about and had no need to prove anything to anyone. *Wonder what that would feel like.*

"Guests to see his majesty," the man said to a guard with extra colour on his shoulders.

"He's almost done in the great hall, but if you hurry, you'll catch him."

"Please send a messenger asking him to wait. These young guests have come from south of the Rehego grasslands."

"Really?" The guard smiled. "I think I will carry that message myself." He headed off at a brisk walk. Then their guide led them down a different hall.

"Why aren't we following him?" Lupji pointed to the where the guard had vanished.

"Because I'm taking you this way. Trust me, it will be worth your while."

"How did you know we were from the south?" Teekja stepped up beside the man. "We didn't tell the guards when we came."

"My dear, it is my job to know. There are rumours going back more than a hundred years about an oasis in that desert, along with a people who looked like cats." He smiled slightly. "I will have to adjust my thinking on that one."

"You didn't ask us about the Confederation," Pounjou said.

"No need. I doubt you have any more recent information than we do, which is they are in a state of flux. Imperial refugees landed there as well as here but have been more aggressive in trying to take control of the government. The present Thilkeen is not yet thirteen, and most of her advisors are from the Empire."

Lupji looked at his friends, and they wore the same expression he knew was on his face.

"What do you know about the Nekku?"

"The warriors who share some appearances with you." The man nodded. "They are divided apparently. Some support the Imperials hoping for new glories and conquest. Others stand behind the Thilkeen and tradition. There have already been new expansions to the south. So far that has kept them occupied. We pushed them back forcefully enough about forty years ago to keep even the most eager warrior cautious about returning here."

"We left before that campaign, but some of our young warriors went to fight." Teekja shook her head. "My grandfather was one. He would never say anything about it, but he joined the peace party when he returned home."

"Peace party?" The man turned to look at Teekja. She glanced at Lupji, and he shrugged. Pounjou nodded slightly.

"Tradition says when our people fled to the oasis, one young man spoke against the violence of the warriors. We are all warriors, it is who we are, but the black jaguar god visited him and told him that he and his descendants were to study peace the way the rest learned to be warriors."

"Most interesting. I would be glad to talk to you more about this as you are comfortable sharing."

Lupji looked at man with even more respect. He'd spotted Teekja's glance.

"I would like to learn more of what you know about the Confederacy." Pounjou said in a tone which suggested he was testing something.

"We could trade information." The man smiled. "I can understand your wanting to know what is going on, even after all this time. After all, the only ways to come north are by the coast or past your oasis. I wonder how many of those young warriors who went to fight truly wanted to. Old men behind doors too often trade in young lives with little thought."

"You're a dangerous man," Lupji blurted out, then his face burned as they all stared at him.

"Perceptive," the man said. "Not all dangerous people carry weapons."

They arrived at a pair of doors which looked like they'd been smashed in, then repaired.

"Eleven years back, there was an unsuccessful rebellion. We left the door as a reminder."

"Did you fight against the rebels then?" Lupji's eyes brightened.

"No, then as now, I'm more comfortable with pen and paper than sword."

"You dealt in information, like you do now." Pounjou tilted his head.

"Correct, information in the right or wrong hands can be devastating."

"Jeremiah!" A young girl ran up. Lupji got the impression she ran everywhere. A quieter boy the same age followed. He nudged the girl.

"Welcome to the palace." She curtsied to them. "I am Princess Thuria, but everyone calls me Fury. This is my friend Nikay."

"Princess?" Teekja stared wide-eyed.

"I'm the king's daughter."

"What am I supposed to do?" Teekja whispered to Jeremiah. Fury laughed.

"It's all right. I'm not very formal."

Nikay laughed, the sound like bells in the hall.

"If you want, you can bow, like this." He tilted at the waist. "But since you're visiting from another country, you don't have to."

Lupji tried a bow, and Nikay applauded.

"I love your hair. Is that face paint?"

"Not paint." Pounjou ran a finger across his swirls. "When we choose, we decide how we want to look."

"That's amazing." Fury shook herself. "But if you're here,

then father will be waiting for you." She pulled the door open and waved them in.

The hall was bigger than the hall at home, but no spiral stairs led to an upper floor. Here tiny balconies dotted the walls with guard holding crossbows.

Down at the far end, a man sat in a chair. A sword stuck into the stone in front of it. *Must be like the door.*

Fury led them to the man on the chair.

"Father, I present guests from far away." Lupji bowed. Teekja and Pounjou copied him.

"Greetings, King Harald." Cameto bowed, a much fancier movement than what Nikay taught them.

"How is Leandra?" The king's voice rumbled in the hall.

"Far away."

Lupji's heart ached. He hoped one day to have someone to miss like that.

"Your Majesty, these are Nekkest. They are particular about names, but you may call them Lupe, Poun, and Teek." Lupji bowed again.

"Let's move somewhere less formal." The king stood and led them back through a door. Another man not in uniform followed. He moved like the best players of the Game.

The room they entered had wood panelling and a wood table. Chairs surrounded the table. The king waved them to sit.

"It's all right. Father likes to pretend he's not king sometimes," Fury whispered.

"Thank you for that, daughter. But she is right, in here for this time, we will set rank aside."

They sat and the king prepared the tea.

"I find that serving people in this small way reminds me of how I serve in a larger capacity." The king put the pot on the table and took a seat, sitting very differently than he had in the big room.

"Why is there a sword stuck in the stone?" Pounjou sipped at the tea and smiled.

"That is a long story, but it will help you understand Belandria better..."

Lupji hung on every word of the tale, as did Teekja and Pounjou.

182

"Your Majesty." A servant stood at the door. "There is a family at the front gate. They sent in this letter."

"I hope you at least brought them into the warmth of the main hall."

"One of the guards suggested it. They are probably having tea served at this very moment."

The king read the letter and went still as stone for so long Lupji began to worry about him.

"We will return to the hall. Please bring them in as soon as they have finished their tea." The king nodded at Fury. "The princess will serve, or you may return to the hall with us." He stood and everyone stood with him. Even Lupji could tell he was king again.

Fury looked at them with eyes full of communication, but Lupji couldn't read them.

"Let's return to the hall." Cameto grinned at Fury, who let a brilliant smile cross her face briefly.

Teekja reluctantly put her cup down, but Lupji exited the room on the heels of the princess and Nikay.

Fury led them over to the side.

"We'll be out of the way here."

The broken door opened, and a guard announced in a booming voice.

"Siana and Tam from the Empire to see his majesty."

Three people walked in. The woman had a mark on her face which made think Lupji wonder if she'd chosen it, but as she got closer it became clear it was a birthmark.

Siana, Cameto guessed. The woman was holding tight onto Tam's hand and a young boy.

"Welcome, Siana." The king stood and walked to meet them.

"Well, Harald, if Rodrigo is a spy and saved the world, it makes sense that you are a king."

Several of the guards stiffened, but the quiet man flicked his fingers and they relaxed.

"It is good to see you." The king embraced Siana, then shook Tam's hand, even leaning down to shake the boy's hand.

"How are Sara and Thuria?"

The princess walked over to curtsy gracefully almost to the

floor. Lupji was impressed that she didn't wobble in the slightest.

"I am Princess Arthuria Sian. Ever since I learned the story about my middle name, I wanted to meet the woman who saved me." Fury wiped her eyes and Nikay stared at her wide-eyed. "I am called Fury."

"Fury." Siana put a hand on the princess' shoulder causing another flick of the fingers from the man behind the king. "You have grown into a beautiful girl."

Fury hugged Siana fiercely.

"You will stay in the palace for now. I will have rooms set up for you. I so want to talk with you, but Father gets precedence." She glanced at her father. "The blue rooms?" He nodded and Fury bolted from the hall, Nikay in hot pursuit.

"Come, we will retreat to the parlour. Sara will be there with the twins." The king looked up at Lupji and the others. "You may come and go as you wish in the castle. There will be rooms set aside for you. We will speak more tomorrow."

He led Siana and her family out of the hall, followed by the quiet man.

"Well, let's go find those rooms." Cameto said.

***

Siana followed Harald, her head still spinning. Deddrick skipped along beside her. Tam, as usual, was her rock.

They arrived at a door which Harald opened and waved them through. The man who had followed closed the door as behind them.

"Siana!" The cry came from the other side of the room. Sara ran over to hug Siana every bit as tightly as Fury. "Harald, you didn't tell me they were coming."

"I didn't know until just now." Harald moved over to a sideboard. "Would you like wine, tea? We have juice for your young one."

Two identical boys came over. They looked as placid as Fury was filled with life. They bowed in unison.

"Welcome to the palace." One of them looked at Deddrick. "What's your name?"

"Deddrick," her son whispered.

"Nurse is telling us a story. Come and listen." They each took one of Deddrick's hands. Siana nodded to him, and he followed the boys.

"Alfaric and Diene," Sara said. "They're six."

"Six and a *half*," came from where they sat.

Siana laughed, then fell into a chair, and for some reason began weeping. Sara knelt and held her until the storm passed.

"I always felt guilty that we didn't tell you who we were, or at least write, but the longer it was, the harder it felt to start." Sara stood, then took the seat next to Siana.

"I understand," Siana said. "I was content to think Thuria was out in the world growing up. She's beautiful, a true princess."

"We'll arrange rooms for you..."

"Fury has already gone to do that." Harald handed Siana a wine glass and one to Tam. "If you prefer beer, I can send for some."

"Wine is good." Siana sipped and raised her brows. "Very good. Not Imperial, better."

"Lord deLanguiers will be delighted to hear your opinion."

"Is this real?" Siana looked around. "I'm not dreaming?"

"It's real." Harald sat across from Sara, beside Tam. "What brings you to Belandria?"

Siana told the story of how she'd met Rodrigo twice since that trip when she'd stowed away on Deddrick's wagons.

"What can we do for you?" Harald asked.

"Rodrigo's daughter gave us the greatest gift we could ask. You know that, but I don't know what we'll do here. We've no money. They put up the ones who come with us in the port. We were allowed to come because we had Rodrigo's letter. I'd like to have an inn again, our friends around us."

"Would you like to be in the capital? Though, to be honest, we need a couple of good inns on the south road. Traffic has increased since the Rehego joined us."

"Wherever is fine." Siana shook her head. "But I'd like our friends to come with us."

"Of course." Sara looked over at Harald. "There's that old seGraine estate. No one wants to live in it as a noble, but it would be good as an inn."

"Perfect. Siana, we'll take a trip out to see the place. If you like it, you can set up there. There'll be room for your friends on the estate or nearby. It isn't nearly enough, but it is a gift. You'll have the royal seal, of course. That way nobles will stay."

"You're giving me an estate?"

"It is the least I can do," Harald said. "It is close enough for you to come to the capital to visit regularly, or we'll bring the boys and Fury out to you." He sat back. "The first thing will be to get your friends here. We've tried to make the welcome as warm as possible, but it is a long way from what it could be."

"Harald." Siana stood, then knelt in front of him. "I pledge myself to your service, me and mine for as long as we live."

"Siana," Harald put his hand on her head, "I will be your King and your friend. You will always be able to talk to me at need." He lifted her to her feet. "Belandria is richer today for your presence."

Siana returned to her seat.

"Tell me more about Aimee." Sara sipped her wine. "We all knew who she was, but I never imagined anything like you described…"

CHAPTER 25

IMPRISONED COMPASSION

Aimee slept in the corner of the old church. Abandoned long before the unrest in the Empire, it had been spared the flames and destruction of the sectarian violence.

"We'll be at Lusia tomorrow." Rodrigo added a twig to the tiny fire which heated the water for their tea.

"Some food would be welcome. I'm getting tired of wild tubers." Milene pulled out the bag of tea.

"It isn't the first time we've lived off the land."

"We didn't have a growing thirteen-year-old with us." Milene smiled over at Aimee. "I'm worried about her. She's pushing herself too hard."

"She knows what she's doing." Rodrigo put mint leaves into the pot.

"That's what worries me." Milene wiped her eyes. "Have you noticed how she is being extra considerate."

"She's trying hard," Rodrigo sighed. He moved around to sit beside his wife and wrap an arm around her. "But yes, I have noticed, and I'm worried too."

"It's like she knows she won't be here much longer." Milene buried her face in Rodrigo's shoulder to muffle her sobs.

"Then it is all that much more important to make what time we have left precious." Rodrigo kissed Milene's hair.

"I think about it…" She hiccupped and sighed.

"I guess I've always lived in the moment. I never worried about the future until I had you, then Aimee. We can spend what remains grieving or celebrating."

"Are you moping again?" Aimee sat up and stretched. "What will be, will be."

"No thirteen-year-old ever talked like that." Milene dried her eyes on Rodrigo's shirt.

"That was the four-thousand-year-old part." Aimee knelt beside Milene and hugged her. "I'm scared too, but to turn my back on the people…" She sighed and laid her head on her mother's shoulder. "I can't, it's too painful. If I can help just a little…"

"We understand." Rodrigo stirred the tea. "But understanding doesn't reduce our fear."

"No, love does." Aimee let go of Milene and dug out the cups. "But it doesn't make it easier."

***

Aimee looked at the city as smoke rose above it. Even from this distance, the carrion stench made her stomach turn.

"There's plague in Lusia." Rodrigo pointed to the flag hanging limply over the gate.

The need of the people tugged at Aimee, an almost physical agony she couldn't ignore. She knew her parents worried and grieved, so she hid behind smiles and her sharp tongue. The more she responded to the call of the world, the further she got from her human presence here.

It isn't fair!

Aimee laughed. When had life ever been fair? Not in four thousand years of existence had she ever seen any justice that didn't come from God or human intervention. But she wanted to experience life, the kiss of a boyfriend, the joy she didn't completely understand which shone from Rodrigo and Milene's bond and the way they celebrated it. She wanted to be a mother, a grandmother.

None of it was going to happen.

"Let's go." Aimee started down the hill.

"Wait a moment." Her mother searched the ground, picking a bit of this, a little of that. She wrapped the bundles with black thread, then pinned them to their clothes before drawing runes over them. "Nothing can guarantee we don't get sick, but this should help. Don't take them off." She looked over at Aimee. "If it is removed, it will stop working. There isn't enough to make a difference in there for others. But if you are healthy..."

"I get it, Mama. Dying of the plague isn't high on my 'wish I could do list.'"

"What is?" Rodrigo lifted a brow.

"I'd like to be a mother." Aimee laughed as her papa tried to think of a response while Milene gave her a measuring look.

"Rodrigo, sweetheart, scout ahead a bit. Aimee and I need to have a little talk."

"Right." He kissed Milene and mussed Aimee's hair, then vanished into the woods.

Aimee could feel the burn on her cheeks as they rejoined her papa, but he only hugged her and led them toward the gates.

"We'll want to stay away from the road. It will be full of predators selling false hope or stealing what real hope is left."

'The cathedral." Aimee pointed to where the strings on her heart pulled her.

"This gate is as good as any." Rodrigo nodded. "It will be a tough walk. Yell for help if you need it. It's hard to help people with a knife in the ribs."

"Yes, Papa." Aimee took his hand. She'd come into the world too old to hold his hand, but today it felt right.

The hot sun beat on them as they reached the gate and saw the source of the stench. A huge open pit was half full of bodies. Men in death masks threw lime on the bodies. A cart pulled up as they walked by, and the men tossed corpses into the pit like they were logs.

"The dead don't feel any indignity, and the living are too exhausted to care." Rodrigo squeezed her hand. "That's why we're here, isn't it?"

"Part." Aimee looked away from the pit. "I guess. All I know is I need to be here."

"Let's go then."

"There's plague in the city." The guards frowned at them.

"We know," Milene said, "but our path leads us here."

"Wonderful." The man rolled his eyes. "The only cure is death. Nothing will change that."

They walked into the city, and as if the plague had vanished, the streets were full of people doing business. The cacophony deafened Aimee. If she hadn't been holding onto her papa, she'd have put her hands over her ears.

In a few minutes, she either become deaf or got used to the noise. Under the sound floated a constant thread of sorrow. Wailing came from everywhere as if the stones of the road and buildings wept.

Almost every building not constructed of stone showed scars of fire. Some had collapsed, others were blackened but standing. The harsh smell of ash fought with the perfume of death.

When they arrived at Margarite and Deddrick's home, they found it gutted and empty.

"They've been gone a while. I hope they got out before the plague." Milene brushed a tiny green shoot which had fought through the ash.

For lack of a better place, they camped there for the night. Aimee slept cuddled between her parents. Dreams of death and light mixed together in her mind, but none of them woke her.

***

Rodrigo woke early and untangled himself from Aimee and Milene. In the dawn light, the city looked almost normal, at least until the corpse cart appeared out of the mist. He shivered. Experience taught him to pay attention to things like that. He crept back to wake Aimee and Milene with a finger on their lips.

"Hoy, we know ye'r in there. Pay the death tax, and we'll leave you alone for now."

A man wearing a death mask swaggered into the ruins.

"Hey, cutie, you have something for the death tax?"

Rodrigo heard the leer in the man's voice. What concerned him more was the man with the club stumbling in behind. They'd both have the plague, who else would handle the dead, and what did they have to fear from the authorities?

"Don't be disgusting." Aimee stepped in front of Milene who looked to be trying to hold her back.

"Aaaah." The one with the club shambled forward. He was covered with sores and so feverish his mind would be permanently delirious.

"Give that one a smack, Arry." The first man pointed at Rodrigo, then turned back to the women. Even with Milene's runes, Rodrigo didn't want to go hand to hand with the plaguish Arry. He pulled out a dagger he wouldn't mind losing.

"Papa, wait." Aimee put a hand on his shoulder. She held Milene's rose dagger. "You poor man. Sleep." She held up the dagger like a shield in front of her. Did it glow for a second? Arry dropped the club and curled up on the ground. His partner had backed up against a wall. Milene drew a rune that settled on his chest.

"Wait until the sun strikes you, and you'll be released."

Out in the street, the city was waking. People gave the cart a wide berth. Aimee had the rose dagger sheathed at her side, incongruous on the light dress she wore.

"Aimee, hand me the dagger for a second." Rodrigo adjusted the sheath, then put it on the small of Aimee's back, held by the sash of her dress. "Try drawing it."

Aimee reached back and slipped the dagger out. He moved it slightly and put the dagger back in. After a few tries, he was satisfied.

"It was fine the first time. What was all the fuss?" Aimee drew the dagger and returned it to the sheath.

"Sure, you could draw it, but in a panic, you wouldn't have a good grip. A dagger's no good to you on the ground."

"Thanks." Aimee looked at him. "I thought you'd be upset, I mean that I had Mama's dagger."

"It is your mother's to hold or give. That is what a true gift is. It is no longer mine. If I told her how to use it, it would be my dagger, not hers."

"Makes sense." Aimee looked around her, then wiped at her eyes. Rodrigo put an arm around her shoulder. "Spill it, daughter of mine."

Aimee laughed and leaned against him.

"The plague isn't a disease, as least not a normal one." Aimee sighed heavily. "It is the manifestation of the despair and chaos around us. People watch their country crumble into civil war, their homes burn, their friends or family murdered. They expect more disaster, and so the plague."

"The cure for it is hope then."

"Sort of. Like that poor man, once it gets into you, it becomes a physical ailment. It's real and won't go away. Then the hope would have been as real to them as the despair."

"Tell me about the knife." Rodrigo loosened his grip on her shoulder and took her hand. Milene claimed her other.

"Mama put a rune on it which made it a hole that magic would fall into. Then when you stabbed the Sword, it overloaded and almost burned up."

"I remember." Rodrigo lifted his arm. He had the gripping 'hand' on it. It had more immediate uses than the hook.

"Mama thinks the magic hole is still there, but now the dagger radiates the absorbed magic back into the person holding the dagger. She thinks it will help keep me strong."

"If she thinks that, she's probably right. She usually is."

"If only you could remember that." Milene smiled at him over Aimee's head. His daughter was almost as tall as Milene. Was she that tall yesterday? Her clothes fit fine, so she had to have been. He just hadn't paid enough attention. Time to remedy that.

The city ignored them, its people too concerned with living and dying to worry about three Rehego. The few who did notice them made a sign against evil and hurried on. He was used to people not liking the Rehego, but this was a new reaction. The back of his mind started churning out ways it could lead to trouble.

"Have you noticed the folk making the sign against evil as we pass?"

"Oh, that's what it is." Aimee frowned. "I don't want them to think I'm bad."

"It isn't about you." Milene brushed the hair away from Aimee's face. "When things are bad, someone needs to be at fault. For most people, it is the Rehego."

"I think it is a bit more complicated than that." Rodrigo felt the balance shifting wildly. "This way." He led them into an alley, then to a tiny courtyard and up steps to the roof. Someone leaned against the wall, their head back. He didn't know how Aisa could still be alive with her body in such bad shape. She was always stubborn.

"Heh, figures it would be you to find me." Aisa flopped her head over. "Still together, I'm glad."

"You're the one the city folk are warding off."

"No one messes with the Rehego, not that there are many left. Either they escape, or they've got the plague." Aisa tried to stand but couldn't. "Never thought I'd say this, but I'm tired. Rodrigo, do you think they can do without me?"

"I'm sure they can." Milene knelt beside Aisa. "Rest."

"Did Leandra make it?"

"She did. Cameto married her, and they have a son named Raphael."

"That's nice. Tell her hello from me." Aisa looked at Aimee. "You're glowing with light. I could never understand. I did what had to be done, but it got worse and worse." Tears slipped down her face. "I did one good thing. I felt the rune when she looked at her baby. Don't know if they are even alive now."

Aimee crouched and took Aisa's hand.

"No matter how dark your soul got, you remembered love." She drew the dagger out. "It is time to sleep. Do not fear the dark." Aimee placed the knife on Aisa's chest over her heart.

The blade glowed until Rodrigo couldn't see for the light, then the light flowed into Aimee. Aisa's sores were gone, the obvious brokenness healed.

"She's alive, Rodrigo, a beautiful little girl. They named her Ais..." Aisa's eyes closed as her body went slack, then disintegrated into dust the wind lifted away.

"Go with the balance restored." Rodrigo dropped his head.

"Go leaving more hope in the world." Milene sat back on her heels.

"Go in love," Aimee whispered and fell bonelessly to the roof.

Rodrigo picked her up and spoke softly, telling the story of Aisa, how she'd served his sister. How in the end she'd found something bigger. Milene added her part. The sun was low in the sky when Aimee's eyes opened. She was taller, older. Her hair hung past her shoulders and pooled on the roof.

***

"The more power you take in, the faster you age." Rodrigo sat beside Aimee as the sun rose.

"I can't stop. I have to help."

"I know, but you may find things confusing. People will treat you differently; some better, some worse."

"You'll protect me, Papa."

"I would give my life for you, but this is beyond me."

"The good thing is you'll be stronger, more able to do what you need to do."

"Let's get started then." Aimee stood up and swayed slightly. "Woah, that's weird." She hoisted Milene to her feet as Rodrigo stood.

They retraced their steps to the street and wound through the crowds to the cathedral.

"This is where I need to be." Aimee headed for the stairs, then two men in legion uniforms stopped her.

"Emperor Striphona sent for you, Rehego who dare walk the streets in daylight. Seems he's got a purpose for you." More legionnaires surrounded them.

"Tell him congratulations for me." Rodrigo met the man's eyes. "But I have nothing else to say to him."

"He don't need your words. It's your blood he's after. Says it will cure the plague." The man put his sword up to Aimee's throat. "You come or she dies now. Don't look Rehego, so she don't matter."

"All right. I'll come, but leave her alone."

"Nah, she's the way we keep you in line. Heard all about how slippery you Rehego are."

"If we go, you'll die." Aimee's eyes were wide with fear.

"If we don't, you will. Once he has what he wants, Striphona will let you go, then you can return to finish your pilgrimage."

The soldiers marched them through the streets to the palace. One wing was destroyed, but the spells on the place were just as strong. They made Rodrigo shudder with an echo of the pain from when Harald had been captured and tortured.

Around a corner, two legionnaires stood guarding a door. They opened it wordlessly.

The hall was bigger than the great hall in Belandria. The legion surrounded the room, shoulder to shoulder, half facing in, half out. Other than that, the room was empty.

They reached the empty throne and waited. A limping step echoed through the hall, and Striphona appeared. He looked almost as bad as Aisa. The plague consumed him. The need for a cure had to be painful.

"Rodrigo." Striphona sat on the throne. "Rumour says your right hand holds the Sword at the bottom of the ocean."

"True, actually."

"I don't care." Striphona glared at him. "If I had the Sword, I wouldn't be dying."

"That's true too. You'd already be dead."

A soldier clubbed Rodrigo to his knees.

"Search them and bind them. Gag the women. If they escape, I'll crucify the lot of you."

Four soldiers carried in a table. They hoisted Rodrigo onto the table and cut his clothes off, checking anywhere a weapon might be hidden.

"I also heard rumours that three Rehego were curing the plague, turning people against me. Now, Rodrigo, you're going to cure me."

"It doesn't work like tha—" Another blow cut him off.

Amunia walked in carrying a stone knife.

"Now, my wife, as you promised, save me from the plague." Striphona's eyes were filled with hate as he looked at the woman.

"I remember you." Amunia smiled coldly. "I can't tell you how happy I am that the spell requires that you take a very long time to die." She leaned over him. "Let's get started."

CHAPTER 26

THE BLACK JAGUAR

Leandra looked down at the Temple. They'd planned to arrive first, but the natural amphitheatre crawled with Nekkest.

"I guessing they are your cousins from the Confederacy."

"They are. If we say we are joining them, they might let us live. You, they'll kill on sight if you were lucky."

"What do I need to do to not die today?"

"Marking your face is likely more permanent than you'd like," Vazee, now Xiuefa said. "Your kitten is young enough that it will fade when he desires it. For an adult, it takes a formal choosing."

"What about a mask like Lichou wore?"

"That might be more acceptable, but you will be expected to have the power of an elder. If someone challenges you, it would be trouble."

"I didn't get to be Rehego queen by being weak." Leandra rubbed the back of her head. "I'll need a mask and a robe. I'm thinking a normal desert robe will not work. Bring me a robe and a chunk of wood, the flatter the better, and a blade, the sharper the better."

"I have Xianju's mask. He had the right but rarely wore it." Xiuefa dug a carefully wrapped bundle out of her bag and handed it to Leandra. "Sorry, but the mask was marked with blood. I didn't have time to clean it."

The dark red of the bloodstain covered half the mask in a diagonal slash.

"What is Lichou going to think when he sees this?"

"His first thought will be that Xianju survived or that I have taken the mask on to declare vengeance."

"Both of which will be wrong." Leandra grinned. "When your opponent begins with bad information, you have an advantage."

"You saw what he did to Hojiam."

"Hojiam never showed up to that fight. I forgot at the time, but I put a rune of endurance on her. Not loaning her power but using my power to bolster hers during the sandstorm when we arrived. If she'd been hit with that kind of power, it would have knocked me over at the very least. It would be easy enough for Lichou to use his mind control to put someone there to smash. He's the kind who would never risk a truly open competition." Leandra fit the mask to her face, then used a rune to bleach the robe they brought her. Chgetke brought her a lizard, and she used its blood to paint the robe, adding another layer of disinformation.

"Shi'iposu, what is your wish?" Mahaloun had lost his glower, most of it anyway.

"You will stay here with Chgetke and Xiuefa. Keep them alive. If things go against us, you will need to warn the Nekkest and Belandria."

He frowned.

"Balance hold me." Leandra stepped into his face. "This is our fallback line. I need you here, not wishing you were down there getting killed. You and Xiuefa are known to Cameto. He will vouch for you. If it weren't for the need for you to take back the clearest picture of the situation, I would have you travelling already."

"Understood, Shi'iposu." Mahaloun pointed to a nearby pinnacle. "We will watch from there. What will be your signal to head to your country?"

"As soon as you have a grasp on the situation. If we fail, there will be very bad things happening. If things look bad, leave. You must not be captured."

Mahaloun sighed. "It would grieve me to leave your fate uncertain, but I see the love of a queen for her people. I will succeed or die trying."

"One last thing, unless you see my body, do not tell Cameto I am dead. He should know anyway since the White and Black heirs would appear almost immediately, but not everyone can be rational in the midst of grief. He must rule the Rehego until I return or the heirs are chosen."

"I will communicate that to him." Mahaloun saluted with his hand on his chest, then he swept up Xiuefa and headed toward the pinnacle.

"Chgetke, you must guide them safely through your territory. No more mistakes. Swear by my blood that you will keep them safe to report to my people."

"I swear." He jogged after Mahaloun.

"The rest of you gather around."

***

They walked into the amphitheatre one at a time, being sure to look at ease. Leandra watched until the last of the walkers had infiltrated the enemy. Now she had to wait. If disinformation were to work against Lichou, she needed to work with the truth. She'd recalled something Milene had said once about loading runes on her dagger, one to shield, one to absorb. The absorption sounded risky, so Leandra altered it. Now that she was thakgoki, she might as well use the power in the blade. Other runes came to mind, and she layered them carefully, leaving one slash or erase to activate them.

"Shi'iposu," the lead walker staggered into the camp. "The whole thing is a trap. Lichou expects you to show up. We never had a chance. My friends are all bound to his service. I was sent to warn you and give you a message. Lichou says the boy is his 'key to the world. The woman may watch him die from here or join him in death on the altar.'"

"Xianju, you think you can hide behind a new name?" Lichou's voice came from the desertwalker. "Bring the woman with you, and I will allow you to live long enough to meet your black jaguar." The walker drew a blade. Leandra made him sleep with a rune, then crouched to draw two more to free him from any compulsion.

"Don't want to keep Lichou waiting." She stood and set the mask more solidly on her face, then strolled toward the temple.

The desertwalkers rushed to the attack, daggers drawn, agony on their faces. A slash of the dagger cut Lichou's control of them. They dropped like empty sacks but still breathed. She walked past, leaving to them the decision to retreat or return to battle.

To survive you must be willing to court not only death but damnation. Aisa's voice whispered in Leandra's mind. It sounded like something she'd say, both dark and pragmatic. Leandra hardened her heart. She'd already broken the law of her people by becoming thakgoki; they'd have no choice but to exile her. No need to fear breaking other laws. She would walk out with Raphael at her side, or she would die.

***

No one moved to stop Leandra as she strode through the streets leading to the central pyramid with its altar built on top. Something lay on the stone. It might have been Raphael or maybe Hojiam. Too early to worry about it yet.

She stepped out into the vast courtyard surrounding the pyramid, and a blast of wind hit her. It should have splattered her against the buildings behind her. She hoped the Confederacy warriors had the sense to get out of the way. They weren't her problem. *Flirt with damnation*, Aisa's ghost said. Leandra drew on the power the blade had sucked in and sent back a blast of her own. Hers was the icy wind of the north sea that would freeze flesh on the bone. Riding on the wind, she sent a creature brought into being through the runes. It would sit on Lichou's shoulder to whisper dread into his soul.

Lichou stood on the bottom stairs of the pyramid, his arms raised theatrically. Leandra rolled her eyes behind her mask. A crack sprang from her feet to run like an arrow at Lichou. He ran to the side and let it expend its force against the stone of the steps. They crumbled and fell halfway to the top.

She followed Lichou, being careful to spring the trap he'd laid for her. If he'd truly aimed it at Leandra, it would have flayed her mind, perhaps killing her, but certainly making response difficult, but Lichou had set it for Xianju - quiet, peaceful, friendly. The images of blood and sacrifice only made Leandra more resolved to destroy the man.

Her return attack showed Lichou stripped naked and powerless, the laughingstock of the Nekkest.

His rage erupted, coming from behind her. He did love his puppetry. Leandra caught up to the priestess with the imp on her shoulder, gray with fear.

Seeing how the imp had grown in mere minutes, Leandra moved to return it to the void, but it fled. Later, she'd track it down and remove it. Its help wasn't reliable enough to run the risk of continuing to use it. She should have known better. She'd have to walk the road to Hel in person.

The priestess fell to the paving stones, a husk with no power. Leandra moved to the next stairs and started up. Time to make things more personal. However many puppets Lichou had in play, he'd be near the center of the ritual.

Lightning struck at her out of the sky. The dagger heated up as it took in the energy then passed it to Leandra. She didn't bother with a return attack, content for the moment to absorb whatever Lichou tossed at her. The top of the pyramid was a wide flat area. The stone altar in the center held Hojiam. Raphael stood motionless with a dagger in his hand. He grinned ferally at Leandra, showing pointed teeth.

"Hello, Mama, you come to watch me sacrifice this failed human."

Leandra sent a bolt to blast the puppet creeping up behind her away down to the courtyard.

"Always the coward, Lichou, sending others to do the work you are incapable of yourself." Another blast obliterated the puppet to the side. She was wasting energy blasting them. The next attack she sucked the puppet dry, then the next. The flow of power was intoxicating.

"Invigorating isn't it, to be the next best thing to a god." Lichou stepped out from behind Raphael wearing his black mask. The grey imp stood just behind the man. It stuck its tongue out at her, then ran away.

Lichou shook himself, then stood straighter, more confident.

"You didn't think your little fear trick would work twice?" He sent panic at Leandra to set her heart racing, her palms slick with sweat. She laughed and brushed it off.

"I know myself. I've lived with fear." A puppet clutched at her, trying to slash at her throat as it fell to dust. "What I wonder is what you know. Fear, of course; you're a coward. Rage, since you think you should own the world when you barely own the skin that holds in your guts. Do you know duty?" Leandra shaped a picture of him setting aside his desires to work for the good of the Nekkest.

"Weakness? You try to best me with weakness?" Lichou laughed.

"Of course, you wouldn't." Leandra ignored his words. "You never were an elder. Even from the beginning you were a fraud, terrified someone would find out." A gust of wind snatched the mask from his face and shattered it on the stones.

The laughter cut off.

"I am power!" His shout shook the stones under her feet.

"Power?" Leandra waved around her. "You think this is power? This is the cry of a little boy who can't have the toy he wants."

"I'll show you power." Lichou's eyes burned. "Raphael, it's time. Offer the cripple to the Black Jaguar." He sneered at Leandra. "You should have protected his name better. He was mine the moment I called him Raphael."

Raphael walked stiffly toward Hojiam, the knuckles on his dagger hand white.

"Raphaello Aida Rodrigo," Leandra let the syllables roll like thunder from her lips. "I'm sorry I took so long to find you."

"The man said you hated me; that's why you wouldn't let me do the runes."

"What do you think?"

Raphael stared at her. "He said I'd be 'portant. Like a king."

"Do you want to be king?"

He lowered the knife. "I don't know. What does a king do?"

"A king kills when he wants, takes what he wants. Kill her!" Lichou screamed, spittle flying from his mouth.

"Do you want to kill her?" Leandra tilted her head. "Mamma

trusts you. You decide. You can be king if that is what you want."

"K'nekket, Raphael." Hojiam rasped from where they lay helpless and broken. "If I am to die, I would be happy for it to be by your hand. If I am to live, let it be by your choice."

"Kill." Lichou jumped forward to hold Raphael's hand with the dagger and lift him and the blade over Hojiam. Raphael kicked and screamed.

"I don't want to. Hoj'am my friend."

"Kill her and be my king."

"NO!" Raphael slammed his head back into Lichou's face. The crunch of Lichou's nose made Leandra wince.

"Cursed brat." Lichou rammed the dagger into Raphael's heart and tossed his body aside. Then he raised the dagger over Hojiam. Leandra screamed, and all her power fled as her heart shattered. She fell to her knees.

Lichou shrieked, and even in her agony, Leandra looked up to see the man held in the mouth of an immense black jaguar. The knife did no more damage than a child's toy as Lichou tried to free himself. The jaguar shook its head and sent Lichou flying. The dagger shattered on the stone, and the man's body rolled off the edge.

The jaguar breathed on Hojiam, and their bones knit and reformed until they lay whole and healthy. The cat padded over to Leandra and growled at her.

"You brought evil into this world." Nekhaize's eyes trapped her.

How did he think to control this being? The demi-god's eyes lightened as if it read her thoughts.

"I did. I feared to be my own evil. I will seek it out and send it back to the void."

"It will not be easy. Even now it gains in strength as it flees south."

"Even so."

"You don't beg for your son's life?" The jaguar lay down and peered into Leandra's eyes.

"It isn't my place to demand his life. Ask him if he wishes to live or die, and I will abide."

The jaguar laughed, a snarl that sent rocks tumbling from the pyramid. He pounced on Raphael's body and stared into the boy's eyes.

Raphael reached up to wrap his arms around the huge animal. "I will try."

The Black Jaguar faded into smoke and drifted away on the wind.

"Raphael!" Leandra couldn't get her legs to work, but he ran to her and wrapped his arms around her.

"The big cat said I did good."

"You did marvellously." Leandra buried her face in his shirt and breathed in his scent.

"K'nekket." Hojiam knelt beside them. "Thank you." She took his hands in hers. "You chose life for me, so I will live it the best I can."

"K'nekket, what's that?"

"It means great kitten." Hojiam put her hand on his shoulder. "Not many would choose their friend over being king. I think if you became king someday, you'd be a great one."

"Do we have kings?" Raphael pushed away so he could see Leandra, and her heart caught. His eyes were those of the Black Jaguar.

"The Rehego have had great kings."

"The big cat said I had to help you catch the bad thing. He said I could see the truth of things."

"That could be a hard thing," Leandra hugged him again, "but I trust you."

They stood up, then picked their way down to the courtyard where Mahaloun, Xiuefa and the desertwalkers waited.

"Lichou wasn't the only one to think of bringing the jaguar back." Mahaloun frowned. "One of them told us about it in exchange for his freedom. The Confederacy sent the tribe to take the oasis. They plan to expand into Belandria. The Imperial advisors are very convincing, especially since they hold the children of the leaders hostage."

"Xiuefa and Mahaloun, go and warn the Nekkest, then travel to Belandria. Cameto will be in the capital. Find him and tell him I'm sorry. I will return if I can."

"We will do as you say, Shi'iposu."

"Chgetke, if your people are willing, have them close the mountain trails." Leandra held up her arm. "Only those willing to pay with their own blood should pass. Let no one pay for another."

"I will carry your words." Chgetke bowed, then looked at Mahaloun and Xiuefa. "For our friendship, I will guide you through before we close the mountains."

"We will pay our way as Shi'iposu declares," Xiuefa said though Mahaloun looked a little green.

"Shi'iposu, we will watch the desert trails. No one will pass without us knowing."

"Thank you." Leandra put her hand on the lead desertwalker's shoulder. "Walk free. Make your own rules. Don't be afraid to love and be loved."

He nodded, turned and led his group away.

"You aren't going with them?" Leandra looked at Hojiam.

"My fate is tied to K'nekket's, so we will travel together a while longer." They bowed to Raphael.

"The bad thing is that way." Raphael pointed.

"Then we must follow." Leandra took his hand, and they headed south.

CHAPTER 27

KING OF THE WORLD

Lydia woke to voices arguing in Vakate's language. She was still getting used to knowing its rhythms and rules, very different from any other language she'd learned.

"I am going," Vakate hissed.

"You will be my woman." The sound of a fist on flesh made Lydia's blood boil. She pushed her way out of the tent. A big man turned to sneer at her as she got up into his face.

"Don't think you—"

Lydia's knee connected solidly with his groin. He groaned and bent over, clutching himself but already straightening. Her other knee drove into his chin, snapping his head back and sending him over into the snow. He rolled over to push himself up as Lydia landed both feet on his shoulders, planting his face deep into the snow.

"Foolish boy," Lydia hissed into his ear. "Do you think the spirits care about your desires? Vakate must meet the King Of the World. If she fails, you will die, your people will die, the world itself might die." She stepped off him and pointed to a couple of men who stared at her mouths gaping wide. "Tie him to a tree. If he follows, there is no hope for your clan. Your hunters will die, your women will be slaves." The men dragged the man away.

Vakate walked over, hand on her face where she'd have a black eye soon enough.

"You might want to put some clothes on."

Lydia looked down at her naked body and laughed bitterly.

"There was only one man destined to be my lover, and he is gone, dead at the hand of a traitor." She shrugged and looked around the camp. "But I guess there is no more need to terrify your men."

When she'd dressed and returned outside, Kristif and his crew were awake, eyes glazed from drinking the night away with the men of the tribe.

"We leave before the sun is a handspan higher." Lydia frowned at them. "You'll just need to keep up."

"We'll rest here another day. There is no rush."

"Suit yourself. It doesn't matter to me whose spear your head decorates." Lydia put her pack beside the tent. "Bring furs, we won't have time for tents and such luxuries." She looked at Vakate. "Carry a sharp knife and sleep with it under your pillow."

She and Vakate skied out of camp a short time later. The transfer of language came with its share of other skills, such as her humiliation of Vakate's would-be suitor and the use of the skis. She'd used skis with Tomak and his friends but not through soft snow for the day. Now she kept up easily with Vakate and took her turn breaking the trail.

"We are being followed." Vakate twisted on her skis. Lydia copied her, working out kinks. She might have the skills, but the morning would bring stiff muscles.

"Kristif and his men, I expect."

"It could be Vundr."

"I hope not. I'd hate to see your people enslaved."

"You're creepy when you do that."

"What?"

"Make statements like that. Do you know all our fates?"

Lydia sighed and leaned back to stare up into the trees.

"I don't know my own fate. The path is clear, but the destination is far away. Still, I can tell when someone is about to step off a cliff." She winked at Vakate. "Or I've learned that being creepy can get things done. Let's go, they'll catch up before nightfall."

***

Lydia and Vakate led the troop south and east. After a week of travel, they arrived at the banks of an immense river. Ice partially covered the black water as it roiled and foamed on its way west. On the other bank, there were no trees.

"This way." Vakate headed east. Lydia followed and the men grumbled as they tagged along after. Kristif no longer gave orders. The others ignored him. At evening, they camped by a dam of huge ice blocks.

At first light, Vakate led the way onto the ice jam.

"I've heard of this from elders who once travelled this way regularly to hunt in winter. None could say why they stopped. Perhaps we wander too far north for it to be reasonable."

Clambering over the ice took every bit of concentration Lydia could muster. Her skis were tied in a large cross on her back. The idea was they would stop her from being pulled under the ice. She didn't trust them. The water threatened her in a way the open ocean didn't. There were caverns and holes in the ice, places it was so thin that a touch would crumble it.

Heart racing painfully, Lydia followed Vakate's steps exactly. A few times, the other woman reached back and pulled her up a particularly steep sheet of ice. The light had all but vanished when they stumbled off the ice onto the snow of the plains. One by one, the men appeared and collapsed. The last was Kristif.

"Where's Oskar?" One of the other men asked.

"Didn't see him." Kristif shrugged.

The man moved to go back, but Vakate stopped him.

"The river has taken its toll. Go back, and it must be paid again."

"Why didn't you say something before we started onto that cursed ice?"

"Would you have crossed the river?" Vakate stared at him. "We need to be on this side, not that, so the river must be crossed. Anyone of us might have paid the toll."

"Neither of you witches were in any danger."

"Perhaps, perhaps not." Vakate shrugged. "Who knows what the spirits have in mind? There are larger powers at work here than our petty human fates."

The man whitened and walked away muttering.

"You are right," Vakate whispered as they huddled under their furs. "Being creepy is effective."

"Be careful, words bind us."

"I'll remember that."

The plain swallowed them as they travelled, only the endless tail of the path showed they'd moved from one place to another. The food ran low, then ran out. The grumbles increased.

"Here is the place of your choice." Lydia gathered them in at the evening. The days were getting noticeably longer, so they were more tired at the end of each cycle of the sun. "You grumble that we've brought you here to this place to die. Well, all must die somewhere. You tore me from my husband's side for this. You left him bleeding on the floor of our home for this. Now you dare grumble at the cost of your actions. Follow us wholeheartedly and obey our words or go off on your own and see if you can do better. Hjoenr travelled this way, and if my ancestor could, then I will."

The men stared at her, but none argued. When Lydia turned to walk back to where she'd dug into the snow, a heavy weight landed on her back.

"You are no northern woman." Kristif spat the words into her ear. He took the dagger from her waist and threw it away. "Now I will take what I have earned." He flipped her onto her back, putting a hand on her throat and fumbling with the other trying to find a way through her furs.

Lydia laughed, making his face grow redder. He squatted, putting a knee on her chest and tearing with both hands at her clothes.

An arrow with fletching as red as blood appeared in his eye as if by magic. It wasn't any of theirs.

"Don't resist!" Lydia shouted as Kristif fell back into the snow.

They didn't listen. As she lay in the snow, tears ran on her face. The men's only real sin was to follow Kristif. The abduction wasn't anything unusual in the politics of the northmen, though

Tomak's death would lead to a blood feud.

The shouts and groans quieted until silence hung over the plain. She waited until a man in furs not much different from hers leaned over and stared at her. His face was strong. High cheekbones highlighted his ruddy complexion.

"You, ours."

Lydia reached up, and the man hoisted her easily to her feet. Another man held onto Vakate.

"Who?"

She put her hand up to her face. "Hoárr." Lydia pointed to Vakate. "Mine."

The men talked rapidly. Lydia picked out a word here and there. Enough to know they weren't in agreement.

"Take me to the King of the World," Vakate spoke up. The men stopped and stared at her, then their argument restarted more energetically. The man who'd lifted Lydia out of the snow eventually won. The other man threw his hands in the air and walked away.

"Come."

They travelled with the men. Lydia thought they'd travelled hard before, but these two drove them mercilessly. They gave the women dried meat and strong cheese to eat.

After three days of travel, they arrived at another river. This one had cut deep into the plain. It roared past them far below. The river widened like an eye. In the centre, an island split the current like a knife. A path switchbacked down the cliff to a tiny flat space where a boat was tied. The men pointed to the boat, and Lydia climbed in, her hands shaking. Vakate held them tight.

"We didn't come all this way to drown in this water."

Lydia nodded and tried to believe her friend.

The men each took a pair of oars and rowed out into the current. The effort they expended might have moved the *Red Wolf* across the ocean. Slowly they won the battle against the current and entered a tiny calm space.

"Don't." The man tossed a bit of meat into the river, and the surface boiled with fish as they fought for the tiny morsel. Lydia hadn't thought anything could scare her more than the black water of the river, but the fish made her skin crawl.

They were let out onto another tiny space of rock.

"Wait."

The men saluted some unseen person, then climbed back into the boat and pushed off. Once more they battled across the river to the cliff.

"Welcome." The voice behind them carried power, but it was soft, as if the speaker had nothing to prove.

Lydia turned to see a man not as tall as the two who'd just left, but she was certain neither of them, nor even both together, could stand against him.

"It has been a very long time since I spoke with a hunter from the taiga." He chuckled at Lydia's puzzlement. "The great forest which circles the world."

"I am Lydia, called Hoárr."

The man raised a brow but didn't say anything.

"I was born to seek the King of the World," Vakate said.

The man shook his head then put his hand on Vakate's arm.

"I am the king and this," he waved his hand, "is my world."

CHAPTER 28

INTO DARKNESS

Nikay ran through the crowd following the laughing Fury. The guards followed. They'd played this game before. No one would harm them. Then the street stretched and twisted. Fury didn't notice, but no matter how hard he ran, he couldn't catch her. He never could, even in his dreams.

Nikay came awake already moving toward his wardrobe. He threw on his warmest clothes and snuck down the hall. Illandria would stop him, and if she did, he'd lose Fury. He had no words for what he felt about her, but he knew he couldn't lose her. Even Illandria had to sleep, and as Nikay moved, he had the feeling that the entire world slept, except for him and three other people.

He didn't bother putting saddle or bridle on his horse, no time. Urgency pulled at him, dragged him into the night. The winter was breaking, and he was hot in his clothes. The horse carried him along the street, its hooves clopping on the cobbles. When he heard a matching sound and the rumble of wheels, Nikay kicked his horse into a gallop.

The wagon looked like any other. A farmer and his wife sat on the bench driving a team of horses. Canvas covered whatever load was in the back. He rode out to block them, pulling his horse to a stop.

"What are you doing out?" The woman's voice was sharp, nervous.

"If you are taking her, you'll take me too." Nikay forced himself to speak confidently. The man held a knife he hadn't been seconds before.

"Why should we?"

"What are you talking about?"

The couple spoke together.

"She's dying." Nikay gave up on confidence. "I can save her."

"What's one more brat?" The woman shook her head. "Shove him in with the other, and let's get on the way before they start looking for us."

The man jumped down as Nikay hopped off his horse and slapped it to send it cantering away.

He crawled in under the floor of the wagon when the man lowered the board disguising the extra space. Fury gasped for breath, having lost a fight for the first time in her life. He squirmed up to her as the board cut off all light. Her laboured breathing guided him.

Nikay followed his fingers up from her bare feet, along the light night dress, to her hair. He put his hands behind her neck, feeling the heat of her fever.

He hesitated briefly, then kissed her, breathing into her lungs, letting her breathe out, then repeating it. He grew lightheaded and began to worry it was just another dream, a nightmare where no matter what he did it made no difference. Then her hand moved to catch his face with an iron grip.

"What are you doing?" Rage echoed in her voice.

"Praise God!" Nikay burst into tears. "You don't know how many dreams you died in."

"Nikay?" Fury's voice softened. "Why are you in my room?" Then she stiffened again. "Where are we?"

"In a wagon heading south."

"Did you tell someone?"

"In my dreams, you died. You died when I called for help, when I tried to rescue you, when I went to wake your father or tried to wake mine." He fought his tears, but Fury's fingers brushed them away.

"So you decided to join me? How did you get in without them knowing?"

"I stopped them on the road and demanded they take me with them." He hesitated, then brushed her hair again. "You were dying, Fury. Whatever they drugged you with was killing you."

"You kissed me back to life like a prince in a story?" Fury hissed laughter.

"I had to breathe for you."

"I'm cold, Nik."

"I have lots of clothes." Nikay twisted and fought until he shed a couple of layers, then started all over again, getting Fury into them. She was the same height, but much more solid, but his outer layers fit all right.

"That's better." Fury lay on her back. "How are we going to escape?"

"I don't think we should." Nikay shook as his terror returned. "I haven't dreamed this. I don't know what would happen, but they want you alive or they would have left a body."

"You're right." Fury went quiet for so long he thought she'd gone to sleep. "What was kissing like?"

"I don't know." Nikay felt his face burning. "I was too worried about saving your life."

"Liar." Fury nudged him in the ribs. "If someone was going to kiss me, I'm glad it was you."

"Really?" Nikay's voice squeaked.

"Really." Fury's hand found his. "Just one thing, Nik. I want you to kiss me when I'm awake. I want to know what it's like. And no little peck. Proper kisses like you were giving me."

He slid toward her and his hands found her hair and the back of her neck. Her arms pulled him to her, and they kissed long in the dark.

"Interesting," Fury said. "I thought it would be grosser." She lay on her back again but held onto his hand. "Thank you for saving me and for the kiss. We'll be fine. There's no stopping the two of us."

Nikay squeezed her hand but couldn't think of anything to say. After a while, her breathing evened out, strong and deep as it should be.

It was dark and stuffy in the space but cold at the same time, too cramped to move.

He couldn't think of any place he'd rather be.

Alex McGilvery

READING ONE

Cover	Knight of cups	Loving thought
Cross	Ace of Wands	New Job/study
Above	Ace of Pentacles	New Financial venture
Below	King of Cups	Keen sensibilities, artistic temperament
Behind	Three of cups	Marriage based on deep affection
Ahead	Nine of swords	Deep personal loss, danger
Now	Ace of Cups	Beginning of Romance, letter from lover
House	Two of Swords	Conflict
Hopes and fears	Two of Cups	Love, happy every after.
Culmination	Queen of Swords	Strong, independent woman, single

Ace of Pentacles

Queen of Swords

Three of Cups

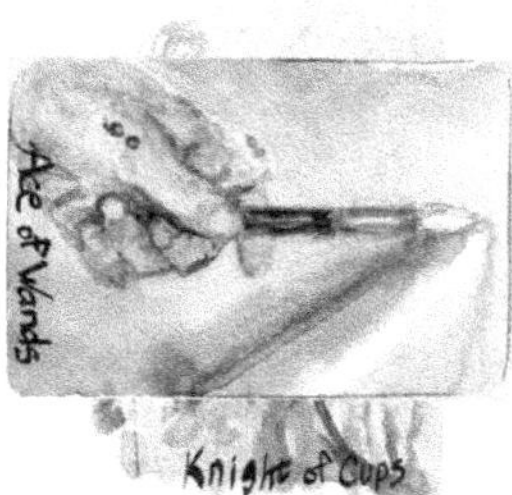

Ace of Wands

Knight of Cups

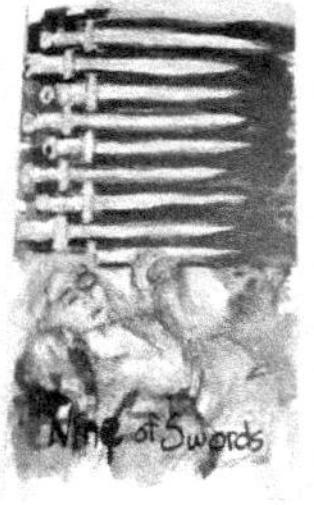

Nine of Swords

Two of Cups

King of Cups

Two of Swords

Ace of Cups

READING TWO

Cover	Strength	Inner Strength
Cross	Ace of Wands	New Job/study
Above	King of Cups	Keen sensibilities, artistic temperament
Below	Nine of Swords	Deep personal loss, danger
Behind	Two of Swords	Conflict
Ahead	Queen of Pentacles	highly organized, businesslike
Now	Knight of Wands	Concerns about career
House	High Priestess	Duality, moody or critical
Hopes and fear	Ten of Pentacles	Financial break or success
Culmination	Seven of Pentacles	Change, business trip

King of Cups
Seven of Pentacles
Two of Swords
Ace of Wands
VIII · Strength
Queen of Pentacles
Ten of Pentacles
Nine of Swords
II The High Priestess
Knight of Wands

READING THREE

Cover	World	Joy and arrival at her goal
Cross	Knight of Cups	Loving thought.
Above	Chariot	Victory
Below	Sun	Paradise found, love of one's life
Behind	Star	hope
Ahead	Devil	fear, division within self, evil influences
Now	Ace of Pentacles	Financial investment
House	Hanged man	Reversal, sacrifice, change in values
Hopes and fear.	High Priest	spiritual fulfillment, wise counsel
Culmination	Death	Change, reaping what was sown

VII · The Chariot

XIII · Death

XVII The Star

Knight of Cups
XXI THE WORLD

XV. The Devil

V · The High Priest

XIX The Sun

XII · THE HANGED MAN

Ace of Pentacles

OTHER BOOKS BY ALEX

Series:

Calliope Books
Calliope and the Sea Serpent
Calliope and the Royal Engineers
The Third Prince and the Enemy's Daughter

Spruce Bay Books
Wendigo Whispers
Cry of the White Moose
Disputed Rock

The Belandria Tarot
The Devil Reversed
The Regent's Reign
The Empire Unbalanced
The World Widens
The Fury Unleashed

Blue in Kamloops
Tranquille Dark

Celticfrog Publishing
Mythical Girls

STAND ALONE BOOKS:

Generation Gap
The Gods Above
Tales of Light and Dark
Like Mushrooms (poetry and photography)
The Heronmaster
Blood and Sparkles, and other stories
Princess of Boring
By the Book
Sarcasm is My Superpower
Playing on Yggdrasil
The Unenchanted Princess

Read short stories and excerpts from his novels at alexmcgilvery.com